SISYPHUS
UNSOLVED

SISYPHUS UNSOLVED

MICK MITCHELL

ABOUT THE AUTHOR

Mick Mitchell has completed an Open University Degree, gaining 2.1BSc (hons) in Arts and Humanities with English Literature. He has always read widely but never mixed in circles where knowledge or erudition was encouraged.

He has an interest in exploring the social history of ordinary working class people, and presenting it in his fiction work. This is a subject he knows well, having been born and bred in a mining community.

He now lives with his wife in South Nottinghamshire and is currently working on a third Sisyphus novel.

First Published in Great Britain in 2019 by DB Publishing,
an imprint of JMD Media Ltd

ISBN 978-1-78091-595-1

Printed and bound in the UK

In memory of Ian Peter Harrison

ALSO BY MICK MITCHELL

SISYPHUS UNLEASHED

CHAPTER ONE

The Golden Hour was playing on the radio. It was the year that the miners' strike finally ended after a year of struggle, the Bradford Stadium fire killed 56 people and the Live Aid concert raised millions of pounds for charity.

'1984,' said Feggy Edwards confidently.

'It was 1985,' I said without a shadow of a doubt. 'We left school that summer, surely you remember?'

Feggy looked up from his machine and had a think, 'No the pit strike was 1984. I remember us kids whose dads were on strike went on a day trip to Skeggy that was paid for by some fundraising thing.'

'Yeah it was the year the pit strike ended: 1985!'

The DJ finally settled the argument by announcing the year. He ended the Golden Hour by playing Tip Topley's surprise hit of 1985, *No Time for Foolery*. The Golden Hour was the only time on Stags FM when you were guaranteed any variety of songs. It would be a repetition of the same five songs for the rest of the shift. *Yes* by McAlmont & Butler proceeded to play – a song that I had enjoyed listening to until I had heard it so many times each day that I was almost nauseated by the sound of it.

There was always the remote possibility that the songs were played as some form of psychological conditioning by the sinister people who ran Tsucol International. The huge multinational company was run like some kind of weird religious cult. Industry, as we had known it in Mansfield, had become all but extinct during the early years of the 1990s. Miners and factory workers who had spent recent years collecting unemployment benefits or signing up for fruitless training schemes were willing fodder for the new regime.

The week before I had started working for Tsucol International, I had been invited to a welcome meeting for all the new operatives. When we arrived, we were led to tables laid with sandwiches and sausage rolls. We were then joined by the previous intakes of new operatives who were encouraged to mingle with us.

The last group who had been inducted before us were all asked to get up and tell us how wonderful it was. I was beginning to expect people to begin speaking in tongues and acts of divine healing to be performed. The Pentecostal fervour was quite entertaining until the new intake were all herded to the front and prompted to tell everyone something about themselves.

'My last job was as a security guard and I hope this will be better than that,' was my contribution, which was met with rapturous applause and exaggerated smiles from the management team.

I was already wishing I was back at home with a library book and my pauper's stipend from the dole office. Since being made redundant from Mansfield Knitwear in 1988, jobs had been hard to come by. I had spent a golden summer the following year, lying beneath trees and composing all manner of villanelles, sestinas and Pindaric odes.

My reverie was interrupted when the employment service decided to press me into one of its training programmes. The employment training schemes were designed to furnish the millions of unemployed with new skills so they could get on their bikes and find work. I spent a year playing cards and drinking tea while waiting for deliveries of concrete to build car parks in local churches.

During another interval in my extended sabbatical, I found several months employment as a security guard. 14-hour shifts through the night, spent in a building-site portacabin, left plenty of time to read but little time for luxuries like sleep and a social life.

Now I was part of capitalism's answer to authoritarianism. Compulsory overtime, the suppression of union representation and daily exercises were all a fundamental part of the new regime. The area was ripe for exploitation by companies like Tsucol; funding from the European Union and financial incentives offered by local government made setting up a plant in Mansfield highly attractive; a global business journal had featured an article that advocated the benefits of Mansfield as a potential goldmine for cheap manufacturing manpower and plant location. New business parks were beginning to sprout in this industrial wasteland, comprising hastily constructed metal factories. The satanic mills were being replaced by purgatorial tin boxes.

Each day I would walk through the soulless collection of identical metal boxes, most of which appeared to be deserted. Some of the huge buildings might only be staffed by half a dozen people. Only Tsucol seemed to display any sign of having a sizeable personnel.

Feggy passed me a panel of car seat cover and I proceeded to sew another piece and threw the completed front seat cushion onto the production belt. I glanced across the belt at Dawn Townroe, who had her head down and was changing a broken needle on her machine. I surreptitiously eyed her canyon-like cleavage while she concentrated on her task. She suddenly raised her head, glancing in my direction, and I hastily resumed my work.

The team leader in the neighbouring cell came dashing out to reprimand one of his operatives, who had just spent a lengthy hiatus in the lavatory, 'You should go to the toilet after you've had your breakfast!' The team leader known as 'Pat the Rat' berated the short, overweight operative nicknamed Doughnut as he waddled back to the cell.

Pat strode around his little fiefdom with the hubris of a king. I had heard that when he had first worked at Welbeck Colliery, the older miners had made his life a misery when they found out he had once played kazoo in the village jazz band. At the end of each shift, while they waited for the paddy train, they would force him to march up and down pretending to play the kazoo.

Feggy was chatting to the material handler, Callum Yates, and I decided to stretch my legs while I waited for a resumption of production. Standing at the sewing machine all day with one leg almost permanently levitating over the foot pedal would have been fine if I was a flamingo. I attempted a quadriceps stretch, balancing on one leg until Feggy tried to knock me off balance. Callum sniggered from behind Feggy's machine, always pleased to find that he wasn't the usual butt of horseplay.

The team leader called break and we all filed out to the canteen for our 20-minute lunch interval. I had already eaten my sandwiches during the earlier 10-minute break, so I would have plenty of time to sit outside and smoke several cigarettes. I walked past the huge banners that hung from the walls which carried the Tsucol logo, with its image of a grasshopper. The banners reminded me of the Nuremburg Rally or May Day parades in Red Square. In the corridor that led to the canteen, a poster hung on the wall with a picture of a soaring eagle and an inspirational quote about the joy of achieving.

In the canteen, people were already queuing for the drinks and food machines, while several others were putting meals into microwave ovens. A muscle-bound body builder was already seated, shovelling pasta into his mouth to maintain his calorie intake. I thought back to the time when factories had canteens that served hot breakfasts and dinners. I remembered Dawn Townroe working behind the counter when I worked at Mansfield Knitwear. One day she let me have my carton of milk for free when I discovered that I didn't have enough money.

I went outside to the tables and benches that were placed for *al fresco* dining and smoking. The September sunshine was still promising an Indian summer and the wasps were making hay amongst the rubbish bins. I went to the table that was furthest from the rest and climbed onto a seat and sat on its back rest. Quasi Wagstaff, Dick Mallory and Scratch King were already seated in an identical manner, all staring vacantly at their cigarettes. With his wall-eyes and stooping gait, Quasi bore a passing resemblance to Victor Hugo's bell ringer. Dick was the lothario of the trio; with his rugged good-looks and roguish charm, he was always popular with the ladies. Scratch was so-called due to his eczema. The brawny, blond-haired youth reminded me of an overgrown Hitler Youth boy in his knee-length shorts.

The silence quickly ended as Feggy approached singing, 'Make a little birdhouse in your ass.'

'Are you gay or what?' asked Quasi, with an expression of genuine homophobic contempt.

'No you're getting me mixed up with Dean's brother,' replied Feggy as he attempted to dry-hump me.

He offered me half a Twix and then added, 'That's your youth's cock that is.'

'Has it just been up your arse then Feggy?' said Scratch, eager to contribute to the day's badinage.

'Hey I wouldn't mind Ian's cock up my arse, the money he must be on, doing all that art bollocks down London.'

It was true that Ian had made quite a name for himself as an artist. He was scheduled to travel to Minneapolis in October for an exhibition at the Walker Art Center. The exhibition entitled *Brilliant!* was an opportunity to showcase the work of contemporary British artists. Ian Swift was part of the new wave of British artists, dubbed the YBA's or Young British Artists. He would be exhibiting alongside fellow visual artists Damian Hirst, Tracy Emin and Chris Ofili.

Everyone assumed that Ian was making a fortune from his work and must be living in the lap of luxury in London. The truth was that he had struggled for his art, living in a small flat in North London. He had been one of the first brave pioneers of the new wave of art, who had paved the way for the burgeoning success of artists like Damian Hirst, who Ian said was tipped to be the year's Turner Prize winner.

Ian and our father had never spoken to each other since they had met at Mother's funeral, where bitter vituperation had taken place between the two. Dad had never come to terms with Ian's homosexuality and Ian accused his father of driving his mother to suicide. Dad also resented Ian's success as an artist. He would have been more proud if Ian had spent his life breaking his back in a labouring job and producing grandchildren like a real man.

'I'd' fuck her,' said Feggy as he nudged me from my thoughts.

Walking along the pavement that ran around the perimeter of the factory were two women who worked in the offices. Office staff were often seen taking authorised 'stress walks' round the site. I was mildly resentful that they were allowed to take time out for stress-relieving activities while the machinists were forced to work all day like battery hens. I recognised one of them as Heidi, the girl I had had a crush on 10 years earlier. She was working her way up the management ladder now, while I was still a mere foot soldier in the global economic war. I hardly dared to look at her now whenever I saw her in the factory. I remembered telling her about my dreams of writing epic poetry and now I was just another underling.

The lunch break ended and it looked as though we would have another 10-minute break at the end of the shift. Several people had phoned in sick and we were short-handed. Targets still needed to be fulfilled, which meant that we would have to work another couple of hours extra to complete our workload. Quasi was delighted that he would accumulate another couple of hours of pay at time and a half.

'I'm coming in on Sunday as well,' he said gleefully. 'Double-bubble for coming in on Sunday.'

There was no way I would agree to coming in at the weekend if I could get away with it. I already felt like a character in a Solzhenitsyn novel without spending my precious free time tied to a machine. Quasi would deliberately work slowly to gain an hour or two of overtime. Quasi and his little cabal worked on the rear seat cushions together. They always complained that theirs was the hardest cover to sew, but secretly relished making a meal of their work when it suited them.

Quasi, Dick and Scratch were three former Shirebrook miners who couldn't come to terms with life without a union. All three of them were of the staunchly militant breed who had supported the pit strike in 1984. It was a man's life in the coal mines but working at a sewing machine was considered women's work for people like Quasi. They compensated for their sense of emasculation by behaving in an overtly masculine manner and were always eager to be the catalyst for any potential industrial action. Dick had already instigated a walkout one day when we had all agreed to refuse to stay late to complete our work quota. It was later revealed that Dick had been granted permission to leave on time on that particular day.

All three of them had the tenuous distinction of being part of the Foot-Long Club during their time as miners. In the depths of the coal mine, toilet facilities consisted of any dark corner where one might find the privacy to defecate. To be eligible for the Foot-Long Club, it was necessary to exhibit the largest specimen of freshly produced faecal matter on a shovel.

Our team leader, Dale Walden, walked up between our machines and attempted to rally us to approach our hourly target.

'Come on I want to hear those machines buzzing!' he futilely commanded.

'Emu!' someone called out in reference to Dale's aquiline countenance.

I drifted into a daydream in which we were all rowing an Athenian trireme at the Battle of Salamis. Dale marched up and down like Themistocles, exhorting us to row harder. We were heading straight for the broadside of the Rover cell, which had taken on the form of a vessel of the Persian fleet. The beaklike metal ram on the bow of our ship was set to crash straight through the timbers of the Persian ship. Already I could see members of the Rover team jumping overboard. I prepared myself to board the ship where a desperate battle would take place; hand-to-hand fighting on the limited space of the ship's deck.

We finally finished our targets around six o'clock and began to sweep the cell. The site of cleaners in factories had become a thing of the past and operatives were now expected to take responsibility for cleaning their workspace. Another innovation brought over by the Japanese, the 5S workplace method, involved five Japanese words beginning with the letter 'S'. Each of the words translated into different forms of housekeeping, which involved tasks like sweeping up and putting things back in their rightful place.

It had been a beautiful day until I stepped outside and mounted my bicycle. The skies had suddenly turned black and decided to cleanse me of the sweat of my labours with a torrent of rainfall. As I pedalled up the steep hill of Hermitage Lane, Dick and his inseparable stooges drove past, highly amused by my wretched condition.

It was fortunate for me that I only had a short distance to travel. I was living in a mid-terraced house on Harrington Street with my old friend Myfanwy. Our street was situated against the old hosiery mills factory on Botany Avenue, where I had worked until its closure. Behind our house was the bus garage and a silo full of diesel stood at the very end of our little yard. The house had been bequeathed to Myfanwy by his grandfather who had died in 1990. After life with my dad had finally become unbearable, the offer of paying board to my best friend had been a godsend.

I pushed my bike into the narrow passageway that led to the living room. Myfanwy was stretched out on the settee watching his *Quadrophenia* video for the umpteenth time. Corky the cockatiel began to repeatedly say 'Good Boy' in the expectation of coming out of his cage and spending some time with me.

'You're going to wear this out before long,' I said, nodding towards the television screen where Jimmy was about to fuck Leslie Ash again.

'This is how I see heaven,' explained Myfanwy, 'me eternally going down that alley in Brighton and getting stuck up Steph.'

'Don't start getting maudlin again,' I chided. 'You'll still be lying there in that Lambretta t-shirt when I'm dead and gone.'

I was beginning to worry about the deterioration of Myfanwy's physical health. It had been a decade since he had been diagnosed with HIV, and there was a time when we'd thought he might live to a ripe old age. He had been in rude health for so many years. The medication he was receiving seemed to be working and his visits to the Terrence Higgins Trust counsellor had given him a new outlook on life.

Lately, he'd been showing signs of flu-like symptoms and was displaying visible signs of weight loss. Whenever he stood up or tried lifting anything he would wince with pain. At first I had been concerned that he had begun to use heroin again, but I had finally ruled that out. He had been clean for 10 years since experiencing an almost fatal drug overdose and had taken on a straight-edged lifestyle that had endured against all odds.

After eating a soggy pizza I'd quickly given a turn in the microwave, I stepped outside for a spot of fresh air. It was cool and the smell of distant bonfire smoke reminded me of Guy Fawkes Night. A waning gibbous moon looked as though it was averting its gaze from Mansfield. The buses purred contentedly as they gathered outside the garage, making the kitchen window vibrate in unison. A lonely German Shepherd dog whined in a nearby back yard. Its slatternly owner left it there all day, too lazy to clean up its mess. Neighbours were beginning to complain that the shit was attracting rats.

I walked to the end of the yard and inspected the rug-sized lawn that nestled between the garden shed and an old coal house. The plaster on the coal house was peeling off to reveal red bricks. The ramshackle yet picturesque effect reminded me of the buildings I'd seen when I'd visited Italy.

I was transported back to 1988, when I had gone on holiday to Yugoslavia with a group of friends. We had visited several locations in Italy as we made our way around the Adriatic. We had made the trip by coach; first spending a night in Austria and then travelling down to Italy to drop off holidaymakers who were staying at a location there. We spent two weeks sleeping in tents, which reminded me of M★A★S★H. Each time we cashed our travellers' cheques, we received more money, as hyperinflation decimated the value of the Yugoslavian currency. The entire country would break up into independent states several years later after a bloody war tore the country apart.

How I wished I could enjoy some of that Adriatic sunshine again. That had been the last holiday I had taken and I was desperate to get away again. I thought about the fragile state of Myfanwy and wondered if we would ever get away for the holiday we had always planned. I was suddenly reminded of the closing scene in *Midnight Cowboy* and Myfanwy in the role of Ratso Rizzo.

I turned around and found my neighbour standing against the garden wall, grinning at me. I had no idea how long she had been watching me; she would often peer through the curtains to see what we were up too. She was a tiny Indian woman called Aashi, who lived alone with her black cat. She was deaf and had learning difficulties and made a living as a sewing machinist at the nearby Remploy Factory. I was acquainted with her father, Piara, who had been a work colleague at Mansfield Knitwear.

'Where's your mate tonight?' she asked, referring to Myfanwy. She had a crush on him which he resisted by attempting to avoid her whenever he saw her, before she saw him. She would often wait for him when he paid a visit to the outside lavatory. He once tried to wait for her to go away but found himself a prisoner in the toilet for 20 minutes and was finally flushed out.

'Myfanwy, someone's asking for you out here!' I called through the back door.

I heard him mutter a string of expletives, which suggested he wasn't available.

'I think he's having his bath now,' I said and did a theatrical shiver. 'It's getting cold out here, better get in before Corrie starts.'

I returned to the living room where Myfanwy was watching *The Cook Report*.

'What did you say to her?' he asked sullenly.

'I told her you like her very much but you always get tongue-tied when you're with anyone you're interested in romantically.'

'Fuck off!' he replied, throwing a pillow at me.

'Don't worry you're safe.'

Corky was growing impatient for me to spend some time with him and began to repeatedly say 'We are the mods! We are the mods!'

I opened Corky's cage, placing my hand in front of him. He joyfully hopped onto my hand and climbed up my arm and sat proudly on my shoulder.

'Well I suppose I should be grateful that you haven't taught him to swear,' I said as Corky climbed onto the top of my head.

'Not for the want of trying,' said Myfanwy, who was distracted by *The Cook Report*. 'You should take him back to the shop, he's definitely faulty.'

I began to take an interest in the topic of *The Cook Report*. Roger Cook was reporting on the emergence of a neo-Nazi organisation called the British Free Corps. The name was taken from a unit of the Waffen SS which had been made up of British volunteers.

'This is that lot that Cuckoo Walsh is supposed to be involved with,' said Myfanwy.

'How do you know all this?' I asked.

'He came round a few times while you were at work; I think he was trying to recruit me. I told him about my HIV status and he's never been back since.'

'If that doesn't work, we'll invite Aashi round to meet him.'

Cuckoo lived in a house around the corner on Spencer Street. I had seen him once, delivering leaflets for the British National Party, so I wasn't surprised about his involvement with the more sinister BFC. I knew he had been a prominent member of the local football hooligan firm that called itself the Coocachoo Crew. Feggy Edwards constantly regaled me with tales of his exploits with the crew and his association with characters like Cuckoo Walsh.

I grew tired of watching Roger Cook chasing thugs, whose only reply seemed to be 'No comment'. I spent an hour reading a dollop of Trollope and then sat outside and played a few reels on my mandolin. Reading Trollope's *Barsetshire Chronicles* would always leave me imagining myself to be Mister Harding, playing his violoncello.

It was beginning to grow cold outside so I decided to go inside and watch television. Myfanwy had gone out for a game of bingo with one of the neighbours, so I made the most of having the television to myself. I switched on in time to see *Have I Got News for You*. Team captain Paul Merton was accompanied by Mike Yarwood, while Ian Hislop's guest teammate was the former Queen's Counsel and Member of Parliament for North Berkminster, Edward Towton. The usual irreverent lampooning of the latest events in world news were on offer. The to and fro of witty badinage was taking place, on topics that included Frank Bruno's WBC world heavyweight championship win; the murder trial of Fred and Rose West; and the defection of a Conservative MP to the Labour Party.

I vaguely remembered Myfanwy telling me that he had once spent a convivial afternoon in the company of Edward Towton. I had been sceptical of his story until later the same day, we had both encountered the former Toy Mistress frontman, Tip Topley. He had spent that morning with Edward and Myfanwy in a drug and alcohol-fuelled party at Trent Bridge Cricket Ground.

Towton was in fine form; quick to produce a scathingly satirical remark on the latest current affairs and comfortable with parrying any witty banter that encroached on his own much-publicised private life. Edward Towton had retired from public life in 1985 after being involved in a media scandal that erupted after the body of a 17-year-old man was found in his hotel room. The young man, whose name was David Read, died of a heart attack which was probably due to the large amounts of cocaine he had taken. A pathologist discovered rectal injuries that suggested a violent sexual assault may have taken place. Another man, who was the son of a peer of the realm, was alleged to have been involved in the incident. No charges were laid against Edward but his associate was charged with the possession of cocaine.

Even though his reputation had been irreparably tarnished, Edward made the most of being a cause célèbre. He spent several years writing three volumes of his memoirs, which became instant bestsellers. His regular appearances on television shows like *Clive Anderson Talks Back* and *The Last Resort with Jonathan Ross* made him an overnight success as a celebrity bon vivant.

Myfanwy returned triumphantly with £20 worth of Iceland vouchers he had won at bingo. He had also returned with an evening repast of delicacies from the An Lushan Chinese Takeaway. Seeing the face of Edward Towton once again brought back a spark of the old Myfanwy; he who had once been wined and dined by that very bastion of jurisprudence, on the day his unsullied reputation in that profession was ignobly shattered.

CHAPTER TWO

On a hilltop where Derbyshire borders the western extremities of Nottinghamshire, perches the little town of Heanor. Amidst the ancient terraced streets of that town, a new housing estate was under construction. Pretty little cul-de-sacs of tiny houses where young families could listen to their neighbours argue through paper-thin walls.

Andy 'Cuckoo' Walsh threw his plastering equipment into the back of his van with the help of his labourer, Josh Hunt.

'Not a bad day's work that Josh,' said Cuckoo as he handed his young apprentice £30 for his 12 hours of labour.

Cuckoo always referred to the lad as Josh; there were still a handful of people who used the cognomen of 'Dog' to address him. When Josh had first sat through a lesson in German at school, his classmates had thought that *hund*, the German word for Dog, sounded like Josh's surname, and the nickname stuck for many years.

Cuckoo drove down the big hill that led from Heanor into the neighbouring town of Langley Mill. He then ascended another hill that brought him into Eastwood and the county of Nottinghamshire. He passed the street where DH Lawrence had once lived but was ignorant of the existence of the illustrious author.

The only thing that interested Cuckoo about the region he was departing was its large percentage of supporters of the British National Party. Working and drinking with locals from the Amber Valley region, he discovered that the area was alleged to be a BNP stronghold.

The legitimate political aims of the British National Party were of little interest to Cuckoo. He had become embroiled in the more radical activities of the neo-Nazi organisation called the British Free Corps. His only interest in those with BNP affiliations was to establish whether they might be suitable for indoctrination into the BFC.

Since the golden age of football hooliganism had passed in the late 1980s, Cuckoo had drifted into far-right politics, along with other disillusioned hooligans. He had been the general of the Coocachoo Crew until a schism in its ranks caused it to disband in 1988. The younger generation of the firm had become loved up on Ecstasy tablets and rave music. They had traded their designer football casual gear for baggy jeans, tie-dye t-shirts and fishing hats.

He had witnessed the tragedy of the Hillsborough disaster of 1989, unaware that 96 people were dead in the Leppings Lane stand, as he stood with the Nottingham Forest fans at the opposite end of the ground. The greatest tragedy for Cuckoo had been the subsequent decision to make English football stadiums all-seater venues. With the old battle grounds of the terraces gone and police surveillance creating more convictions for hooligans, football was turning into a family spectacle which was anathema to Cuckoo and his kind.

Cuckoo's involvement with the BFC had recently led to a reprise in his role as a football hooligan. In February he and some of his BFC associates had travelled to Dublin for a friendly football match between England and the Republic of Ireland. During the game, which took place at the Lansdowne Road stadium, they had instigated a riot. The disturbances were planned and executed as a demonstration of support for the group's loyalist associates in Northern Ireland and a protest against the activities of the Provisional IRA.

Young Josh had come along with him on the trip to Ireland and had given a good account of himself. Cuckoo had big plans for Josh, in whom he saw great potential. The boy was malleable enough to take orders from Cuckoo without asking questions. He was certain that Josh would keep his mouth shut if he was questioned by the police. It was just a matter of time before he decided where and when he would initiate Josh into the messier elements of the BFC agenda.

Glancing at himself in his rear-view mirror, Cuckoo was pleased with the new look he had adopted. He had finally shaved off his moustache after someone had suggested that it made him look like Freddy Mercury. He had been a fan of Queen in the 1980s and had even taken his wife to see them at Wembley Stadium. He had always admired Mercury's macho image and had been shocked when he had discovered that the Queen singer had been gay. His mane of black hair had been given the chop, along with his moustache. He could no longer hide the growing bald patch that was spreading across his pate, so he decided to shave it down to the wood.

Josh put his Screwdriver cassette on and Cuckoo turned up the sound of *Hail Victory*. The title track of the album began meandering along with an acoustic guitar-led, country feel. Cuckoo felt a surge of patriotic pride each time he listened to the lyrics. *Hail Victory* had been Screwdriver's final project before the band's leader, Ian Donaldson, had died in a car crash. Donaldson's Blood and Honour organisation had raised funds that helped to make white power concert events possible.

The song erupted into a faster, hard-rock style and Cuckoo and Josh began to rock backwards and forwards like a racist parody of *Wayne's World*. It had been during a Screwdriver concert that Cuckoo had first met Josh and spotted his potential. The concerts had become a regular recruiting ground for the BFC and Cuckoo had enjoyed the task of grooming Josh as a foot soldier for the cause.

Josh had been a keen fan of punk rock during his teenage years. Unlike some punks, he hadn't seen any distinction between bands like Disorder and OI! Bands such as Combat 84. His best friend Sammy had drifted off into the world of rave music while his older role model, Spike, had shaved off his Mohican and joined the army. The Pakistanis who owned the bottom shop had banned him after catching him shoplifting a packet of Scampi Fries. Since that day, he had harboured resentment against anyone whose countenance was not of the purest white complexion. Left alone in the village of Meden Vale without a job, he had found belonging amongst the crowd he met when he went to a Screwdriver concert one evening. His meeting with Cuckoo had been even more fortuitous when the renowned hooligan had offered him regular employment.

CHAPTER THREE

Life for the Freeman family had finally begun to settle down for the first time since Kevin Freeman had sacrificed his life in the service of his country, during the Falklands War. The marriage of Alex and Maggie Freeman had been torn apart by the premature death of their son. Communication had broken down during the grieving process and Maggie had found solace with another man, while Alex's life spiralled into an inner world of pain and despair that bought him to the precipice of suicide.

Their other son, John, had been caught in the cross-fire of his parents' crisis whilst trying to make sense of his own grief issues. After fleeing to the streets of London to make a new life for himself, John found a new vigour for life when he embarked on a relationship with a homeless girl. After being reconciled with his parents, the family slowly began to mend their tattered relationship.

John and his girlfriend, Sally Hodge, known by the soubriquet of 'Podge', cemented the cracks in the family dynamic with the birth of a son in 1994. They tied the knot at the Mansfield Registration Office on St. John Street. Alex Freeman recorded the entire event for posterity on his precious VHS camcorder.

John and Sally lay on their well-worn settee and watched the video for the first time since Alex had brought them a copy. Their little boy, Kevin, was crawling around the floor bare-arsed in his Incredible Hulk t-shirt. The antiseptic smell of baby cream, blended with shit, filled the air.

'When are you going to get your dad to borrow us his camera?' asked Sally as she lay between John's legs. 'We could have some fun making our own home videos in the bedroom.'

'You're insatiable woman!' said John as he smiled at his best friend Spike on the wedding video. 'I thought you were supposed to go off that sort of thing after having a baby?'

'I might be getting broody again,' said Sally, rubbing her hand between John's legs.

John watched Spike standing beside him during the wedding. He wore an ill-fitting grey suit that was two sizes too small for him. Since his time in the army, Spike had put on a lot of weight; the consequence of drinking a regular surfeit of Guinness. John turned his attention to the ravishing figure of his new wife. She was dressed in the same trousseau his mother had worn for her own wedding and he hoped that it would bring better luck for them than it had for his parents.

'You didn't look half bad that day,' said John as he picked up Kevin, who had announced his wish for attention by biting John's toes.

'You didn't look bad yourself,' said Sally, stroking her son's hair as if it were the finest silk.'

'We would definitely have needed some spare video tapes during the honeymoon,' said John as he began the task of putting a fresh nappy on his son.

He smiled as he reflected on their honeymoon in Ibiza. They had spent most of their time robustly consecrating their marriage and eating Jaffa cakes. They had managed to find the time to spend a night dancing to the Balearic Beat at the Amnesia nightclub, which had become a mecca for dance music enthusiasts.

A sharp noise on the window interrupted John's reminiscences. He recognised the sound of stone hitting glass and rushed to the front door to confront the culprit. He walked over to the front gate in his bare feet, wearing nothing but his jeans. He leaned over the gate in time to see two youths of about 14 years old walking casually down the street. One of them looked round to see if they were being watched and then he nudged his friend.

'Did one of you just throw something at my window?' John called out with stentorian authority.

One of the pair, a podgy youth with red hair and freckles, fearlessly called back, 'Yeah what are you going to do like?'

Sally stood in the doorway holding Kevin and said, 'Come inside, they're just kids!'

Ignoring his wife, John athletically leapt over the fence and began to give chase. The two youths immediately began to sprint away. Several people were standing in their gardens watching with interest and John began to feel foolish chasing a couple of silly kids. He halted, realising he wouldn't catch up with the much fitter teenagers. Turning around and seeing that he had given up running, they stopped and began calling out a string of expletives that John couldn't make out. He turned around and walked back to the house, the sound of the two boys egging him on to continue the chase still audible in the distance.

Sally was still waiting in the doorway nursing Kevin, who had begun to cry for his father.

'You just play into their hands when you try to chase after them.'

'I'm not taking that from anyone!' he said, projecting his anger onto his wife.

Sally walked back into the house, opting to leave John to cool down on his own.

He was still shaking and felt light headed when he sat down in the kitchen. He didn't get angry very often but could erupt into violent retaliation if he felt under threat. He sat with his head in his hands and tried to take deep breaths. His doctor had given him a prescription for beta-blockers to help with his anxiety but he was sure he needed a higher dose. Regular 12-hour shifts at the double glazing factory were taking their toll. One day the stress had overwhelmed him and he had thought he was having a heart attack. The doctor had told him that what he had experienced was a panic attack.

He continued to work at controlling his breathing and he began to feel a little calmer. The unpleasant tightness in his chest and the light-headedness he experienced were all symptoms of hyperventilation which he had learned to recognise.

He knew what kids could be like; he himself had gotten up to all kinds of mischief during his childhood. He remembered every year, on the evening before Bonfire Night, he and other boys would go out and celebrate Mischievous Night. The annual festival of roguery would involve daubing people's windows with butter and lifting gates from their hinges.

When he had been a boy he knew he'd get a good hiding if he was caught in the act of any misbehaviour. Since he had moved to Mansfield Woodhouse, there seemed to be a new breed of feral youth stalking the streets. They had worked out that there was little that parents and adults in general could legally do to them if they misbehaved. Kids were becoming bold enough to be disrespectful to anyone they pleased without fear of reprisal. He had seen wooden fences smashed where youths had kicked them in, while frightened pensioners had looked on in disbelief. A neighbour had told him that a teenage boy had jumped up and down on her flowerbeds in front of her while his friends watched with amusement. She had told him that there was one particular boy who seemed to be the ringleader. The others were emboldened by his audacity and attempted to emulate his acts of delinquency. The neighbour told him that the ringleader was a 14-year-old boy named Sean Cain, who lived with his long-suffering grandmother, and she struggled to keep him under control. She would try to lock him in his bedroom sometimes but he would just escape through the window.

John returned to the living room where Kevin and Sally were watching *Rugrats*. Sally smiled at John, relieved that he had evidently calmed down. His anxiety attacks were a constant worry to her and she feared for his mental health. She knew that his dad had been recovering from serious bouts of depression when they had first moved to Mansfield together.

Since the day she had met John, her life had changed for the better. She remembered how vulnerable and worthless she felt before they had met. Her low self-esteem had led to her falling into the clutches of a controlling and psychotic maniac who had almost succeeded in ending her life. The day that John had leapt in front of her ex-boyfriend's car to save her had made Sally realise that her life was actually worth saving. Although the dangerous sociopath named Fritch was dead and buried, she still occasionally entertained the irrational fear that he would come back and get her. She would often awake in feverish sweats from dreams in which Fritch would be standing over the bed with a shovel raised, ready to stove in her head, in the same way he had disposed with Sally's friend Suze.

John left her alone with Kevin and went upstairs to paint the damp wall in his and Sally's bedroom. One of the walls was so black with mouldy dampness that John had been forced to give it a regular coat of paint. They had informed the council about the dampness and it had been suggested that they paint the wall until such a time as repairs could be arranged. The house was so affected by mining subsidence that a crack ran up the entire rear wall of the house from top to bottom. Rats had found entrance into the loft through the narrow crack. It had been fortunate that the council's pest control department had been quicker to respond than those concerned with the repair of local housing.

John and Sally had tried on several occasions to request a transfer to a house more suited to a family with a young child. The lack of double glazing was another major factor in the dampness of the residence. The old windows might easily have been pushed out by their damp and rotting frames with a modest shove. The old front door frame was alternately difficult to open and easily pushed in, depending on the capricious whims of the seasons.

Nevertheless, Sally counted her blessings. She remembered when she had been forced to flee from Fritch and learnt to survive on the streets of London. Things had improved for her since the days when she thought a bench on Primrose Hill had been a desirable residence.

CHAPTER FOUR

Heidi Marsh stepped out into the car park of Tsucol International and watched the wind blowing the company flags that fluttered atop their white poles. She saw the head of production, Les Johnson, getting into his red Mazda MX-5 and she picked up her pace to try to reach her own car which was parked in the next space.

She arrived beside her metallic grey Ford Fiesta in time to see Les pulling on his brown leather driving gloves. He put on his dark glasses and glanced at Heidi, giving her a barely perceptible nod of the head. *Roll With It* by Oasis erupted from his compact disc player and he began to pull away. Heidi made a pretence of looking for her keys in her handbag to prolong the moment. Feeling slightly disappointed with his lack of acknowledgement, she hastened to get into her car. As she pulled out her car keys she almost dropped them on the floor when Les gave a blast on his car horn as he pulled away. She turned around a little too quickly and waved to him. He glanced at Heidi from above his dark glasses, before pushing them up the bridge of his nose and condescending to offer a perfunctory wave.

As Les drove away, Heidi hopped into her car, satisfied that he had taken notice of her. She began to replay the incident as she drove away through the business park and its identical neighbours on Hermitage Lane. She switched on *The Great Escape* by Blur and *Country House* began to play. She couldn't listen to the track anymore without seeing Keith Allen in a bowler hat doing a poor imitation of the Ministry of Silly Walks sketch. She changed the track to *Fade Away* and decided that it was time to give Oasis a try. The Battle of Britpop had recently taken place between the two bands and Heidi had placed her loyalties firmly in the Blur camp. After noting that Les was listening to Oasis, she decided it might be time to give them a try. She had always thought them a little scary looking compared with the clean-cut boys from Blur.

She drove onto Sutton Road and passed the Sir John Cockle pub. She saw Les walking into the pub and wished she had the nerve to go inside on her own. She concluded that it might look a little too obvious if she walked in alone, two minutes after he had arrived. She didn't want to appear slutty like Angie Seddon on reception, who was always shamelessly trying to get off with anything in trousers on the management team. The Cockle was a regular watering hole for Tsucol employees and Heidi decided that she would bide her time until a group of her colleagues went there for a drink. It wouldn't be long before Christmas and then she might get an opportunity to get closer to Les.

As Heidi passed Kwik Save she saw Dean Swift emerge with a two-litre bottle of Strongbow. He looked quite cool with his little goatee beard. Dean's face had once had an epicene quality, now tempered by the incipient growth of facial hair. He had always adopted a bohemian look and Heidi thought it suited him. She remembered when she used to talk to him sometimes when they were teenagers, drinking at Harvey's and Brigadoon. He had had great ambitions as a poet in those days but he didn't seem to have had the confidence to realise his dreams. She saw him most days whenever she walked across the shop floor; his head down at his machine, lost in his own thoughts. She had heard about his mother committing suicide and felt sad for his loss. He had a brother who had become quite successful in the art world and she wondered if Dean felt like a failure in comparison.

Heidi considered herself fortunate to have been nurtured by her parents during her school years. She was glad that she had worked hard and hadn't thrown away the opportunity to succeed like her old school friend Jeanette Wallace. Since dropping out of college, Jeanette had already been married and divorced. She was now a single parent with two children. The first birth had been the main reason Jeanette had made the decision to get married when she was 19. The second had been the result of an affair which had left her in her current position as a single parent.

Heidi had still maintained her friendship with Jeanette, even though their paths had diverged a decade earlier. She would often visit Jeanette in her semi-detached house on the Ladybrook estate. Since Jeanette had become a mother, Heidi had found a fresh motive for visiting her old friend. She loved spending time with Jeanette's two children. Little Gemma was now six and Robbie would soon be two.

Sometimes Heidi thought that all the advantages she took for granted in her own life were shallow in comparison to the miracle of being gifted with a couple of beautiful children. Heidi always admired the fact that despite being a consummate slattern and a strumpet, Jeanette had a natural aptitude for motherhood.

Heidi's journey took her to her parent's bungalow which was tucked away in Littlewood Lane, on the outskirts of Mansfield Woodhouse. Since retiring, her parents, Tony and Elaine Marsh, had moved from their home on Nottingham Road in search of somewhere quieter. Now that Heidi and her brother had both flown the nest, the old house had seemed too large for the two of them. The new residence was situated close to a golf course and ideal for enjoying rural walks alongside the River Meden. The area had been a perfect place for the couple to repair their damaged marriage.

Heidi parked her car at the front of the house and could see her father peering through the window. She had begun to make regular visits to her parents since her mother had been diagnosed with early-onset Alzheimer's disease. It had been a tragic blow to the family since the couple had been on the brink of divorce ten years earlier and had finally been reconciled and were settling down to a comfortable early retirement.

'It's only me!' Heidi called out politely to announce her arrival, even though she knew her father had seen her. She walked through the hallway, past the framed graduation photos of herself and her brother, Andrew. Her parents were sat in their easy chairs; Dad's slippered feet were stretched out on his foot rest. Anne Robinson's face dominated the television screen. *Watchdog,* the investigative consumer programme, was staple viewing for Heidi's parents. Heidi had always preferred *That's Life*'s approach to consumer investigative journalism and had once visited the BBC Television Centre to watch Esther Rantzen and the team record an episode.

'Look who's come to see you Elaine!' Heidi's father called out enthusiastically, hoping that his wife would show immediate signs of recognition.

Heidi gave her father a kiss on the forehead and then did likewise to her mother.

'So how are things going at work?' her father asked, as he did each time she visited.

'Well I'm not quite running the place yet but it feels like it sometimes,' said Heidi as she made herself comfortable on the settee.

'Remember what I always tell you—' he began.

'Yes I know,' said Heidi who knew this aphorism off by heart, 'you don't want to take orders from the boss, you want to be the boss.'

Heidi went into the kitchen to prepare something to eat. As she was leaving the living room she heard her mother whispering, 'Who's that?'

'That's your lovely baby daughter, Heidi!'

Heidi tried to force back the tears as her mother's words sunk into her consciousness. Andrew had visited a few weeks earlier with his girlfriend, and Elaine had seemed delighted to see her son. She had produced the obligatory embarrassing baby photos and regaled everyone with the story about when Andrew had got lost at Disneyland.

Spreading some mustard on a ham sandwich, Heidi wiped a tear from her eye. She didn't notice her father walk in.

'It's okay,' he said, putting his arm around her, 'she has trouble recognising me some days.'

Heidi dropped the knife and flung her arms around the only man who could make everything seem okay.

'She was fine when Andrew came around the other week; why is it always me she doesn't recognise; she always did hate me!'

'Andrew popped round yesterday lunchtime and she thought he was me,' he said with a smile, trying to put a brave face on things for his daughter.

'Oh Dad what are we going to do?'

'Well she certainly isn't going in any nursing home. I've heard lots of bad things about those places.'

As she began to eat her sandwich, Heidi digested her father's words with each bite. She couldn't help thinking about him having a life of his own, enjoying a few rounds of golf and everyone going round to the nursing home to visit Mum every few days. She imagined the nursing home to be something like the retirement village in *Waiting for God*. Mum playing the irascible and rebellious Stephanie Cole character, having lots of adventures and giving hell to the penny-pinching manager.

She finished her sandwich and then made a cup of tea for everyone. They all watched *Coronation Street* together just like the old days. Phyllis was trying to make Percy Sugden jealous by seeing a widower called Louis. Heidi watched the delight on her mother's face as she watched the machinations of Phyllis unfold.

'I think they've got some good characters in the show at the moment,' said Heidi in an attempt to gain a rational response from her mother.

'Oh they'll never beat Ena Sharples and Mini Cauldwell,' Elaine replied. 'I remember when Arthur Lowe used to be in *Coronation Street*. He used to play Leonard Swindley and ran a clothes shop called Gamma Garments. He even had his own spin-off programme called *Pardon the Expression!*'

Heidi's father looked at his daughter and gave her a wink.

'I can only remember starting to watch *Coronation Street* as far back as when Ernest Bishop was shot during a robbery,' said Heidi.

'Oh I remember you sitting with me and watching *Coronation Street* from when you were very small Heidi,' said Elaine. 'You always loved Stan and Hilda.'

Heidi left her parents' house feeling a little better after her mother had shown so much of her old lucidity. She decided to drop by at Jeanette's house and stopped at an off-licence to buy the kids some Jelly Tots. It was nearly half past eight but she knew that Jeanette's children would still be up and about.

She pulled up outside Jeanette's house which was tucked away in a corner of a small cul-de-sac. A tricycle was strewn across the garden path and an old cement mixer that had been left by the previous occupant was the sole garden ornament amidst the untended grass and discarded toys.

Heidi let herself into the house through the front door, which never seemed to be locked. She was greeted by Gemma, who was sat on the stairs playing with another little girl who lived next door. Gemma's friend had curly red hair that looked as though it needed a good wash and ice cream around her mouth. Gemma held her arms out for Heidi to lift her from the stairs. She was wearing the *Animaniacs* t-shirt that Heidi had bought her for her birthday. She had blonde hair, just like her mother, tied up in a ponytail, which reminded Heidi of Pebbles from *The Flintstones*.

With Gemma still in her arms, Heidi pushed open the door that led to the living room. Robbie was jumping up and down on the sofa in his Power Rangers pyjamas. Jeanette was stretched out in her favourite armchair, oblivious to the chaos. Heidi was always envious of Jeanette's slim figure, which she had retained effortlessly after giving birth to two children. She was engrossed in that evening's episode of *Eastenders*; one of the few occasions when Jeanette's volubility wasn't manifested. The usual dreary melodrama was taking place in Albert Square. Phil Mitchell was sat in a car kissing Kathy Beale.

'I thought Phil was supposed to be doing the dirty with Sharon behind Grant's back?' said Heidi with a baffled expression.

'No Grant found a tape with Sharon confessing to Michelle about her affair with Phil, and played it full blast in the Queen Vic during Phil and Kathy's engagement do,' explained Jeanette, the *Eastenders* aficionado. The drums kicked in to announce the closing credits and Heidi shook her head in disbelief. She always thought that *Eastenders* took itself too seriously and lacked the humour of *Coronation Street*.

'Gemma looks cool in the t-shirt,' said Heidi proudly.

'Oh she won't take it off, she loves it,' said Jeanette as she lit a cigarette.

'Did Greg come round for her birthday?' asked Heidi, referring to Jeanette's ne'er-do-well ex-husband.

'No he forgot again. At least he remembered to get her a Christmas present last year, that's something I suppose.'

'Oh yeah I forgot about the Rubik's Cube; how did she get on with that?'

'I think Robbie preferred it really; Gemma just peeled all the stickers off.'

'I remember having one of those about 15 years ago,' mused Heidi. 'Did you ever have one?'

'No I think I was already more interested in playing with boys by that time.'

'Oh Jeanette, you're incorrigible!'

Gemma had disappeared once again to re-join her playmate. Heidi played with Robbie, wishing that she had a couple of children of her own. Her experiences with men had been few and unhappy; she doubted whether she would ever meet a man who she would want to raise children with. She had worked so hard, studying assiduously at school and then at Bradford University. While people like Jeanette were partying and having casual sex, she had kept her nose to the grindstone.

Heidi had been assistant manager at the Mansfield branch of the Ackroyd's department store chain. She was later side-lined for the manager's job at the much larger Nottingham branch, until the entire company went into liquidation in 1992. When Heidi had been studying, her father had set aside some money for her to go travelling during her gap year, as her brother had done. Not wishing to break the momentum of her focus on studying, Heidi had declined the gap year option.

After being made redundant from Ackroyd's and depressed that she had been cruelly denied her chance of running her own branch, she decided to finally go travelling. She chose to go backpacking in Australia with a group of other young travellers. She soon found the stifling environment of sharing hostels and coaches with a group of people unbearable. As the entire group began to gradually disintegrate into bickering and backbiting, she bowed out gracefully with a young man called Gerald.

During her years of schooling, Heidi had resisted the temptation to become involved in relationships with members of the opposite sex. She had seen where long-term relationships could lead at first hand, listening to her parents argue on a regular basis. Her coquettish friend Jeanette had almost been raped and murdered after blindly copping off with a psychopath.

Heidi's real problem was that she had always set her standards too high. She had always pictured herself finding love with the school prefect or the store manager.

On several occasions she had become friends with young men who had been kind and made her laugh but she had always ultimately rejected them due to their failure to live up to her high standards.

Gerald belonged to the latter category but had come along when Heidi's spirits were at a low ebb. Homesick and upset by hurtful remarks made towards her by fellow travellers, Heidi found solace in the company of Gerald. During their stay in Melbourne, Heidi enjoyed reading and sleeping in a hotel bed while Gerald watched Australia play the West Indies in a test match at the Melbourne Cricket Ground.

Feeling relaxed and refreshed, Heidi finally succumbed to Gerald's easy charm, on Christmas Day of 1993, with the aid of a cork-tainted bottle of Shiraz. She fell head-over-heels in love with Gerald and her feet didn't hit the ground until they reached Adelaide and he had left her for a trainee dental technician from Redcar. Alone and with her funds dwindling, she was forced to spend a month gutting tuna in a fish processing plant in Port Lincoln.

As if reading Heidi's thoughts, Jeanette asked, 'So how are you getting on with this Prince Charming character at work; what's his name, Len?'

'Oh Les, no we're "just good friends" at the moment,' said Heidi, her cheeks beginning to glow. 'Do you remember that programme?' she asked, in an attempt to change the subject.

'No' said Jeanette, who was now engrossed in *Stars in Their Eyes*. The hirsute figure of Matthew Kelly was introducing an obese car insurance salesman with a cleft palate who announced proudly, 'Tonight Matthew I'm going to be Tip Topley.' The plucky contestant waddled away towards the rear of the stage where a huge star rose up to reveal a triangular doorway. He disappeared into a cloud of dry ice and then instantly, with the magic of editing, re-appeared in the guise of Tip Topley. Heidi was always reminded of *Mr Benn* whenever she watched this ritual take place.

The transformation was quite breathtaking, 'This bit always reminds me of the final scene in *The Fly*,' said Jeanette.

Wearing a long flowing auburn wig, a denim jacket and tight leather trousers, the contestant looked more like Tina Turner than Tip Topley. He began to gyrate his hips and launched into a flat approximation of *No Time for Foolery*.

'Oh wow!' said Jeanette. 'Is he supposed to be Rod Stewart?'

At that moment, Gemma and her friend came into the living room with Robbie toddling along behind them. Gemma walked into the middle of the room and produced a large purple vibrator.

'Look Heidi!' she said triumphantly, 'I've found Mummy's favourite toy.'

Jeanette moved for the first time that evening and grabbed the vibrator from Gemma.

'What have I told you about going into Mummy's bedroom!' she screamed. 'Right, bedtime! Time for you to go home now Ellie.'

She grabbed Gemma by the hand and led her out of the room with the vibrator in her other hand. Heidi sat with her mouth open in amazement and then concluded that it was a pretty ordinary event in the life of Jeanette.

CHAPTER FIVE

Crossing the road from the Sandy Lane Workingmen's Club, Sammy returned to the little Portakabin that served as his base. It was nearly time for him to make his bi-hourly call to headquarters to establish that he was still awake and in one piece. He had been reluctant to tear himself away from the convivial atmosphere of the club. It had been worth the small fee to make himself a member and he considered himself fortunate to have been posted in such a convenient location.

He was disappointed that he had missed the chance to play the Snowball bingo which would have been worth eighty pounds if he had won. At least he wasn't riding his bike as far as South Normanton to guard the creepy abattoir.

'Sandy Lane checking in; everything okay here,' he said without waiting for a reply and then put the telephone down. He could settle down again for another two hours.

He thought about his boss, sat in his nice warm living room with his beloved Doberman Pinschers. Sammy was sure that his boss preferred those evil looking dogs to his wife. Every week Sammy was forced to make the journey to the premises of Leonidas Security to collect his wages. The sinister figure of his employer, Ben Froggatt, would sit at his desk scrutinising Sammy with his Dobermans either side of him. The door to Frogatt's house where he ran his business would always be opened by his wife. Behind her medication-addled smile her eyes seemed to be crying out, 'Get me the fuck out of here!' The ex-copper had an albino quality with his deathly pale skin and hair. Sammy thought of Froggatt as a cross between Ralph Fiennes in *Schindler's List* and the ghost of Jacob Marley.

Sammy put on his headphones and proceeded to roll a big joint. After about half an hour he was beginning to grow bored, calculating that he had another seven hours of purgatory to endure. When he arrived earlier in the evening at seven he had his session at the club to look forward to. Once he had relieved his colleague on the day shift, he would always be there in time for the first bingo session. It would always take ages for him to get rid of the officious Malc Cromwell, who would have to brief him on every single youth he had seen roaming near to the site. They were only keeping an eye on a new community centre. A trip round the back for a piss every hour or two was enough surveillance as far as Sammy was concerned.

Cromwell was Ben Froggatt's favourite security guard; almost an honorary Doberman. He was practically the only member of the team who had been presented with a proper security guard uniform. The quick turnover of employees gave Froggatt cause to be reluctant to spend money on uniforms when the average tenure of his guards was around three months. Malc Cromwell was a retired traffic warden who subsidised his meagre pension by working as a security guard. Some said that he was massively in debt and continued to work to pay off his creditors. Either way he seemed to live for his job, always preferring nightshifts so he could sleep for most of the night and then get back home in time to do his job as a lollypop man. Malc had requested a week on the day shift so he could take part in a dominoes tournament in his role as captain of the Park Hall Tavern dominoes team.

Sammy decided to ring around his friends to see if anyone was available to come over and keep him company. The construction company's phone was only meant to be used to contact headquarters but the guards would regularly phone each other to help pass the time on their lonely shifts.

A sudden knock on the door caused Sammy to almost jump out of his skin. Still feeling the after-effects of the joint, he was feeling slightly paranoid. It was always a strain on the nerves for Sammy, sat alone all-night, wondering if a crazed junkie might be lurking around. He had already gotten into trouble when thieves had waded across a river and stolen an entire roll of copper cable from another site while Sammy had been inside his office asleep.

He pusillanimously peered around the door and was relieved to find that it was only, Jess Durward. Old Jess lived several doors from the site and was a regular visitor to Malc Cromwell whenever he was on shift. Malc would always make the octogenarian a cup of tea.

Jess scrutinised Sammy as though he might be some kind of imposter who had usurped Malc by some despicable means.

'Where's Malc?' he asked curtly, peering past Sammy to see if Malc might be tied up and gagged inside the Portakabin.

'No mate he's playing dominoes tonight, do you want to come in for a cuppa mate; get a warm?'

'No I don't want a cup of tea!' said Jess, thinking it might be another trap.

The head of a Jack Russell terrier poked out of Jess's overcoat and growled at Sammy.

'Nice dog mate,' Sammy offered lamely, 'My gran's got a Jack Russell.'

'When's Malc back again?'

'I think he's back again tomorrow night. I'm off this weekend; first time I've had a proper weekend off since I started this job.'

Without another word, Jess turned around and began shuffling back to his bungalow.

'That's it fuck off you smelly old twat!' said Sammy, just loudly enough for the old man to hear.

Free of his unwanted visitor, Sammy once again picked up the phone. He rang up his friend Luke Walsh to see if he was going to the Vibealite rave on Saturday night at Venue 44. The phone was answered by Luke's younger sister, Lorna. Luke's sister was only 16 and had a crush on Sammy. After finally stopping her from talking, he ascertained that Luke was out and would probably be hanging out with the rest of the boy racers on the circuit. Sammy was delighted to discover that Luke had purchased a Motorola mobile phone.

After jotting down Luke's mobile phone number, Sammy dialled the number. After receiving no reply on the first attempt, he was about to hang up the second time when Luke finally replied.

'Who's that?' called out a voice that Sammy could barely discern amidst the sound of happy hardcore music.

'It's me Sammy! Turn the fucking sounds down man!'

'Sammy! How's it hangin' bro?'

'Sweet mate, sweet. Are you on for Vibealite tomorrow?'

'Can't hear you mate!' called out Luke, competing with the sound of Slipmatt. 'We're down on the car park on Toothill Lane. Where are you?'

Sammy was having trouble hearing Luke as the mobile phone signal began to break up. He heard Luke revving up his Nova SRI and then the line went dead.

Several minutes later the phone began to ring and Sammy grabbed the handset, expecting to hear the sound of Luke's voice. He was disappointed to hear, not the melodious tone of his friend, but the nasal whining of Clive McLain.

'Where's Malc?' said Sammy's work colleague after shrewdly deducing that it wasn't Malc answering the phone.'

Sammy's heart sank as he anticipated a long, tedious account of Clive's shift so far. As Clive began to drone incessantly on the other end of the line, Sammy began to wish he had studied harder at school.

'And then Ben Froggatt said to me you're at the abattoir tonight and I said no because he knows I hate and detest the place and then…'

Sammy looked out of the window and tuned out while Clive continued talking at him. He watched a couple walking home from a night on the town. They were arm in arm, loved up. *I bet they will be going bang at it when they get home*, thought Sammy. He began to think about Judy and the baby. Having a great girlfriend and a child had probably been the best thing that had happened to him but he had thrown it all away. He had to confess that he had been immature and totally incapable of commitment. All he had really wanted to do was go out with his friends occasionally, but Judy had constantly put her foot down. In the end she had grown tired of his indolence and puerile nature and sent him packing.

'Because my brother went off with Ben Froggatt's son's woman and he gives me all the shit sites and I said…'continued Clive in his interminable diatribe.

'Shit!' exclaimed Sammy, unable to continue listening any longer. 'Ben Froggatt's just arrived, I'd better hang up.'

'Well he got there quick then, he's only just…' said Clive before Sammy slammed down the phone.

Sammy decided to take a look outside. He didn't really need a piss but he was so bored already that he decided to patrol round the site. Once outside he began to enjoy the fresh autumn air. He decided to pay his neighbour a visit on the Bath Lane site. It was only a short walk down to the sewage treatment works on Bath Lane. The entire site was undergoing major redevelopment and Leonidas security guards patrolled its gloomy environs. With vast areas of the site resembling the Somme and the sulphurous smell of the sewage works, the place resembled Milton's vision of Tartarus. It had been here that thieves had crossed the river and stolen the copper wire while Sammy was asleep. The site and all its equipment was constantly being scrutinised by local villains.

The gates to the site were open when Sammy arrived. He could see the lights of the construction firm's offices casting a beacon amidst the all-enveloping darkness. Sammy was expecting to find Albert Nash, probably sound asleep or watching his portable television. Albert was one of the few guards who Sammy could endure for more than a few minutes.

Albert was a sanguine character, the antithesis of the irascible Malc Cromwell or the resentful and vindictive Clive McLain. He had held a regular post guarding the Renault showroom on Sutton Road until he had witnessed an attempted robbery. After being called as a witness to the crime, he had been subjected to intimidation during his shifts and had been consequently moved to another site.

Sammy surreptitiously crept towards the window beside where he expected Albert to be sitting asleep. Crouching beneath the window sill, he prepared to leap up like a jack-in-a-box and give Albert the fright of his life. Springing up from his crouched position with all the agility of a frog, Sammy discovered that a different guard was seated in Albert's usual spot. The stranger was sat with his back to the window and hadn't even noticed Sammy's unexpected appearance. Sammy couldn't make out much of the new guard, but he appeared to be much younger than the sexagenarian Albert Nash. His hair was styled with frosted and gelled tips of blond which contrasted with the darker hair at the base that revealed his natural colour. He seemed to be lost in his own thoughts, staring into space.

Sammy tapped on the window but the stranger was so absorbed in his own meditations that he didn't take any notice. Sammy decided to walk round to the door and let himself into the office. He opened the door and was greeted by the sound of loud music, which explained why his tapping hadn't been heard. He walked through the kitchen area and prepared to open the door into the office without startling its sole occupant. As he stood before the door he suddenly recognised the music he was listening too – a song that he hadn't recognised ended and a conversation began between a couple of cockneys about going out for a drink. Sammy thought that he was listening to a clip from *Eastenders* until he recognised a familiar punk rock power chord sequence. The unmistakable lyrics to *Hurry Up Harry* by Sham 69 brought back a flood of memories for Sammy. He recalled hearing an album called *That's Life* by the band, which had been a favourite amongst the punk crowd he used to hang out with. The album's songs were interspersed with snatches of conversation, telling the story of a day in the life of a teenager, struggling to come to terms with adult life. Sammy had once heard someone refer to *That's Life* as a punk version of *Quadrophenia*.

Intrigued by the musical taste of the new guard, Sammy burst through the door. Totally unfazed by this sudden unexpected visitor, the occupant of the swivel chair merely swung the chair round to get a better view of the new arrival.

There was something decidedly familiar about the face that smiled at Sammy. Behind the beer belly and the hair gel lurked an anarchic Achilles who Sammy had followed like a punk Patroclus. He was face to face with a man he hadn't seen for 10 years.

'Where have you been all me life?' said Sammy

'Here and there,' replied Spike.

CHAPTER SIX

Spike had indeed been here and there since the days in which he had been the punk prince of Meden Vale and Sammy and Dog his devoted squires. He followed his best friend John Freeman to London in the summer of 1985 and stayed there for a year, residing in various squats. He had a brief fling with a new age traveller who lived in a converted ambulance until she decided that it was high time that they raised a drove of tiny hippies.

Spike searched far and wide for some deeper meaning in his life like a latter-day Candide. In 1989 he surprised everyone by taking the Queen's shilling and enlisting in the army. He spent several years stationed with 40th Field Regiment of the Royal Artillery that was part of the 1st Armoured Division in the town of Verden in West Germany. He trained as a loader as part of a crew that manned a Challenger 1 battle tank. He soon grew disenchanted with army life as he settled into a routine and spent his free time drinking the local beer and drifting into relationships with German women.

Everything changed in 1990 when the armed forces of Iraq invaded neighbouring Kuwait. A United States-led coalition force began a build-up of troops in Saudi Arabia in preparation to liberate the people of Kuwait. Spike took part in the heroic confrontation known as the Battle of Norfolk. The British tanks of the 1st Armoured Division supported the much larger United States contingent by guarding its right flank from the possibility of a counter-attack by the tanks of Saddam Hussain's Republican Guard. Like the armies of the Hellenic League under the leadership of Alexander the Great at Gaugamela, they won a decisive victory.

Spike came home with a Queen's Gallantry Medal and an assortment of mysterious mental and physical ailments that would come to be known as Gulf War Syndrome. He returned to Mansfield after his time in the army, greeted by a piece in the local newspaper about 'The former punk rocker turned war hero'. His return was hastened by the death of his grandfather, whose lungs were decimated by Emphysema.

The skills Spike had learned during his time in the armed forces weren't easily transferred to civilian life and he took a job as a retail security guard until he was caught allowing a young homeless girl to walk out of the store without paying for a packet of biscuits. With his references somewhat in tatters, he found a job with Leonidas Security where few questions were asked during his interview.

'I heard you were in the army,' said Sammy. 'What's up, did it do your head in?'

Spike continued smiling at his young friend. Sammy had altered considerably since the days when he bunked off school in favour of going on poaching trips with Spike and John.

'Aren't you cold dressed like that?' asked Spike, checking out Sammy's worn looking blue shell suit.

'It's all I've got for this job, I don't want to get my best stuff dirty. The tight bastards are supposed to supply a uniform by law or something aren't they?'

Spike was dressed in clothes that didn't look that different to the ones he used to wear for poaching expeditions in his punk days. He still had his old camouflage jacket and a pair of 14-hole Dr. Martens. He was wearing the blue crew-necked pullover he had been given during his time as a retail security guard.

'So, did you see any action when you were in the army then?' asked Sammy.

'Not much,' said Spike, reluctant to discuss the harrowing scenes he had seen during the Gulf War. 'Boring really. Not much has changed around here has it?' he said, attempting to change the subject.

'Yeah, Dog still lives in the village and hangs around in the garages all the time playing football.'

'I can think of worse things to spend your life doing. I heard you had a kid?'

'Yeah I soon binned that off,' replied Sammy without any trace of emotion, 'I like my freedom too much.'

'So have you got anything else lined up or are you planning on doing this for the foreseeable?'

'I can't see me lasting much longer to be honest. Froggatt is always on my back for one thing or another. Have you had the pleasure of meeting him yet?'

'Yeah,' said Spike, yawning with boredom and fatigue, 'typical fucking ex-copper.'

After an hour of reminiscences about the old times, Spike was growing tired of Sammy's company and felt desperately in need of a nap. He walked with Sammy as far as the gates and returned to the site office. He settled down in his chair with the sound of a BBC World Service programme about the Putney Debates lulling him into a peaceful sleep.

The sound of the telephone startled him into consciousness and he suddenly realised that he had forgotten to make his call to headquarters.

'You weren't asleep were you?' Ben Froggatt asked in an agitated tone of voice.

'Sorry I've just been for a look round the site and I thought I saw some lads hanging around the perimeter fence so I've been keeping an eye on them.'

'Okay,' said Froggatt, reassured by Spike's ostensible vigilance. 'Just be careful they don't lull you down one end of the site while they have someone else rifling the site office. You lock the door each time you go out, don't you?'

'Yeah every time,' replied Spike. 'I'd better get out there and make sure they're not still hanging around.'

He replaced the receiver and settled down once again for another catnap. He looked at the clock and was pleased to find that he only had two hours left until his shift ended.

His doze took him almost to the end of the shift. It was becoming light outside, still a week till the clocks went back and the light of day would be rationed to school hours. Spike felt refreshed after his long rest. Since coming back from the Persian Gulf he had regular bouts of fatigue and aches in his joints. He was regularly afflicted with headaches that he often had to endure through bouts of insomnia. No logical cause had been singled out for the various symptoms that thousands of Gulf War veterans had contracted since the conflict. Spike suspected that some kind of nerve agent had been used by the Americans; a strategy which had somehow backfired when the wind direction had changed or the speed of the coalition advance had brought them into contact with chemicals intended for the enemy. He figured that if Saddam Hussain had ordered the use of nerve agents or chemical weapons, the whole world would have soon known about it.

Spike walked outside and found to his surprise that it was pleasantly mild for the time of year. He had missed the temperate climate of England when he had been stationed in Saudi Arabia. The scorching hot days in the desert would quickly be transformed into cold nights. Night time would descend in those tropical regions with the rapidity of a cover over a budgie cage. Spike preferred the gloaming of long British summer days.

A sudden dryness in his mouth instilled a raging thirst for the beer, which he would drink when he got home. A 3-litre bottle of lager would usually help him get some sleep. Quenching his thirst in the hot and dry climate of Saudi Arabia had been the hardest part of being stationed in a country where alcohol is forbidden. Occasionally whisky had been smuggled in in shampoo bottles. The soapy aftertaste had somehow made him feel nostalgic for the beer he used to drink in the Blue Boar in Mansfield.

He took a last walk around the perimeter of the site and checked that all the plant-hire equipment was still all present and correct. Remembering the telephone conversation he had had with Ben Froggatt, Spike went back into the office to fill in the report book. He added an entry for 05:00 hours to the effect that he had monitored the movements of three youths who seemed to be attempting entry to the site from across the river.

It was nearly time for Spike's opposite number to arrive and he decided to greet him by appearing to be diligently patrolling the site. He walked over to the riverside where the copper cable had been purloined several weeks earlier. A large wooden cable drum was still sat in the middle of the river, bereft of its copper. Elsewhere a shopping trolley protruded from the murky water.

A pile of black rags suddenly caught Spike's attention. At first he thought he was looking at some old clothes that were caught amongst the detritus that mingled amongst the rocks and weeds of the river. A white line down one side of the black bundle appeared on closer inspection to be the stripes on the side of an Adidas track suit. Spike, who was still half asleep, shook himself out of his groggy lethargy and waded into the water. With only preservation of life on his mind, he grabbed the body that lay face down on the shallow river bed. He grabbed the tracksuit-clad figure by the arms and attempted to turn over the body. Finding no immediate signs of life, he grabbed the body beneath the arms and dragged it to the riverbank. Panicking, Spike quickly tried to remember the first aid course he had attended when he had been a member of the Boys' Brigade. He looked down at the face of a young man in his mid-20s and the face of Sergeant Mick Riley stared up at Spike, life draining out of him amidst the fog of battle, screaming, 'Don't let me die!' Spike suddenly remembered that he needed to check whether the youth was breathing. Pulling himself together he checked for a pulse and, unable to find any sign of breathing, Spike took a deep breath and braced himself to administer mouth-to-mouth resuscitation. As he placed his lips against the cold mouth of the young man, he heard the sound of an approaching car.

CHAPTER SEVEN

John slammed the front door and marched into the kitchen where Sally was ironing.

'You're early,' she said with an expression of concern, 'are you sick? You don't look very well.'

'Where's the *Chad*? I need to start looking for another job.'

'Don't tell me they've laid you off; they can't have. What's happened?'

'They put me on a new job where you have to put coloured paint into bevelled window panes,' explained John. 'This powder that you have to mix is really toxic and it can blow up in your face if you mix it wrong. Anyway they said you're supposed to wear a special breathing mask to do this job safely, but they said it wasn't working properly so I'd have to do the job without it.'

'So did you ask them to put you on another job?' asked Sally, sensing that their fragile world was about to collapse again.

'No I said I wasn't going to do it without the mask, so they said if I wouldn't do the job they would get someone else who would.'

'They can't do that!' screamed Sally. 'Surely you can take them to a tribunal or something?'

'They've been trying to get rid of me for ages; they can shove their job up their arse.'

'Oh fucking great!' Sally shouted as she stormed out of the room, slamming the door behind her. 'Great fucking Christmas it's going to be this year!'

The little black and white portable TV that sat on the top of the fridge was showing an episode of *Fifteen to One*. William G. Stewart was asking which English monarch was the subject of a play by Christopher Marlowe. John switched off the set and then unplugged the iron. He sat down at the dining table pushing a pile of laundry that needed ironing to one side so he could read the *Chad*.

He turned the pages of the *Mansfield and Ashfield Chronicle and Advertiser* in search of the situations vacant section. The local newspaper was better known as the *Chad;* an acronym that suggested that the writing was on the wall. Finding the job vacancies in the *Chad* could be as laborious a task as finding a sex scene in *Lady Chatterley's Lover.* He searched through endless pages of real estate adverts, photos of scout jamborees and smiling councillors. Finally, he found a single page devoted to job recruitment. Amongst half a dozen vacancies for skilled overlockers and Mig and Tig welders, he found only one job vacancy that stated no previous experience was necessary. Unfortunately, this position was situated at the double glazing factory that he had just walked out of.

He turned to the front page and read the lead story about the murder of a 24-year-old man who was identified as Stephen Andrews and lived in Clipstone. The man had been found lying dead in the River Maun, next to the sewage works on Bath Lane. A coroner's report concluded that the death had been caused by several blows to the head with a heavy object. A security guard who had found the body was helping police with their investigations.

John didn't immediately recognise the name of the murder victim until it occurred to him that Stephen was the christian name of a local junkie known as 'Nappy' Andrews. He had been responsible for a series of burglaries in the Forest Town area. One of John's work colleagues had been amongst those who had had their homes broken into. Andrew's, who was the son of a milkman, would check his father's order book to find out which of his customers was on holiday and then break into the empty property. Consequently, Nappy's father began to lose custom and was forced to quit his round. Nappy continued to obtain money for heroin by any means possible.

A pile of letters lay on the table, almost obscured by the washing that John had previously moved. He looked through the bills for gas, electric and council tax, recalling the old expression that it never rains but it pours. He was surprised to find a small blue envelope with a hand-written address and an Irish postage stamp bearing the image of a goldcrest. He opened the envelope which was addressed to himself and found a hand-written letter inside. John proceeded to read the neat italic handwriting on the pale blue writing paper. The address on the top right side of the letter revealed that it was from his old friend Ray Keaton.

'Hello my auld flower, how are you?

Hope all is well with you and Sally. Sorry I didn't see you before I departed but everything happened so quickly that I barely had time to say farewell to anyone.

Anyway, since I've returned to the "Auld Sod" it's just been work, work and more work! I've been teaching at a school called Clongowes Wood College, where James Joyce himself once studied. (Read *A Portrait of the Artist as a Young Man*.) I've found the time to write a new collection of poetry and I'm scheduled to do a tour of the United Kingdom soon. Would you believe, on the list of tour dates I'm performing at Mansfield Arts Centre on the 26th of November. I was hoping we might be able to meet up and maybe you could even put me up for a couple of nights and save me a few quid on a hotel.

Congratulations on becoming a daddy by the way. Hope Podge is well and I can't wait to see the wee fella. How's yer man Spike these days? Is he still living the dream bless him?

Anyway you've got my number so let me know if it's okay for me to come over next month.

Best Wishes

Ray'

John's spirits were raised considerably by the unexpected correspondence of his old friend. When John had moved down to London in 1985 to make a new life for himself, Ray's friendship had been a lifeline. Ray, who was already a published poet back then, had nurtured a love of literature in John. It had been John's wish to study arts and humanities with the Open University, but he had been forced to quit after only one module due to the commitments of work and parenthood.

Sally returned to the kitchen and had evidently been crying.

'Look don't worry I'll sort it out,' said John reassuringly. 'I'll get a job with that security firm that Spike is working for; he says they'll take on anyone and aren't fussy about references.'

'Oh fucking brilliant. So then I'll never see you, working 14-hour nights and then going to bed when you get in.'

'I'll have to get some sleep when I'm on the job, like Spike does. Then I'll have plenty of time to spend with you and Kevin in the daytime.'

Sally sat down at John's feet and rested her chin on his knee. She was already feeling depressed and her sense of hopelessness was now heightened by John's latest piece of bad news. It seemed as though she had nothing to lose when they had first met and now she couldn't believe she was reduced to worrying about buying Christmas presents and paying the council tax.

'What time is Mum bringing Kevin back from the swimming baths?' asked John.

'They didn't go out till just before you came home so they should be a couple of hours yet.'

'Why don't we go down to the Sunnydale for one before they get back?' suggested John naively.

'Yeah and then we can go for an Indian,' said Sally with barely concealed sarcasm. 'We haven't got any fucking money!'

They sat in silence for a while, John stroking Sally's hair as if it might somehow solve all their problems. Sally found John's grooming quite therapeutic and felt a sudden urge to drop to sleep. She began absent-mindedly rubbing John's thigh and as her hand strayed towards the crotch of his jeans, she discovered that she was unintentionally arousing him. She hadn't felt like having sex for ages and John's erection was the last thing she had been expecting as a consequence of the current crisis.

'You can forget that as well you dirty bastard!' she snapped.

'Whaaat?' replied John like a schoolboy caught with his fingers in a jar of sweets.

'Anyway your mum will be here with Kevin in a bit, so we haven't got time.' Sally said as she stood up and prepared to put the ironed laundry away.

'Hey Dad's supposed to be lending me that video camera. We could make those videos you wanted to do and make a fortune selling them,' suggested John with a cheeky grin.

'Oh come on then, it's been ages since we've had a good fuck,' said Sally, taking John by the hand and leading him to the stairs. 'At least it's free and I need something to cheer me up.'

While Sally was leading the way upstairs. John grabbed her and began to pull down her jogging pants. She wasn't wearing any knickers and began to giggle as John started to kiss her buttocks and teased her with his tongue. She playfully pushed him away, pulling up her pants and continuing up the stairs.

Once in the bedroom she went over to the window and closed the curtains. She felt John's hands grabbing her by the waist and then lifting up her faded black Fred Perry polo shirt. He pulled the cups of her bra down to reveal her breasts and began to tease her nipples and kiss her neck. She sighed with pleasure as all the tension in her neck and shoulders began to evaporate. His right hand began to stray down her naval and beyond and then Sally grabbed his hand and turned around, pushing him onto the bed.

Sally undid John's belt and jeans and watched his erection spring from his boxer shorts as she yanked them down to his knees.

'Remember the first time I did this to you behind that pub in London?' she remarked as she planted kisses along the length of John's penis.

'Mmm,' was all that John could come up with in response. He was lost in a world of pleasure, far from the troubles of reality.

He was about to enjoy the pleasure of Sally's mouth encircling the tip of his penis when a loud knocking on the door put a dampener on their brief respite.

'Shit, their back already!' said Sally, springing up from her kneeling position and adjusting her clothes. John hurriedly pulled up his jeans and boxer shorts, trying to find room for his redundant erection.

Sally had already bounded down the stairs before he had carefully zipped up his jeans, anxious not to cause any accidents. He made his way downstairs and heard Sally speaking to someone at the door. When he arrived in the hallway he was surprised to see, instead of his mother and son, the towering figure of Spike.

Disappointment quickly turned to joy as he invited Spike into the kitchen. He recounted the events of the day to his friend who it seemed had also lost his job earlier that day.

'Have you read about this murder on Bath Lane?' said Spike, pointing at the *Chad*. John nodded in the affirmative and Spike explained, 'Well I was the security guard that found the body. I've been in and out of the police station answering questions all week. They keep asking me the same things, trying to trip me up as if they think I've got something to do with it.'

'So are you out on bail then?' asked Sally, leaning against the wooden surround of the electric fire.

'No they haven't charged me but they've told me I've got to stay in the area because they will probably have some more questions for me. I was only trying to give him the kiss of life and they think I'm the murderer.'

John sat in silence, trying to think of something helpful to say.

'How come you've got the sack then?' asked Sally. 'That can't be right can it if nothing has been proved?'

'Well the thing is I fell asleep and missed my call to the gaffer. I'm supposed to call in every two hours to let them know I'm okay,' Spike explained. 'I told him there were some lads hanging around and I was outside keeping an eye on them. Then I had to write down in the report book that I had seen people hanging about and the police checked it and it turns out that the coroner's report has the time of death at about the same time I reported seeing these lads.'

'Why didn't you just tell them you were lying to your boss?' enquired John.

'I did and now I'm out of a job as well as a fucking murder suspect.'

'Looks like you're both looking for a new job then,' said Sally.

Spike turned over the pages of the *Chad* in the hope that he might find a job vacancy.

'I wouldn't waste your time looking in there,' said John despondently, 'unless you fancy giving the shithole I've just walked out of a try.'

'I saw Feggy Edwards in town earlier on,' said Spike. 'He's working at that Tsucol place on Hermitage Lane.'

'Yeah,' replied John cynically, 'it's down the road from where I was working. I can't see us as sewing machinists somehow.'

'Well Feggy says it's not that bad apparently. There are a lot of ex-miners there and they're crying out for workers.'

The conversation was interrupted by the arrival of John's mum, Maggie, and Kevin. The pair of them were flushed from their exertions at the Water Meadows swimming complex and their damp hair was combed greaser style.

'He's worn me out this little monster, chasing him up those stairs and down that water chute,' said Maggie Freeman in a tone that could barely suppress her adoration for her grandson.

'Was it busy?' asked Sally.

'Oh it was snided with dole scroungers,' replied Maggie querulously, 'it's free to get in apparently on a Wednesday if you show them your signing-on card.'

Kevin was busily laughing and farting as John tickled his belly.

'Ooh John, take him to the toilet if he wants to do a dirty!' said Maggie as the smell reached her nostrils. Spike seemed to find this remark hilarious and began to snigger.

'And you're not too big to get a smacked arse!' said Maggie, playfully slapping Spike on the arm.

'Is that a promise?' said Spike, blushing like a schoolboy with a crush on his teacher.

Maggie coquettishly smiled at Spike and concluded that he didn't look too bad since shaving off his mohican and smartening up a bit.

'I'll have you know I'm old enough to be your mother,' said Maggie as if it might come as a surprise to Spike.

'You know what they say,' said Spike, who was enjoying the flirtation, 'there's many a fine tune played on an old fiddle.'

Maggie flirtatiously pushed herself against Spike. 'Cheeky sod. Hark at him Sally!'

'You want to watch him Maggie, he's a dark horse that one,' said Sally who knew a thing or two about Spike's sexual prowess.

It came as a relief to John when his mother announced that she needed to get home and get ready for her and Alex's line dancing class. Watching Maggie's embarrassing attempts to display her mature sexuality never failed to make him cringe. The memory of her drunken bump and grind routine on the dancefloor during his wedding reception was still a source of neuroses for John, worthy of hours of psychoanalysis.

'So, are we going to see about this Tsucol place then?' asked Spike as he prepared to leave.

'Doesn't look like I have much choice,' replied John, looking sheepishly at Sally.

'Looks like we've got a couple of budding seamstresses here son,' said Sally as she picked up Kevin.

'I'm not bothered whether I'm a sea mistress or a sewist, I'll try anything once,' said Spike as he stepped out into the November gloom.

CHAPTER EIGHT

I had been unable to pursuade Myfanwy to accompany me to the arts theatre for the poetry reading, so I decided to go alone. I mentioned to Heidi at work that I was interested in going to see Ray Keaton. It had been the first time we had spoken for 10 years and she asked if I was still a budding student of the art of poetry. I didn't bother to explain that my father had shattered my confidence with his withering remarks about it being a load of bullshit, just like the rubbish that Ian called art.

I had decided to renew my passion for verse and brought a ticket for Keaton's poetry reading in the hope of gaining some much-needed inspiration. I wasn't sure whether there would be a great deal of interest in the event and was surprised when I walked along Leeming Street towards the arts theatre to find a group of people waiting outside.

On closer inspection I discovered that there seemed to be a disturbance of some kind taking place. A police officer was attempting to calm down a group of surly looking men, several of whom I recognised as local football hooligans. The police officer was surrounded by half a dozen men and was face to face with a man I recognised as Cuckoo Walsh. Walsh's associates seemed to be egging their leader on as he lambasted the policeman about their right to make a peaceful protest.

While the thugs were occupied with wasting valuable police time, I took the opportunity to enter the arts theatre unmolested. The droning rendition of 'No surrender to the IRA' led me to believe that they were targeting the poetry of a peaceful Irish poet for their protest against the latest Republican bombing campaign. I recalled watching the documentary about the far-right group known as the British Free Corps and Myfanwy's revelation about Walsh's involvement with that organisation.

I bought a drink at the bar and browsed through some of the literature that was on sale. Keaton's new book of poetry, *Fall of a Tartar*, was on sale. I bought a copy of the slim paperback book which fitted neatly into my wax jacket. I made my way into the small auditorium that would probably accommodate no more than a hundred people. I looked around and saw the usual arts theatre clientele; school teachers and students mostly and the usual local characters who would turn up for any event rather than stay at home alone.

I was surprised to see an old face that I recognised from my days growing up in the village of Meden Vale. John Freeman was several years older than me and had played with me when I was a little boy, when our fathers had been close friends. I hadn't seen him for some years and he had altered his appearance since his days as a punk rocker. I was more surprised when I suddenly recognised the man who sat next to John as Ray Keaton himself. The two were engrossed in conversation and clearly knew one another quite intimately.

A bespectacled middle-aged man in a corduroy jacket and jeans appeared on the small stage and announced Ray. He had the look of a comprehensive school history teacher, who one minute might tell you about his misspent youth listening to Jethro Tull records and the next throwing a blackboard rubber at you. As he spoke he wrung his hands nervously and his prominent Adam's Apple bounced up and down with excitement. An obsequious contingent of culture lovers laughed and applauded every excuse for a witticism that he uttered. They were the kind of people who always laugh a little too loud during a Shakespeare comedy to display their knowledge of early modern language.

After the interminable introduction came to an end, Ray Keaton ambled onto the stage. He humbly nodded his appreciation for the warm welcome and apologised for the behaviour of the rambunctious critics who had been present outside the theatre.

Keaton had an easy manner and spoke with a broad Dublin accent. He was casually dressed in a blue chequered shirt and cream coloured chinos. He began with a poem from his latest collection, which he said was inspired by 'An auld German fella called Heidegger'.

I find myself in the clearing of being,
but leave behind fragments, that might have been.
The essence of truth is always illusive.
Chasing butterflies with a broken net,
we skip through life's meadows, to the water's edge,
where a weeping philosopher dips golden toes.

I was mesmerised by his performance and the music of the words he spoke. The meaning of each poem eluded me, but he could create alchemy with his choice of words. As he threw back his head and spoke each line in a robust, declamatory style, I was reminded of the Celtic bards of ancient Britain.

The reading lasted for an hour and the reverent silence that accompanied each poem was replaced by rapturous applause when the performance ended. Several people approached Keaton to shake hands or get a copy of his book signed. I considered asking him to sign my own copy but felt too shy to speak to him.

I made my way down the aisle between the seats as Ray patiently answered a string of pedantic questions about the metre and rhythm of his verse. I noticed John Freeman still occupying his seat, patiently waiting for Ray to finish talking. As I passed John, he looked up and I noticed a gleam of recognition in his eye.

'Is that Dean Swift?' he said, obviously feeling somewhat left out of the intellectual discourse taking place between the poet and his fans. 'You've altered a bit since I last saw you.'

'Ayup John I thought I recognised you. I didn't think this was your scene; I thought John Cooper Clark would be more your thing.'

'No I'm just working as Ray's roadie, I carry his books to the car and back.'

'Wow nice job! I bet you're swamped with groupies all the time.'

'Yeah as you can see they're constantly trying to rip Ray's clothes off,' replied John, nodding towards a corpulently built lady in a pashmina, who was asking Ray whether he thought *The Waste Land* was the greatest poem ever written.

'Well I think I'm going to head across to the Masons for some refreshment,' I said, trying to sound cool.

I left the stiflingly pretentious atmosphere of the arts theatre and crossed the road to the Masons Arms public house. I opened the door and was greeted by the familiar sound of *Radar Love* by Golden Earring on the jukebox. I expected the lounge to be empty at ten o'clock in the middle of the week, but there were probably a dozen people scattered around the room. As I stood at the bar I could see through to the games room where an old Teddy Boy in a wheelchair was playing pool with a bearded man who wore a top hat and a black waistcoat.

I nodded to a man dressed in a long leather overcoat and a broad brimmed hat and sunglasses. He was a fan of The Mission and liked to dress in the iconic attire of the band's singer, Wayne Hussey. Unfortunately, his stocky build and snub nose made him look more like a gothic version of John Belushi in *The Blues Brothers*.

At the far end of the lounge sat a group of bikers who wore leather vests emblazoned with the insignia of the Robespierre's Barbers Motorcycle Club. Malcolm the convivial landlord came over and served me. He was a short, rotund man with a luxuriant moustache. His wife was of similar build, always wearing black, with her dark, greying hair tied back. The pair had the appearance of a couple of Italian peasants who might crack open a bottle of chianti and string up a dictator at any moment.

I sat on a stool at the bar and drank my pint of Guinness and settled down for the lengthy guitar break on *Freebird*. I eavesdropped on a conversation between a man with a leonine head of blond hair, who wore a Marillion t-shirt, and an older man with grey hair, tied in a ponytail. The older man wore a denim jacket that looked as though it had been borrowed from Jim Ignatowski from *Taxi*. The younger man was enthusiastically eulogising *The Doors of perception* by Aldous Huxley. I always thought that whereas Evelyn Waugh was just a pissed-off P.G. Wodehouse, Huxley was the Waugh of the Worlds. My attention switched to Desmond Lynam interviewing Frank Bruno on *Sportsnight*. I imagined myself discussing my latest test century at Lords with the slick, moustachioed Lynam.

My reverie was interrupted by the arrival of two new customers and I was surprised to find myself next to none other than Ray Keaton himself. He was accompanied by John Freeman and I heard Keaton offer to buy the drinks in return for John's hospitality.

'Ray let me introduce you to an old friend of mine who I used to play with when we were little kids,' said John. 'This is Dean Swift.'

Ray shook me firmly by the hand and offered to buy me a drink as he ordered refreshments for himself and John.

'Dean Swift eh?' said Ray with a playful smile. 'You have a fondness for eating Irish children then do you?'

'Err I don't think I could eat a whole one,' I replied, rather puzzled by the remark.

Ray seemed to find my extempore retort quite hilarious and seeing that both John and myself were both drawing a blank, attempted to explain, 'You must have heard of *Gulliver's Travels* by Jonathan Swift for fuck's sake. Are all you English a bunch of philistines or what? Swift was the Dean of St. Patrick's Cathedral in Dublin. He wrote a satire in the style of Juvenile called *A Modest Proposal*. It's supposed to be a serious pamphlet that proposes eating Irish children to alleviate hunger.'

'I think that one passed me by somewhere along the way,' remarked John.

'Maybe your parents are interested in literature, Dean?' asked Ray.

'I think Wilber Smith is about my Dad's limit. More likely he was listening to Dean Martin while everyone else was listening to Procol Harum when I was born.'

'How is your dad these days by the way?' asked John.

'Oh about the same as usual,' I said, rolling my eyes. 'Still sits in front of the telly moaning all day.'

'Sounds about right,' John reflected. 'My old man sits watching the cricket all day when it's on and just moans about how shit England are. Then he moans when there isn't any cricket to watch. Oh sorry to hear about your mum; I know it's been a while but I haven't had the chance to speak to you. It was a big shock I can tell you; my mum was always on about how well turned out your mum looked when she was dancing at the club.'

It wasn't until John mentioned my mother that I realised I hadn't even thought about her for what seemed like months. After she had taken her own life, there had hardly been a day for many years when I hadn't reflected on what had possessed her to slash her wrists. I often thought about the final morning that I had seen her. She had fallen out with dad and had decided to stew herself in sherry. I had attempted to make some polite small talk but she was already spitefully drunk.

I remember the day before she had killed herself; everything had seemed okay. I gave her my board money and we watched *Grange Hill* together. She had asked me if I was courting yet and I told her all about the girl called Heidi who I had been getting to know.

'Just don't bring a black woman home!' she said jovially.

It was strange how she accepted Ian's homosexuality but her worse nightmare was that one of us should marry someone of a different race.

Ray and John were getting ready for another round and I supped up and offered to pay for the next drinks. I waited at the bar and saw Malcolm serving a group of men who had just walked into the games room. I sat on a barstool and took out Ray's book and began reading one of the poems at random. I was considering whether to ask Ray to sign the book when Malcolm came through from the games room to serve me. I ordered three pints of Guinness and waited patiently for the black velvet liquid to trickle into the glasses. In my peripheral vision I noticed the group of men who had just been served walk into the lounge.

The new arrivals seated themselves around a table that was situated in a booth near the door. As I carried the drinks across to the corner beneath the television set, I was suddenly reminded who the newcomers to the bar were. For the second time that evening I was invited to hear a tuneless version of the 'No Surrender' theme.

As I placed the drinks on the table I glanced at the nervous expression on Ray's face. I sat facing the set of thugs and saw Cuckoo Walsh in their midst, grinning apishly. I recognised the Scotsman, Strachan, wearing a blue and white striped polo shirt bearing the Glasgow Rangers badge. He glared through his slit-eyes; his pale cadaverous face disfigured by scars. On his neck was a tattoo that said, 'Fuck the Pope'. Amidst the cacophony I heard him call out, 'Yah Fenian bastard!'

I began to quaff my stout, eager to bow out gracefully at the soonest opportunity. Only John seemed unfazed by the confrontational manner of Walsh and his cronies. He was staring incredulously at the young lad sat next to Walsh, who I knew by the cognomen of 'Dog'. I remembered he used to follow John and his friend Spike around the village and would always try to beg cigarettes from me if ever he saw me smoking.

Suddenly, with delicious irony, *The Irish Rover* by The Pogues & The Dubliners started to play on the jukebox. Ray drained his pint in one Charybdian swallow, then slammed his glass on the table and stood up.

'Okay which one of you gobshites is going to come over here and call me a Fenian bastard?' He roared like Mad King Sweeney.

All hell was about to break loose as Walsh's crew all rose to their feet after a few moments of stunned hesitation. John rose to the aide of Ray, smashing Ray's empty pint pot against the edge of the table and brandishing it like a poniard. I was ready to crawl underneath the table and could see no way of escape without losing face.

What can only be described as a *deus ex machina* arrived in the form of half a dozen of the Robespierre's Barbers. Rollo, their illustrious leader, marched over from the other side of the room to find out what all the fuss was about. Rollo and the rest of his club had spent the entire day taking part in a wake held in honour of a recently deceased member. Tony Wolfe was an Irishman from Skibbereen and a long-serving member of Robespierre's Barbers. He had ended his life in a collision between himself and his Vincent Black Lightning motorbike and an articulated lorry.

'Keep it down lads or I'm going to have to knock the fuck out of you all,' said Rollo with authoritative firmness.

'Get tae fuck Yeti!' said Strachan.

The sound of Strachan's retort brought back a distant memory in Rollo's mind. A recollection of a confrontation, in which a feral Scot vainly held out against superior forces, from the meagre fortification of a pool table; a memory of Tony

Wolfe wearing a scar on his nose until his dying day; the tenacious Scot doggedly clinging on to Tony's nose as he was set upon by Rollo's myrmidons.

Cuckoo Walsh stepped in front of Strachan and stood face to face with Rollo, 'Right then, me and you, right here, right now!'

I decided that it was time to discreetly retreat as Ray and John joined the morass of bikers and BFC members. I stepped through the rear exit and hastily retreated across the car park and the quiet of Clumber Street.

CHAPTER NINE

It was the Friday before Christmas and the workers of Mansfield were stirring with anticipation of the biggest bacchanal of the year. The old days of breaking up for a week off with holiday pay had given way to a more Dickensian break. Christmas Day took place on Monday and everyone would be back at work by Wednesday.

I remembered my first Christmas at work, when it was obligatory for factory girls to be paid to spend the morning drinking and terrorising any young males who dared to show their face on the shop floor. Anyone foolish enough to stray too near the debauchees might later find Polaroids of their penises available for posterity.

Work didn't stop at Tsucol until the last car seat cover had been sewn and each area was swept clean. It was a frenzied rush to complete targets in order to be ready at the starting line for the commencement of the Christmas drinking marathon.

Feggy Edwards and I managed to get a lift with Dawn Townroe to the Sir John Cockle pub. Dawn intended to join the party in the evening after she had secured a child minder for her two teenage daughters. I had grown fond of the mature charms of Dawn and had high hopes that I might succeed in a dalliance with her later that day.

We were fortunate to arrive at the bar before the greater portion of Tsucol's workforce began to fill the Sir John Cockle. It had been some years since the pub had seen so many people cross its threshold during the festive season, when the Etam factory had done business across the road.

I managed to drain a pint of Guinness and order a second before the majority of the throng had arrived. I was joined by Sammy and Spike, who were amongst the latest batch of Tsucol neophytes.

John Freeman was absent from the party as he still hadn't yet received his first month's payment. It would be a lean Christmas for John, trying to find the money for presents for his little boy and completing a month's work without seeing a penny's wages. He would have to complete a six-week trial while still receiving unemployment benefits. If he was considered suitable after that time, he would still have to wait another four weeks before he received his first month's salary.

Sammy, on the other hand, had no such concerns about making ends meet. He had moved in with his older sister and was living rent free. He had scraped together some cash for the day's drinking session and was blissfully ignorant of his own paternal commitments.

'I'm living the dream at the moment,' he proudly announced.

'What about you're young 'un?' asked Feggy cynically. 'Don't you have to give your lass ought?'

'Her mam and dad are loaded; he's an ex-copper and she gets anything she wants. Besides I haven't got any spare coin after getting the sack last month.' Sammy had been fired from his job as a security guard a month earlier and had found himself fresh employment with Tsucol. He had a natural aptitude for sewing and had been the first in his training group to be transferred to a production cell. I was given the privilege of 'buddying up' with Sammy while he learned the ropes. He had latched on to me like a barnacle since being assigned to my sub-cell and I had taken quite a shine to him.

'Oh shit Sammy!' said Feggy with an expression of exaggerated consternation. 'The rozzers have come for you!'

Sammy casually glanced behind him and saw two suited, middle-management types walking towards the bar.

'Yo bollocks!' he replied, as Feggy collapsed in a fit of puerile laughter. Each time *Set You Free* by N-Trance played on the radio, Feggy would call out, 'Go on Sammy!' I dreaded the moment that *I Fought the Law* was included in the playlist.

On the night that Nappy Andrews had been killed, it had been brought to the attention of the Nottinghamshire Police Constabulary that Sammy had been seen in the area, at the approximate time that the murder had taken place. Sammy, who had been posted at a nearby site as a security guard, was seen leaving his post by an elderly man called Jess Durward. The ever-vigilant Durward had taken it upon himself to keep watch over the construction site while it was left unguarded. After hearing about the murder in the local paper, he informed the police that Sammy, who Jess had considered a suspicious individual, had been absent from the site for over two hours. Sammy had become a suspect in the murder case and had lost his job after revealing his true motives for being absent from his post.

'This will be your arsehole when you've been in prison a few weeks,' continued Feggy as he held up my empty glass of Guinness and showed its creamy interior to Sammy.

'Well I was reading in the *Nottingham Post*,' I said in an attempt to intercede on Sammy's behalf, 'that the police are investigating the murder of someone called Richard Bosworth in connection with Nappy's murder. Remember that guy they found chopped into bits and stuffed into a dustbin on the Carsic Estate in 1986?'

'Were you in Carsic at any time during 1986?' Feggy asked Sammy with mock solemnity. 'Remember this could be very important when the case goes to trial.'

'From what I read there might be some kind of underground connection with the killings,' I continued.

'What like the Mafia and shit like that?' said Feggy spitting his lager all over my face.

'Something like that; organised crime; drugs and rent boys, that sort of thing.'

'Woah Sammy you used to be a rent boy before you came to Tsucol didn't you?'

Sammy walked away, shaking his head, and joined Dick Mallory and his gang, who seemed extremely pleased to see him. Sammy had supplied them with some ecstasy tablets, which, judging by the incongruously demonstrative manner of Quasi, were beginning to kick in. Quasi enveloped Sammy in a bear hug, almost causing asphyxiation in the process. Dick and Scratch were locked in a passionate embrace, singing along to *All I Want For Christmas Is You* by Mariah Carey.

After an hour of drinking, the atmosphere was beginning to grow increasingly obstreperous. Les Johnson arrived in a taxi, accompanied by Heidi and a couple of other girls from the office. As soon as Johnson entered the doors of the Sir John Cockle, a huge barrage of jeering and booing greeted his entrance. He posed in the doorway a moment, trying to look cool and remain unfazed. As he smiled and took a theatrical bow, he was mentally taking note of some of the faces he might reap retribution upon at a later date. As he walked towards the bar, I noticed that Heidi appeared to be totally embarrassed by the attention that the arrival of Johnson and herself had aroused.

After a couple of hours, many were making their excuses that they needed to get away and concentrate on Christmas shopping. Others were beginning to migrate towards the town centre, and Feggy and I followed Dick and his loved-up troglodytes to the next port of call. We arrived at the Wheatsheaf and discovered that last orders were being called. A cooling-off period had been instigated, lasting from three until six pm. The Four Seasons shopping centre was also closing its doors rather than have a horde of drunks descending upon its businesses.

I took the opportunity to go home for an hour and eat, wash and change before the evening session. I found Myfanwy reading the *Nottingham Post* when I arrived home. Since hearing about the Nappy Andrews killing, Myfanwy had become somewhat distraught that he hadn't been able to be around to help his old friend. He had always held an avuncular affection for Nappy and felt indebted to the youth after he had saved his life during a heroin overdose. Myfanwy had managed to eventually kick his own drug addiction but had felt it prudent to avoid Nappy before he descended into the same abyss.

'It says here that the police seem to think Nappy's murder might be connected with Boz's killing,' Myfanwy said to me as though I might be able to offer the correct answer.

'You knew them both better than me,' I said shrugging my shoulders, 'what do you reckon?'

Myfanwy gave this question some thought and then answered, 'Well Boz always was a dodgy fucker and I wouldn't put anything past him, but Nappy; how could he be connected with something that happened nearly 10 years ago. No, poor old Nappy made himself a lot of enemies when he started robbing for his skag money.'

The last time Myfanwy had seen Nappy, he had visited him in hospital after someone had taken a baseball bat to him after a break-in. Nappy was adamant that he hadn't burgled the house, but his reputation had preceded him and fingers were pointing in his direction for any local robberies

'You still feel guilty about not being able to do anything to help him don't you?' I said as Myfanwy gazed morosely at the newspaper.

'If it wasn't for him I would have been dead and buried a long time ago.'

'If Boz had had his way with you that night, you would have probably ended up with your head caved in the same as Nappy; who it was, by the way, who led Boz straight to you.'

'I know but if I'd just kept an eye on him, he wouldn't have got involved with that prick in the first place,' Myfanwy said as he removed a couple of sheets from the newspaper. 'I only picked up the fucking paper to line Corky's cage, now I'm on a right downer.'

'You should come out with me tonight,' I said in an attempt to raise Myfanwy's spirits.

'We need a holiday,' Myfanwy replied as he rose gingerly from the settee.

After managing to persuaded Myfanwy that a night out might do him some good, I waited while he got ready. We had recently had cable television installed and I amused myself by watching an episode of *The Wheeltappers and Shunters Social Club*. Myfanwy and I were still enjoying the honeymoon period of cable television and would stay glued to the set for hours, watching anything from sumo wrestling to topless weather girls.

I decided that it might not do me any harm to change from the clothes I had been wearing since I got up for work that morning. The white polo shirt I had worn to the Sir John Cockle had a huge Guinness stain on it that resembled Australia. I changed into a striped Farah shirt that I had bought from a charity shop and splashed on some of the Joop aftershave my brother had sent me for my birthday.

'Fuck me!' said Myfanwy as he inhaled the odour. 'You smell like a tart's armpit.'

'Yeah well you should know,' I replied. 'You should look at home in those old bowling shoes where we're going.'

Ten minutes later we were approaching the Mansfield Superbowl that had recently been built beside the shoe factory.

'We're going for a drink at the bowling alley!' Myfanwy said incredulously. 'When you said I'd be at home in my bowling shoes I thought you meant that we were going to a Northern Soul all-nighter or something.'

'It's just somewhere to meet up that's all,' I tried to reason with him. 'it's close to the bus station.'

'So's the Wheatsheaf,' he whined. 'Well don't expect me to play fucking bowls.'

Inside the bowling alley, some of my Tsucol colleagues had already arrived. They were sitting in a balustraded bar area that overlooked the bowling lanes. I had spent an evening at the Superbowl a few weeks earlier when our team had been awarded a free night there for completing a month with the least absenteeism in the factory.

A bunch of office workers were raucously enjoying a game in one of the lanes. A corpulent, red-haired youth, with his tie fastened round his head, Rambo-style, staggered down the lane, dribbling a bowling ball as far as the pins. His effort to push the ball into the pins was greeted by cheering from his colleagues. They began to chant his name as he knocked over a couple of pins and then kicked the rest over before falling flat on his back.

Dick and the gang were all waiting for Sammy to arrive with more ecstasy tablets. Myfanwy sceptically scanned the assembled group as I mingled and introduced him. A huge cheer erupted when Callum Yates arrived wearing a red bow tie and a sky-blue tuxedo. He looked as though he intended to win the heart of Molly Ringwald in an 80's teen film.

Dawn Townroe arrived next, looking stunning in a black off-the-shoulder dress with a flared skirt. I was highly aroused by the sight of her Rubenesque figure in her outfit. I noted the sniggers emanating from some of the male members of the team and felt a twinge of anger. Callum was quick to join in the derisive whispering and I was baffled how a man as ugly as him could criticise any woman.

Dawn bought herself a gin and tonic and came over to where Myfanwy and myself stood on the periphery of the group.

'You look absolutely stunning,' I said with a surprising degree of confidence.

'You don't look bad yourself,' she replied coolly.

Les Johnson arrived shortly afterwards with Heidi. I noticed that she still wore the black puffed sleeve dress she had been wearing during the lunchtime session and wondered if they had been making a day of it. Neither of them looked as though they had been drinking a lot. Les was looking very pleased with himself, while Heidi wore a sheepish expression of guilt, as though she had just committed a murder.

Heidi went to the ladies' while Les was queuing for the bar.

'Have you cracked it yet Les?' called out Dick from his table.

Les sauntered over with a smug 'that would be telling' expression. 'A gentleman never tells,' he said proudly.

'You dirty bastard,' said Quasi in a congratulatory tone.

'It's always the quiet ones,' said Callum, like the man of the world he thought he was.

Heidi returned a couple of minutes later and joined Les, who had recommenced ordering drinks.

'I'd get yourself checked out duck after going with that dirty bastard!' called out Dick.

Heidi gave Dick an embarrassed smile and nodded her head. She usually just switched off when any of the machinists tried to draw her into factory-floor banter. Then she turned to Les and caught him making a shushing motion with his index finger.

'Ignore them,' he said as he registered Heidi's hurt expression. 'They can't get their heads round the idea of a man and woman just being friends.'

'Did you tell them about what we did this afternoon?' Heidi asked indignantly.

'No, like I said, they're just a bunch of cavemen. They haven't learned any manners since they finished at the pit.'

Dick suddenly appeared behind Les and pushed his way to the bar, 'Mind out stallion,' he said, patting Les on the back.

Les gave Heidi an embarrassed shrug of the shoulders and drained his glass of Southern Comfort and said, 'Come on let's go somewhere else.'

Hearing Les, Dick slapped him on the back and said, 'He's insatiable this lad; tonight's your lucky night duck. You'll go far at Tsucol you will.'

Heidi looked around and felt as though everyone was looking at her and laughing, 'You bastard!' she said to Les and threw her glass of red wine in his face.

A huge cheer erupted from the Tsucol contingent, who all despised Les.

'What are you doing you mad bitch?' shouted Les as he wiped wine from his face. 'Look at the state of this shirt!'

'I can't believe you could use me like this,' roared Heidi as she struggled to hold back her tears.

Les's embarrassment turned to anger as he began to realise he was being made to look a fool in front of his minions, 'Look you've had your fill what more do you want. I wouldn't have bothered if I'd known you were some kind of bunny boiler!'

Heidi couldn't take anymore and ran out of the bowling alley without a backward glance. I felt awful as I watched my workmates doubled up in fits of laughter. I watched Les Johnson wiping wine from his shirt and felt like going over and punching him in the face. Dawn looked similarly unimpressed by his behaviour and I suggested that we go outside and see if Heidi was okay.

We found Heidi kneeling down outside the Superbowl, being sick.

'That's it, get it up duck, then you can start again,' a passing reveller helpfully called out.

Dawn tried to put her arm around Heidi but she pushed her away and collapsed against the wall and began to sob. Dawn gave me a concerned look and I shrugged my shoulders, unable to think of anything helpful to say.

'I can't believe I've been so stupid,' Heidi said between fits of uncontrollable sobbing.

'They're all a bunch of twats,' said Dawn, putting her arm around Heidi again. This time Heidi didn't attempt to push her away and she continued to sob on Dawn's black dress.

Myfanwy came outside to see what was happening. I just looked at him and shrugged my shoulders again, feeling useless.

'I won't be able to show my face at Tsucol again,' Heidi groaned.

'Don't worry it will all be forgotten about by next week,' Dawn replied. 'Everyone thinks Les is a prick and they'll all think you were great, throwing your drink at him.'

'I want to go home,' Heidi whimpered.

'Why don't we go over to the taxi rank and get you home then?' said Dawn. She carefully lifted Heidi up and began to walk arm in arm with her towards the taxi rank. Heidi's eye makeup had run down her face, making her look like Alice Cooper.

'Wait for me at the Wheatsheaf,' Dawn said to me as she crossed the road towards the bus station.

Myfanwy and I continued towards the Wheatsheaf and surveyed the scene of debauched chaos that was already unfolding on Stockwell Gate. A man lay in the middle of the street, clutching his bloody nose; a group of girls staggered down the street, one of them attempted to walk with her knickers around her ankles; groups of men emerged from the stairs that led from the bus station, glaring confrontationally at anyone they passed.

We had arrived at the Wheatsheaf just as everyone was arriving in town and the place was heaving with bodies. The Wheatsheaf was awash with all manner of wassailers, topers and inveterate Brahms and Liszt artists. I would have turned around and left if it hadn't been for Dawn asking me to wait there for her. By the time we were being served, Dawn had arrived. She announced her arrival by squeezing one of my buttocks.

We found a small space near the pool table and discussed the deplorable behaviour of Les Johnson.

'I was married to a bloke just like him,' said Dawn. 'She's better off finding out what sort of a shit he is before he really hurts her.'

'Well I just hope she will be okay,' I said.

'She'll get over it,' offered Myfanwy. 'She'll have a big headache in the morning. I'm guessing he's been plying her with drink to soften her up a bit.'

Dawn went to the ladies' and Myfanwy produced a wallet from the pocket of his Harrington jacket, 'Well that Les bloke might be walking home tonight now he hasn't got the taxi fare home,' he said, taking out a wad of bank notes and stuffing them into his jeans.

'Oh for fuck's sake what did you do that for? He might think Heidi took it.'

'No he won't, he was buying that Dick character a drink after she ran out; he'll probably think it was him if anyone.'

Myfanwy shoved the empty wallet behind the back of a radiator before Dawn returned from the ladies'. Feeling somewhat pleased that Myfanwy had picked Les's pocket, I raised my glass in a silent toast.

By the time the party had got as far as the Swan, we were reunited with the rest of the Tsucol brigade. Feggy and Sammy had finally re-emerged and Les had apparently gone home after his wallet had gone missing. Myfanwy paid a visit to the toilet shortly after we arrived at the Swan and didn't appear again.

'Your mate can't take his ale can he?' Callum slobbered in my ear.

'Why's that then?' I asked reluctantly, not wishing to be drawn into one of Callum's pedantic conversations about work.

'He was puking his guts up in the toilets 10 minutes ago and then I saw him sneak out of the back door.'

It seemed odd to me that Myfanwy should be ill after only drinking a couple of pints. He had seemed subdued all evening and I knew the Nappy Andrews's murder was weighing on his mind. Stealing Les's wallet and then disappearing with the money indicated to me that he might be sliding back into using heroin.

Dawn brushed against my hip and started to gently sway to the sound of *Disco 2000* by Pulp. There was little I could do for the time being if Myfanwy had relapsed into his old ways, so I concentrated on letting my prematurely thinning hair down.

By 10 o'clock Dawn and I were discussing whether to spend the remainder of the evening at Valentino's or the Village. We had already established that we would definitely not be going to Limited Editions on Westgate, where most of our workmates were destined to go.

'Shall we go to Valo's then?' I suggested with a lack of preference for either nightspot.

'Oh you fancy a bit of a grab-a-granny night do you?' teased Dawn as she threw her arms around me.

The others had just gone into the Portland Arms and we were left on our own on Albert Street.

'What are we going to do now, Mister nice guy?' Dawn asked, gazing meaningfully into my eyes.

I kissed her modestly on her lips and then pulled her close and our kisses became more passionate. I could hear groups of drinkers passing by. Everyone was too drunk to care what anyone else was up too and we continued fondling each other in the doorway of an estate agent.

Dawn brushed her hand up my leg and explored the hardness beneath my jeans. I responded by running a hand up her thigh causing her to shudder with excitement.

'I want to take you to bed,' she whispered.

'What about your kids?' I croaked. 'Won't the babysitter be waiting?'

'The kids are at their nana's for the night. Do you want to take me home or what?' she said emphatically.

'Well if you're going to insist, then I suppose I'd better do as I'm told.'

We hurried under the viaduct towards the Midland Hotel. Dawn lived nearby on Princes Street and it was only a matter of five minutes before we would arrive at her home. We passed where the new railway station was being completed and were so aroused that we were forced to stop and embrace passionately against a wall. Unable to control our desires any longer, I led Dawn by the hand to where a new pedestrian tunnel had been built beneath the railway line.

The area was completely deserted and the tunnel and walkway to the station were shrouded in darkness. I pushed Dawn up against a wall and ran a hand up her skirt. I placed my hand underneath her knickers and fondled her buttocks as we kissed with violent intensity. With my other hand I began to explore between her thighs, pushing my fingers beneath her damp knickers. I soon came into contact with her clitoris and began to stroke my thumb against it, feeling it pulsate and throb. Dawn's breathing quickened as I accelerated my pace and explored her most intimate recesses with my free fingers. She held on to me and began to gasp and shudder in the throes of a violent orgasm.

Dawn grabbed my hand and pulled it away from her, unable to take anymore.

'It's a long time since anyone has done that for me,' she whispered appreciatively in my ear.

We held each other silently for a few minutes. I could hear shouting and singing coming from the direction of the town centre. Someone shouted, 'It's Chriiistmas!' in a spirited imitation of Noddy Holder.

'Come on,' said Dawn, taking me by the hand, 'it's getting cold out here, take me home and keep me warm.'

CHAPTER TEN

The evenings were starting to grow lighter again and a rare blessing of early spring sunshine shone through John Freeman's car window. His dad had helped him to pay for the old Ford Escort which had previously been owned by a dodgy looking character named Colin. Since buying the old wreck, he had already arrived at work late on several occasions due to its unreliability. He would pick up Sammy every day on Debdale Lane and they had been forced to give the car a push start earlier in the week.

John drove home alone on this glorious March evening. Leaving work on time was often a luxury at Tsucol but since taking command of his own team, John had the responsibility of staying behind and completing the paperwork, which he hated so much. He was struggling to get used to the computer on which he was meant to log all his daily targets and machine down-time.

Since commencing employment with Tsucol, he had displayed qualities of leadership that had been noted by his superiors. He had loathed using the sewing machines from the moment he had set eyes on one. He found it hard to sew anything but the straightest panels and constantly had work brought back to him with needle damage or wide seam margins.

He had been fortunate to work alongside Dean Swift, who patiently attempted to mentor him in the finer points of sewing. John's ineptitude had been overlooked by his team leader due to the stoicism of Dean and the ambivalence of Feggy Edwards.

There had been talk of getting a union involved at Tsucol and he had been one of the militant faction who had championed that cause. Workers were joining the Transport & General Workers' Union in the hope that if a majority became members, representation on the shop floor couldn't be resisted by the management.

As more and more people had joined the union, representatives from the T & G had parked a bus on the roadside outside the factory. Employees had been encouraged to visit the bus where they could join up or where existing members could speak to union representatives. More importantly to many were the union badges that were given away to anyone who visited the bus. Callum Yates was one of the first to proudly display his badge, though many were sceptical as to whether he'd actually signed up as a member.

The sudden mania for union activity had made the management of Tsucol very nervous. Their entire method of doing business relied on non-interference by organisations that might empower its operatives. The crisis reached a critical point when the management called a meeting in the canteen. Les Johnson stuck out his chest and delivered a polemical speech, in which he condemned certain individuals who had reportedly bullied operatives into joining the union. John had expected some kind of 'Gang of Four' type show trial to take place. Things had quickly quietened down after the Tsucol propaganda machine had rolled over the catalysts of the intended coup.

The worst thing about John's new job was the poor pay which hardly covered the monthly expenses of his family. Things began to change for him one day when Dale Walden took him up to the office known as 'The sty in the sky'. An office had been built for the team leaders, which had been christened 'The pig pen'. An upper-storey space had been added to the structure, and the team leaders had been up-rooted to the sty in the sky so the downstairs area could be used for storage space.

John was greeted by Bill Green, an affable and prepossessing group leader, who John had known at school. John had no idea why he had been called into the presence of Green and wondered if his poor work had been brought to the attention of his superiors.

'How's it going mate?' asked Green in a disarming tone, 'Don't worry mate you're not in trouble; I just wanted to have a chat to find out what you want to do here.'

John was confused by Green's amiability and wondered if there was some kind of good cop, bad cop scenario taking place.

'I've been hearing a lot of good things about you John and I'm sure a bloke with your intelligence isn't satisfied with just standing at a sewing machine all day.

Is this the bit where he sacks me, thought John, 'I just like to get my head down and get on with the job Bill,' he said with as much conviction as he could manage.

'Oh we've seen you're a grafter mate but I think we can put your talents to better use. Production will soon be starting in the new Ford cells that are being set up. We're going to have another 200 operatives here soon and they're all going to need team leaders.'

During John's time as a sewing machinist, he had been one of the most militant operatives in his team. Before he knew it, John had been reprogrammed into a Tsucol robot, loyal and committed to the company. Only a month earlier he had been complaining about being kept back for compulsory overtime; he was now telling people to, 'Show some commitment!'

His new role had already brought him into conflict with his best friend, Spike. After receiving a second written warning for his absenteeism, Spike had been transferred to John's cell in the hope that he might turn over a new leaf. He had turned up late on several occasions, imagining that John would turn a blind eye for an old friend. John had been forced to take Spike to one side and verbally warn him, before the other operatives began to see him as a soft touch.

It was seven o'clock according to the radio, by the time John was driving into the heart of Mansfield Woodhouse. John was momentarily distracted from his worries by the top news story. A gunman had shot dead 16 primary school children and their teacher in Dunblane in Scotland. John reflected on what could possess someone to do something so horrific. He thought about his own little boy and couldn't bear to imagine anything similar happening to Kevin. He knew he could lose his temper when he was stressed, but for someone to snap and go out and kill people, there had to be some serious mental problems. As he drove up Vale Road and turned onto Brown Avenue he couldn't get *I Don't Like Mondays* by the Boomtown Rats out of his head. He remembered reading in a newspaper that the song had been inspired by an incident at a California university campus, where a teenage girl had gone on a killing spree with a gun. He could hardly comprehend anything so horrific occurring in the British Isles.

When he arrived home, he opened the gate and saw that Sally was on the back garden with Kevin, fetching in some washing. Kevin's eyes lit up when he saw his dad and he ran straight into John's arms. The boy seemed to be growing with the rapidity of a bean stalk and could hardly be kept still, till he was too tired to scamper about any more. During John's precious free time there was nothing he liked more than taking walks with Sally and Kevin through the countryside that led to Pleasley Vale.

Sally warmed up John's dinner of liver and onions in the microwave. A can of continental strength lager helped take the edge off after another stressful day at Tsucol.

'Is Spike still being a twat?' asked Sally, who always enjoyed receiving the latest work gossip from her husband.

'Yeah he's digging a hole for himself,' replied John, reluctant to talk about work. 'One more strike and then he'll be out.'

'He's never really been the same since he came back from the Gulf though has he?' remarked Sally.

John shrugged his shoulders and wrinkled his nose, 'He always was a funny fucker. I can understand one or two mardy bastards at Tsucol resenting me getting made up to team leader but I thought I might be able to count on Spike. Oh well, that's mates for you innit.'

'I was watching this thing on *This Morning* where they were talking about something called combat stress disorder, or whatever it was called. I reckon that's what Spike has got.'

'Well he's always been cagey about discussing anything to do with his time out there,' said John as a gang of youths passed by the front gate.

'Makes you wonder though doesn't it?'

'Makes you wonder about what?' said John as a figure came flying through the privet hedge. *Ignore them* he thought *don't let them wind you up.*

'Well what if he did lose it with that lad on the building site and ended up killing him?' continued Sally.

Before John could reply that the idea seemed ridiculous, another figure tumbled through the privet hedge onto the lawn and then leapt back through the gap he had made. John jumped to his feet and ran straight for the front door and then marched up the drive. Leaning over the gate, he saw Sean Cain and a couple of his followers. Sean was wearing the blue and white Manchester United away top that seemed to be the only shirt he owned.

'Get off that hedge!' yelled John.

Sean looked at him without any sign of fear and said casually, 'It wasn't us mate, it was them lot who just ran up Oak Tree Avenue.'

'Don't lie to me,' replied John as he tried to keep his temper under control, 'I just saw you jump onto my garden.'

One of the group who John recognised as the red-haired youth he had pursued several months earlier, looked up without any hint of remorse and said, 'Just fuck off inside mate and there'll be no more trouble.'

John was so stunned that he turned around and walked straight back into the house. He closed the front door and leaned against it, taking deep breaths. *They're just kids* he tried to tell himself, *it's the same for everyone else around here. They're not trying to take you on. Don't take it personally.*

Sally stood in the doorway of the kitchen with Kevin in her arms and said, 'Come away from the door, they'll soon move on to someone else.'

John was about to walk away from the front door but turned around to reassure himself that the lads had walked away. He opened the door slightly and peered through the gap. They were now standing in front of the gate, obstinately holding their ground.

'He's hiding!' John heard the red-haired boy exclaim euphorically.

Then something snapped inside John's mind.

The next thing John knew he was charging like a bull at Sean Cain, who had decided to walk onto the garden and pull up the newly sprouted daffodils. Sean looked up, and, slightly startled by John's reaction, took a step back. John was almost face to face with Sean when Sally grabbed him from behind in an attempt at averting a catastrophe.

John could hear Sally scream, 'Come inside, I've called the police.'

Suddenly everything began to swim before his eyes like a dream. He could see Sean brush his long fringe from his eyes, grinning contemptuously with no intention of relinquishing any ground. Neighbours were gathering at various points along the street. The fat boy from the neighbouring house was peering through his bedroom window, laughing with his friends.

'Look at him, he's shaking.' One of Sean's friends commented.

John was indeed shaking, but with rage rather than fear. Seeing the unhinged expression on John's face, the boy's countenance changed from amusement to uncertainty.

'Come on let's just fuck off,' he suggested, taking a step back.

Sean responded by slowly stepping away, reluctant to concede a defeat, but bemused and slightly afraid that he had finally overstepped his mark.

A grey Austin Metro pulled up near the house and a blond-haired man with a Geordie accent began to berate the youngest of the three delinquents, 'Get in that house now! What have I told you about causing trouble?'

The small, blond-haired replica of his father stormed away, muttering that he hadn't done anything wrong.

A few minutes later, John was standing near the front door attempting to calm down. He suddenly felt foolish reacting in such a way to a bunch of kids. He could see the faces of the neighbours starring at him like a lunatic.

Sally stood holding Kevin in her arms trying to divert John's attention, saying, 'There's Daddy look. We love Daddy don't we.'

John looked up and smiled weakly at his son. He felt a sudden urge to collapse on the floor and burst into tears.

Turning around to face the front door, he saw the blond-haired man marching purposefully down the garden path. John opened the door, expecting another confrontation. He stepped outside, ready to take on an opponent who was old enough to take a good hiding.

'Look I'm sorry mate,' said the Geordie with his hands held up in a gesture of supplication, 'I've tried everything, but I just can't do anything with him. I'm going to make sure he stays away from that lot in future.'

Another neighbour, Howard Stokes, came down the path next, Stokes was an amiable, middle-aged man who wore big tinted spectacles and tried to conceal his bald pate with a combover, 'They're bastards aren't they?' he began to rant, 'I've told the police no end of times, but they won't do anything! They said if you're going to give them a good hiding, just make sure you do it where no one can see you.'

Several other neighbours began to emerge and join the discussion. It was the first time that most of them had made the effort to speak to John. Mrs. Taylor from the next house, came over to speak from behind the garden fence. It had been her son and his friends whom John had seen laughing from the bedroom window. It seemed that her son was the victim of bullying by Sean Cain and he had evidently been amused by the sight of his tormenters being put to flight.

It became apparent that the problem of anti-social behaviour on the estate had reached a critical level. A meeting had taken place at the community centre on Vale Road where concerned residents had discussed the problem with representatives from the police force. Elderly residents complained about being reluctant to visit the local shops due to intimidation by gangs of youths; acts of theft and vandalism were on the increase; there was a sense that the police had lost control of the area and the teenage delinquents were being given a free rein to run riot as they pleased.

It was the first time that John had felt part of the community that evening as he and Sally discussed the problem with their neighbours. Mansfield Woodhouse had seemed to John to be a place where it was hard to fit in if you hadn't lived there all your life. Most of the perceived animosity and reluctance to talk seemed to be linked with the sense of discontent due to lawlessness.

After Sally had put Kevin to bed, she and John finally managed to relax with a couple of glasses of wine. After three hours, they both concluded that Sally's telephone call to the police had gone unheeded and they agreed that it would be best if the whole incident were forgotten.

CHAPTER ELEVEN

It was the last day of the football season and Cuckoo Walsh had travelled to Chesterfield with a group of Notts County supporters. With Mansfield Town languishing in the bottom division of the Football League, a ceasefire was taking place between the more bucolic factions of Stags fans and Spireites.

Cuckoo sat in the main grandstand at Saltergate, near to the terraces of the Cross Street stand, where the away supporters were gathered. County had brought a decent following of supporters, who packed the small, uncovered away area. Directly opposite where Cuckoo sat was the Compton Street Stand. A contingent of the Chesterfield football hooligan firm that called itself the Khmer Blues was picketed at the far end of that stand; here they could closely watch their rivals from opposing firms. A fenced off area of terracing, patrolled by police officers, acted as a kind of no man's land between the two warring tribes.

Cuckoo could remember the first time he had travelled to Saltergate in 1979 for his first local derby between Chesterfield and Mansfield Town. It was a cold November day and he had seen his team lose two-nil. The score had been of minor importance in his memory, but the day had been his first opportunity to whet his appetite for football hooliganism.

He was 16 and had only left school a few months earlier. He had begun working at Warsop Main Colliery but was commencing another apprenticeship with some of Mansfield's leading hooligans. Lester Downie and Barry Parks were bootboys of the old-school of football hooliganism. Shoulder-length hair, Dr. Marten boots, denim jackets and turned up jeans, had been the standard uniform of Downie and Parks since the early 1970s.

Cuckoo had lived in Shirebrook back then; a town on the Derbyshire border, where football loyalties were split between Chesterfield and Mansfield Town. Cuckoo had nailed his colours to the mast a few years earlier, when he had seen the Stags hold Tottenham Hotspur to a 3-3 draw at Field Mill. His aversion to the Spireites came about during that time, when he climbed off a bus one afternoon after a match, wearing his blue and yellow scarf. A gang of youths a couple of years older than himself were coming home from a match at Chesterfield and saw an easy target in Cuckoo. After leaving him bruised and bloody, Cuckoo vowed that he would one day have his revenge.

Both Downie and Parks worked at Warsop Main and Cuckoo found it hard to refuse when he was invited to join them for a trip to Saltergate. He hadn't anticipated that he would be expected to infiltrate the Spion Cop end of the ground, where Chesterfield's hardcore fans congregated behind the goal. Told by Barry Parks to tuck his blue and yellow scarf under his pullover, Cuckoo followed the two veterans into the lion's den.

Lester Downie found a spot near to one of the floodlights. The area was at the extremity of the Spion Cop and a few steps down the terracing would take them onto the pitch if they needed to make a hasty retreat. At a given signal Downie pulled out his scarf and, holding it aloft, he began to sing, 'I'm only a poor little spireite'; his own extempore version of a tune he had heard on *Tiswas* earlier that morning. Barry Parks revealed his own scarf and Cuckoo took out his own with a certain amount of trepidation.

He expected to be set upon by boots and fists at any moment, but to his surprise the spectacle only received a muted response from the home supporters. Before he knew what was happening, Cuckoo was being hurled over the advertising hoardings by an aging copper who'd seen it all before. He expected to be thrown into a black Mariah and locked up for the night. The three offenders were marched alongside the length of the pitch and were met by jeering from the home crowd in the Compton Street stand. They were deposited amongst the Mansfield Town fans in the Cross Street stand and met with a hero's welcome.

'Make sure you get home in time for Basil Brush tonight,' was the world-weary copper's advice. 'You'll stay away from that lot, if you know what's good for you.'

Time proved that Cuckoo didn't know what was good for him and he never once regretted ignoring the sage advice of the ancient plod. He still harboured a passionate animosity for Mansfield's local rivals, and would happily have burned to the ground the tinderbox of wooden benches and seats where he sat at that moment. He vacantly watched the match progress, ambivalent to the fortunes of Notts County.

He contemptuously watched Mambo Lambert pacing anxiously at the rear of the stand, with his mobile phone glued to his ear. Lambert was the general of the Notts County hooligan firm that called itself 'The Fucked Up Humbug'. Lambert was marshalling his troops on the terraces, communicating with his fancy phone and sporting the latest Stone Island designer gear. He would be calculating the chances of his FUH foot soldiers successfully undertaking an end-of-season pitch invasion and breach of the enemy lines.

Cuckoo reflected on how things had changed since people like Lester Downie had terrorised the terraces in bootboy gear. Cuckoo himself had adopted the football casual style of the mid-80s, wearing the designer label sports gear that he and his contemporaries had brought back as bootie from European Cup trips.

He had always scorned the baggy look that the drugged-up next generation had brought to British hooliganism. He had a grudging respect for the more rugged looking styles that were becoming the uniform of the aspiring football thugs of the new era.

It all seemed a shallow façade to Cuckoo; all style and no action. Police surveillance techniques had all but killed the genuine game of football violence. When he had first been bloodied, Cuckoo had taken part in medieval-style pitched battles, where hundreds of youths would charge at each other and take part in combat that would only be broken up by the police after a fair amount of mayhem had taken place. In the football stadiums of the 1990s it was more likely to be assailed by someone wielding an inflatable banana, or a sixth-former peddling fanzines.

The new breed of hooligans were forced to out-manoeuvre the police in order to meet in battle. With CCTV cameras in operation and helicopters watching in the skies, skirmishes could be averted whilst the warring parties were still streets apart from each other.

Cuckoo had little time for the cat-and-mouse games that took place between hooligans and officers of the law. He had become a dinosaur, a remnant of a golden age, which the new breed could hardly imagine. He scanned the seats to his left and saw one of his own generation, who had capitalised on the new wave of hooligans.

Further along the main stand sat a well-groomed man, dressed in a loose fitting, cream coloured Armani suit. Behind a pair of designer sunglasses was Cuckoo's erstwhile nemesis, Paul 'Pol' Potter. It had been Cuckoo's folly that Potter had evaded many a well-deserved beating during his time as the top boy of the Khmer Blues.

Cuckoo envied Pol's subsequent success as an author and screenwriter. His series of mystery thrillers, featuring the hooligan and sleuth Touchstone Addison, had become award-winning best sellers. The offer to write a screenplay for a film based on his novel, *Murder on Chip Alley,* sealed Pol's reputation.

The half-time whistle distracted Cuckoo from his bitter musings on Pol and reminded him that he had other business to attend to. He made his way up the wooden aisle, to the area behind the stand where he made his way to a refreshment stall. He ordered a cup of scalding hot Bovril and found the first available space he could to put the cup down before burning his fingers. A plastic dustbin served as a makeshift table and Cuckoo sucked the traces of hot liquid from his fingers. Nearby, a short man in his late-30s with an enormous paunch, covered by a black and white striped Notts County shirt, tucked into a hot dog. Tomato ketchup and onions spilled onto the zebra-hewed shirt, as the man stuffed the bread and sausage into his mouth.

Cuckoo knew the man by the soubriquet of Doberman; so-called for his resemblance to the corpulent character from *The Phil Silvers Show.* A smaller version of Doberman appeared by his father's side with a can of Tango and inquired whether he could have a Mars bar. Doberman Senior produced a pound coin from his jeans and the teenage boy joined the queue.

Doberman wiped the ketchup from his shirt and without looking at Cuckoo said, 'We're meeting up at a pub called The Wife of Bath an hour before the Netherlands match.'

Cuckoo didn't respond, but understood that Doberman referred to the forthcoming European Football Championship match between England and The Netherlands at Wembley Stadium.

'A few of the Scottish BFC lads are coming down as well,' continued Doberman, 'and we've arranged to have a row with a bunch of Dutch lads who want to know what we can do.'

Doberman was interrupted by the arrival of his son, who was clearly bored and restless.

'Go and wait for me at the seats, I'll be back in a minute, I've got a surprise for you,' said Doberman, affectionately ruffling the boy's hair.

He watched as Doberman Junior trudged away and then pulled out a match programme from his back pocket, 'We need you to get your new boy to torch a house down in Islington, when we meet up with the Dutch,' said Doberman as he studied the programme. 'A couple of reds are getting a list of all our members and planning to make it public. Two former Angry Brigade members with links to the Provos. They're a married couple called Alicia and Dominic Hammond. Get your lad psyched up for it and memorise the address, written on this.'

Doberman turned around and dropped the programme as he made his way back to the stand, Cuckoo picked it up and began to follow Doberman as though he intended to return it to its owner. Once inside the stand again, Cuckoo ceased the cloak-and-dagger routine and returned to his seat. He made a pretence of reading through the match reports and team line-ups and then studied and memorised the address that was written at the bottom of a page full of advertisements for double-glazing and taxi hire firms. He then tore out the address and shredded it into small pieces which he scattered beneath his feet.

The match ended with the home team winning one-nil and the anticipated pitch invasion was quelled by a cordon of stewards and policemen. Cuckoo filed out of the stand with the Notts County fans. Those who were corralled in the Cross Street enclosure were retained for 10 minutes so that no breach of order would take place with the home supporters.

Outside the main stand on St. Margaret's Drive, Cuckoo watched Doberman and his son hurry away to the supporters' coach. At the end of St. Margaret's Drive, a police van was parked across the road to guard against a confrontation between rival supporters on the Saltergate road.

Dressed in a neutral red England shirt and knee length shorts, Cuckoo hoped to avoid recognition as he casually turned onto Saltergate and headed towards the town hall, with Mambo and two of his lieutenants. Cuckoo was growing irritated by seeing Mambo chatting on his phone like a lovesick teenager.

'Some of the lads have taken the Sun Inn!' Mambo said triumphantly, 'we need to get a dash on before we miss the party!'

They crossed the town hall car park, where Cuckoo saw Pol Potter getting into a white Audi Quattro Coupe.

'There's Pol Potter!' Cuckoo said, nudging Mambo excitedly. 'Come on let's trash his wheels!'

'No way man,' said Mambo resolutely, 'he's promised me a part in that film he's working on. Anyway, we'll blow everything if we start kicking off here.'

Mambo nodded his head towards the Saltergate Road, where a couple of mounted police were patrolling. There had never been a more tempting prospect of messing up Pol Potter, and Cuckoo resentfully followed the others across the Shentall Gardens.

They arrived at the Sun Inn just in time to be greeted by a chair, which came flying through a window. Inside the pub, 40 or 50 of the FUH were drinking and singing triumphantly. Cuckoo made his way through the throng, contemptuous of their swagger. Taking over a pub wasn't his idea of a victory, unless it followed a successful skirmish with the opposing firm.

He watched as Mambo hugged and shook hands with his associates, as though he'd just succeeded in masterminding the Battle of Waterloo. Cuckoo decided to sneak out through the back door, while Mambo was distracted with his cronies. It would be only a matter of time before the police appeared and he had no intention of attracting attention to himself before commencing the European Football Championship campaign.

A door at the rear of the pub led to an enclosed beer garden. More of the Notts County mob were carousing outside and Cuckoo slipped through the crowd and over a wall that led onto West Bar. He walked on into the busy market place where stallholders were packing up their wares. He took a roundabout route through the town centre, which eventually led him back to the bus station.

As he waited for the Nottingham bus that would take him into Mansfield, he regretted his decision not to drive to the game. After what seemed like an eternity, the bus finally arrived and he wearily found an upstairs seat where he proposed to sleep throughout the journey.

He leaned against the window and watched as the last of the passengers finally boarded the bus. He sighed with relief, as he looked round at the empty seats and stretched out and made himself comfortable. He heard the doors shutting downstairs and was preparing to nod off, when all of a sudden the engine stopped once again.

With growing impatience, Cuckoo looked through the window to see what was delaying the bus this time. He banged his head against the window in frustration at the sight that met his eyes. A procession of around 30 Notts County supporters were being shepherded by two police officers towards the bus. Cuckoo was forced to wait another 10 minutes as each new passenger fumbled through his change to pay his fair. The entire upstairs section of the bus was besieged by the very same firm that Cuckoo had escaped from in the Sun Inn. The police had escorted them to the bus station and were now intent on staying on the bus to keep order.

Trapped next to a flatulent, 23-stone hooligan, Cuckoo endured his purgatory, until Rosemary Street finally came into view. He had a splitting headache and wished never again to hear the 'I'm Only a Poor Little Spireite' song.

CHAPTER TWELVE

On the evening of 26 June, England's hopes of winning the European Football Championship ended. Another penalty shootout against the Germans sealed the host nation's fate in the semi-finals, as had been the case six years earlier in the World Cup. Despite the orisons of Baddiel and Skinner, football was not coming home to England in 1996.

Myfanwy and I returned to Mansfield on that same evening, after a coach holiday to Italy. As we collected our bags in the bus station, windows were being smashed on Leeming Street. The painted faces and family fun that had characterised the new face of English football during the tournament had been replaced by a swansong from the barbarian brigade.

We jumped into a taxi and the driver updated us on the latest news about the aftermath of the game. There were already reports of disturbances in London and the stabbing of a Russian student. My memories of watching some of the matches in a bar, in a little village in Tuscany, seemed like a dream on my return to reality. We had cheered with the locals for Italy, in a bar that also served as a post office and general store. We celebrated England's progress with chianti, while the Italians bewailed their early exit from the tournament.

The *Midnight Cowboy* scenario had become an option when Myfanwy booked the trip. In May he confessed to me that his medication wasn't working anymore, and he had developed non-Hodgkin lymphoma. Myfanwy's doctor informed him that he might only have a few months left to live, so he decided to enjoy one last hurrah in Italy.

It had become evident that Myfanwy's health was deteriorating for several weeks before he told me the fateful news. During the Christmas holidays he had managed to put on a lot of weight; so much so in fact that he could no longer fit into his boating blazer. Then in the spring his weight had dropped rapidly.

He began to suffer with fevers and when I changed his bedding one morning, I concluded that he had either pissed the bed or he was suffering from night sweats. I began to suspect that he had relapsed into his heroin addiction again and was attempting another surfeit of cold turkey. So much time had passed since he had been diagnosed as HIV-positive that it seemed to me as though the AIDS hysteria of the 1980s had all been exaggerated, due to lack of knowledge about the disease.

Italy had been chosen as the location for Myfanwy's trip, after he learned that his father had fought at the Battle of Monte Cassino. Over the years, Myfanwy had told me many stories concerning the illustrious life of the father he had never known. He had at various stages been a great train robber, a showbiz impresario and had played professional football for Wrexham.

The latest incarnation of Myfanwy's begetter suited me, as I'd always dreamed of visiting the homeland of Dante and Caravaggio. It was just a case of whether Myfanwy could hold out for the duration of the pilgrimage, and I was plagued by visions of Dustin Hoffman in a Bermuda shirt. I watched him physically disintegrate before my eyes, which he did with a great deal of panache. Bowie's Thin White Duke persona paled in comparison to the denouement of Myfanwy's final performance.

I had made inquiries about train schedules that might take us to Monte Cassino. Myfanwy had already grown bored with the idea by the time I had returned to the hotel with the timetables and information I had received at the tourist office. Before we had even arrived in Rome, he had decided that he wanted to do a tour of the Eternal City on a Vespa.

Florence had held little interest for Myfanwy, apart from the Ponte Vecchio. The old medieval bridge seemed to capture his imagination. He dreamed of being a Machiavellian double agent, playing off the Medici and Pazzi families against each other. The cathedral, with Brunelleschi's gigantic dome and Giotto's bell tower, left him equally underwhelmed. He preferred to share a bottle of wine with the beggars who congregated outside the huge bronze doors of the cathedral.

We spent several days in Rome and spent a whole day exploring on a rented scooter. When Myfanwy set eyes on a silver Vespa GS scooter, almost identical to the one that Sting rode in *Quadrophenia*, it seemed like kismet. Riding on the pillion around the chaotic Piazza Venezia, I seriously believed that Myfanwy intended to take me with him into the next world. The monument of Vittorio Emanuele II might have seemed a majestic place to end one's days, but I hoped to see more of the historic Italian capital.

The experience of Rome was overwhelming for me; both for its illustrious past and my awareness that Myfanwy would soon no longer be with me anymore. While we sat outside a café, a bored-looking young American student at a neighbouring table, made an attempt at conversation.

'So what do people do around here?' he asked with a shrug of his shoulders.

While I watched the Swiss Guards on duty outside the Vatican, wearing their familiar plumed morion helmets and parti-coloured uniform, another American tourist called out, 'Hey they've got clowns!'

As the taxi made its way up Sutton Road, the contrasting gloom of Mansfield cast me into a melancholy and lachrymose depression. I felt in my pocket for the bottle opener I had bought for Dawn. The souvenir from Rome was my last attempt at re-igniting the relationship with her which had realistically run its course.

After spending the night together, after the Christmas night out, we had continued to see each other in clandestine secrecy. In the workplace, we had evaded the inevitable puerile comments of our team mates by strictly avoiding each other. Dawn had been reluctant to commit to introducing me to her teenage daughters, for fear of exposing them to the kind of domestic discord that had characterised her relationship with her ex-husband.

I had been too eager to tumble blindly into a full-blown relationship with Dawn. I would have loved to shout from the rooftops that we were an item. As always, whenever I had met a woman, I had fallen hopelessly in love. Dawn, on the other hand, was happy for us to meet once a week at her house for sex, when her daughters stayed with their grandma. I didn't think that the 10-year difference in our ages mattered, but she seemed to be convinced that I should find someone younger, who I could raise a family with. I knew deep down that if I'd have moved in with her, I wouldn't have relished taking second place to her daughters and the whole set-up would have been a disaster.

The taxi turned right, past the William IV pub and onto Spencer Street. The red and white St. George's flag still hung from Cuckoo Walsh's window. Tommy Randall was sitting in his wheelchair in the doorway of his house, with stumps where his legs had once been. Sometimes living in Mansfield made you feel tethered to the spot, like Tommy with his amputated legs.

All was well on Harrington Street and the house hadn't been burgled while we'd been away. I was anxious about fetching Corky from across the Road at Mrs. Blower's house, where he'd been in residence during our holiday, but decided that the old lady would probably be in bed after 10 o'clock.

Myfanwy went out into the back yard to use the outside toilet and I opened my case and tried to locate the bottle of Pusser's rum, which I had bought on the ferry. I poured two generous measures of the potent spirit, which had been the chosen brand that the Royal Navy had used for its daily rum ration.

I switched on the television and browsed through the channels, until I settled on *Never Mind the Buzzcocks*. Along with the sports-based *They Think It's All Over* and the current affairs quiz *Have I Got News for You*, *Never Mind the Buzzcocks* was the latest in the new wave of irreverent panel game shows.

Team captain Sean Hughes was accompanied by our old friend Tip Topley. Phill Jupitus had Peter Stringfellow on his team, and the similarity between the nightclub owner and Topley was being lampooned by the show's presenter, Mark Lamarr. Stringfellow wore a leopard skin design on his shirt, which was undone to reveal a gold medallion. Topley's black silk shirt was also undone, revealing similar adornments and an abundance of chest hair. Both wore their hair in an extravagant mullet of bleached blond.

I was about to call out to Myfanwy that his hero was on TV, when I heard him shout from outside, 'Dean, get here quick!'

I leapt up from my chair and rushed outside. Myfanwy leaned on the wall that adjoined our house with that of Aashi's property. He pointed to where smoke was billowing out of a small window in one of the bedrooms. Myfanwy climbed over the wall and began to hammer on the back door. I stood dumbstruck, watching the black smoke pour from inside Aashi's house.

'Phone the fire brigade!' Myfanwy shouted to me.

I snapped out of my daze and rushed to the telephone.

After making the call, I hurried outside in time to see Myfanwy kicking in Aashi's back door. We had always said that the old door would be easy for a burglar to gain entry through. Once he had breached the door, Myfanwy ran headlong into the living room, where he was confronted by dense smoke. I hesitantly followed him, awed by his fearlessness. He began to shout out Aashi's name, but was repeatedly greeted by silence.

I found a couple of tea towels in the kitchen and ran some water over them. I remembered seeing an episode of *London's Burning* where I had seen someone put a wet towel over their face during a fire, to protect their lungs from the smoke. I had no idea whether this would have any effect but I held one of the towels over my face anyway.

I made my way through the thickening smoke of the living room with the other towel in my hand, but I couldn't see Myfanwy. My eyes were already stinging from the smoke and I had difficulty seeing ahead. I wasn't sure if Myfanwy had gone into the front room, or whether he had gone upstairs. As I neared the passage that led to the front door I was met by a surge of heat from flames that enveloped the front room. There was no chance of anyone leaving through the front door. I moved across to the doorway that led to the narrow passageway, which contained the staircase. Once again thick smoke and intense heat hindered my progress.

'Myfanwy get the fuck out!' I screamed.

I could hear the sound of Myfanwy choking but received no other reply. I could hear the sirens of the fire engine outside and then the sound of the front door being forced open.

I was about to follow Myfanwy upstairs, imitating his bravery, but the heat and fumes forced me back. I began to choke and retch and felt as though I might black out when I felt someone grab me and drag me away. Several moments later I emerged from the suffocating miasma of Aashi's house and was met with the most heavenly fresh air I had ever tasted. Hellish looking figures wearing breathing apparatus, passed me by. The sound of sirens had multiplied and my oxygen-starved brain perceived dozens of flashing lights and fire engine noise as I emerged onto Harrington Street.

Sitting beside a fire engine with an oxygen mask on my face, a few minutes later I began to get a clearer picture of the scene that was unfolding. Neighbours watched from their doorways and from behind windows, like toddlers enthralled by their first Bonfire Night display. A fireman stood atop a ladder, aiming a fire hose into the front bedroom of Aashi's house. An ambulance had arrived on the scene and I wondered if Myfanwy had been badly burned. I was sure he must have been too late to save the life of our neighbour, amidst the raging inferno that I had barely been able to approach.

'Do you know how many other people were in the house?' asked a burly fireman with a goatee beard.

'Our neighbour,' I began, trying to compose my mind, as it competed with the confusion of shock. 'She lived alone. My friend went upstairs to rescue her. I couldn't see anyone.'

I broke down in tears and the fireman just nodded and went back to his duties. His colleagues were now going in and out of the house quite freely and it appeared that they had dealt with the worst of the fire. I began to panic about the effect of the fire on our own home and wondered if we would have a roof over our heads that night.

Paramedics entered Aashi's house and came out several minutes later with a stretcher, which they carried to a waiting ambulance. The bearded fireman approached me again wearing a puzzled expression.

'Are you sure there was one person in there when you and your friend entered the building?'

'I'm sure the lady would have been on her own. Her dad only ever visits in the daytime and she never goes anywhere.'

'The thing is, we have only found a single male in there; there is definitely no one else inside.'

'You've found my mate!' I croaked. 'Is he okay?'

I looked deeply into his eyes and could see he wasn't optimistic, 'He's suffering with some very severe burns and he's inhaled a lot of smoke,' said the fireman, taking off his helmet and wiping his forehead. 'I'm sure the ambulance service and the hospital staff will do everything in their power to take care of him.'

I felt a sudden surge of adrenalin and pulled myself up onto my feet. I needed to get to the hospital and find Myfanwy.

'Sir you need to sit down,' the fireman said as he steadied me by the arm, 'another ambulance is coming, and they'll check you out to make sure you're okay. Then you can see your mate.'

I began ranting, trying to make sense of everything, 'He's inhaled more smoke than a laboratory beagle that lad,' I said to nobody in particular, 'His lungs have sucked in and spat out more than that each day, before he's even had his breakfast.'

A taxi turned onto Harrington Street and quickly stopped when the driver saw the road cluttered with vehicles of the emergency services. I watched a figure in the back seat, passing the driver his fare. I staggered to my feet once again and steadied myself as I recovered from a bout of dizziness. I began to walk briskly down the street, signalling to the taxi driver to wait. I had to get to the hospital and see Myfanwy; I wasn't ready to say goodbye just yet.

The passenger emerged from the rear door of the taxi. A small, stocky Asian woman climbed out and smiled at me as I approached. It was Aashi, dressed in an orange saree and adorned with henna and golden jewellery. Her mountainous midriff was exposed for all to see.

'I've been to a wedding,' she said with one eye on the flashing lights behind me.

'Your house has burned down,' I said sympathetically and climbed into the taxi. I suddenly realised that I hadn't even locked the back door.

CHAPTER THIRTEEN

The sound of mail dropping through the letter box produced a churning in Heidi's stomach. She didn't want to get out of bed but she needed to see if there might be a summons to appear at court. The irrational fear that Tsucol would sue her for quitting her job without due notice constantly plagued Heidi's troubled mind.

She hurried down the stairs in her Snoopy nightshirt and felt a moment of panic when she set eyes on the pile of mail that had arrived that morning. She shuffled through the letters; a postcard from Malta, sent by her brother; several official looking envelopes, which bore her surname spelled incorrectly, which singled them out as junk mail. Finally, she opened an envelope with a handwritten address and a second-class stamp. She anxiously tore it open and was relieved to discover that it was just a letter from the health centre to remind her to make an appointment for a review of her medication.

It had been two months since Heidi had walked out of her job at Tsucol. Since returning to work after the Christmas break, her career had taken a downward spiral. After the debacle at the Superbowl, she had gone home and spent most of Christmas crying. The thought of returning to work in the new year and having to confront Les and the gossips at Tsucol made her feel like never going back again.

The holiday had been the worst she could remember at home; even worse than the years when her parents had argued throughout the festive season. Heidi's mother's dementia was manifesting itself in a more aggressive manner. The days when Heidi had worried that her mother had forgotten who she was had been but a prelude to the horrors to come. It was growing more difficult each day to get her to eat the food Heidi and her father tried to place in her mouth. She could hardly articulate any rational language anymore, let alone recognise her children. Elaine grew more aggressive and lashed out at anyone, when her confused brain became frustrated with the effort of trying to make sense of the strange world she woke up to each day. The one morsel of comfort was that Heidi's father was now entitled to several days respite each month, while Elaine spent time in a nursing home.

The fact that Heidi's own mental health issues had made it difficult for her to help her father only strengthened the hold in which her depression gripped her. She had begun the year with a new year resolution to be stronger and focus on succeeding in her career in management. The first day back, she had noted that Les had distanced himself from her. She had told herself that everyone would have forgotten about her outburst at the bowling alley. The first time that Heidi had needed to cross the shop floor, she had been met with cheers and whistles from certain areas. She decided that it would all die down sooner or later and they would find something new to gossip about.

Things didn't get any better for Heidi and life in the office gradually became unbearable. She noticed Les on several occasions in conversation with colleagues and she was convinced that they were glancing in her direction and sniggering. Les began to criticise her work and no longer complimented her when she did well.

Promotion and a pay rise had seemed inevitable a few months earlier, but it was becoming clear that Heidi was now being overlooked in favour of other candidates. Jill Blunt had always been a character that Heidi had given a wide birth. Jill always flirted with Les and resented Heidi's diligence and work ethic. She would spend all day talking to whoever would listen to her. She was always the last in and would not stay a minute over her contracted hours.

Everything came to a head one day during a meeting about proposed changes to the structure of the administration department. Heidi had previously made suggestions that would bring greater efficiency and a more productive environment. Les had praised Heidi's new system when they had discussed it in December.

During the meeting, Les was now displaying a large degree of ambivalence to Heidi's ideas. Most of the other staff were taking on board what was being proposed. Everyone had expressed their desire to spend their time in a more productive and rewarding way. Jill's indolence was a constant source of irritation to everyone, especially since she was on a higher salary scale to many.

It was clear from the outset that Jill would not find the changes agreeable to her, as they would require her to work as hard as everyone else. She bided her time while everyone else enthused about the new system, until it was time for her to have her say. Heidi kept quiet, always slightly afraid of Jill. But the more outspoken Melanie Davenport argued the toss with Jill. Eventually Jill erupted, but it wasn't Melanie she aimed her polemic at, it was Heidi. She began to jab her index finger towards Heidi and yelled across the table that the whole thing was a counter-productive farce. Heidi shrank into her chair, terrified by the palpable violence of Jill's acrimonious onslaught. Melanie attempted to calm Jill down but she carried on relentlessly, crucifying Heidi with her invective. At no point did Les try to intervene during the tirade, remaining impassive throughout. Despite several imploring glances from various people for him to intervene, Les sat with his arms folded, staring vacantly into space.

Tears began to run down Heidi's face and she felt physically sick. Her fight-or-flight response was screaming at her to run for the hills. Unable to take the unchecked verbal battering any longer, Heidi rushed out of the meeting room with the sound of Jill's voice still reverberating in her ears.

Heidi hid beneath the bedclothes for several days after fleeing from her job. Each time the phone rang it felt as though her superiors at Tsucol were physically reaching through the line to bring her to justice. She received a letter written by Les, imploring her to speak to him about her absence. He wrote in a diction that suggested a sense of empathy for Heidi, from himself, and expressed concern from her colleagues.

When Heidi finally plucked up the courage to speak to Les, she was beginning to feel more confident about returning to work. She imagined that Les had seen the error of his ways and might be concerned about how the incident at the meeting would impact on his own career. She entertained herself with visions of Jill being ceremoniously given the sack and a triumphant welcome from her colleagues.

As soon as she heard Les's tone on the other end of the telephone receiver, Heidi knew that she had deceived herself.

'What did you think you would achieve by storming off in a huff during a meeting?' he asked reproachfully. 'Come back in tomorrow and we'll see if we can start again. Onwards and upward and all that. Maybe this is the kick up the arse you needed.'

This was not what Heidi had expected at all, 'I'm not sure I can come back after everything that has happened,' she said through her sobs.

'Well maybe that would be the best thing for everyone concerned,' was his curt answer before abruptly putting down the phone.

Heidi's P45 came through the post two days later, along with a letter accepting her resignation. She was paid her full salary up until the end of the month. It was fortunate that she had put aside enough money to get by for a couple of months. Depression and anxiety forced her to stay indoors for many weeks. The anti-depressants she had been prescribed by her doctor made her feel more anxious than before she had begun taking them. They made her stomach sensitive and kept her from sleeping at night.

Only Jeanette kept Heidi from doing something truly desperate, with her regular visits with her children.

'You should take the bastard to court for sexual harassment,' Jeanette would say, but Heidi just wanted to walk away and never see Les or Jill ever again.

'He must be fucking that Jill,' Jeanette said angrily. 'Either that or she's got something else over him.'

It pleased Heidi that her friend supported her in such a partisan manner, but she knew that she didn't have a leg to stand on.

Six months later Heidi was filling in the forms so that she could receive unemployment benefit. Dole money had been given a new facelift and Heidi found that she was eligible for *contributions based* Jobseeker's Allowance. Filling in the forms for her claim had involved writing a lengthy statement about her reasons for leaving her previous job. When she was asked what she had been doing to find employment since leaving her last job, Heidi wrote down a list of employers she might have contacted, if she had felt sufficiently confident enough to venture back into full-time employment.

It was a perfect summer's day outside, and as Heidi opened the curtains she had a sudden urge to break free. It was quiet outside in the street, with most children still at school and many of the adults in the neighbourhood out at work. During England's campaign in the European Football Championship, the street had been uncomfortably noisy. The long June evenings had been warm and brought out the barbeques and kids with footballs. Heidi had hidden herself away, while everyone else seemed to be enjoying a street carnival. The sound of drunken revelry outside, felt intimidating and Heidi was relieved when the inevitable torrents of rain finally called time on the party. For many months during her reclusion, Heidi had craved solitude but she was finally growing weary of being alone. Her father was struggling to care full-time for her mother and Andrew was busy with his new career down in Taunton.

Jeanette's visits had diminished since she had started seeing her new boyfriend. Heidi had only met the man once; a sly and narcissistic character called Colin, who said he was part of the management team at the Barr's soft drinks factory. Heidi was sceptical about Colin's actual role at Barr's as he had been evasive when she had asked him questions about the management of the factory.

A young mother pushed a pram down the street and Heidi wished that she could have a child of her own. *I would probably make a rubbish mum*, she thought. When she had dreamed of being a successful businesswoman like Melanie Griffiths in *Working Girl*, the last thing Heidi had wanted was to be tied down with a baby. She had looked contemptuously at those old school friends who had become parents when they could have been enjoying their salad days. Heidi now realised that no amount of travel or worldly pleasures could match the life experience of giving birth to a child.

The little house on Oak Tree Lane was growing claustrophobic and Heidi made her mind up that it was time to get out and breathe some fresh air. She changed into her jeans and a light blue smock blouse. While she was searching through her drawers, she found her old Tsucol polo shirts neatly folded. She decided that they might make decent dusting cloths. She decided that some spring cleaning might prove to be good therapy at some stage.

Heidi picked up her car keys and marched purposefully to her car. She had no idea where she was going but she started the car and pulled out of the drive before she had the chance to change her mind. There had come a point where she had considered selling the car. Her father persuaded her that it would prove indispensable if she needed to travel to a new employer.

Driving up Nottingham Road, Heidi slowed down to take a look at the house where she had spent her teenage years. It had been a turbulent period, where her parents' marriage had almost imploded and Heidi had been forced to make new friends after the family had moved from Essex.

The urban creation that was Mansfield soon gave way to the trees and fields of rural Nottinghamshire. The sunshine streamed through the trees of Harlow Wood, in the heart of Robin Hood country. The car weaved its way through the sylvan splendour, passing through the picturesque villages of Ravenshead and Papplewick. Driving aimlessly around the beautiful countryside, Heidi once again found herself heading towards Mansfield. The gates of Newstead Abbey beckoned her unto a romantic region which had been the ancestral seat of the Byrons.

After paying five pounds to enter the grounds, Heidi drove along the drive that led to the place where the illustrious poet George Gordon Byron had once lived a life dedicated to the art of poesy. Passing the rhododendrons and the cricket pitch, Heidi parked near the old gardener's cottage.

She sat in a courtyard that overlooked the old house and the gothic ruins of the priory. The atrocities of the Reformation had left little of the old monastic buildings. A huge arch invited the imagination to picture it adorned with stained glass. Fragments of pointed architecture still boldly displayed the splendour that had been created by the genius of medieval craftsmen.

The majestic lake and serene Japanese garden brought a refreshing calmness to the stormy seas that raged inside Heidi's mind. The peacocks that spread their Argus-eyed fans reminded her too much of the posturing of Les. At the rear of the ruins, she found a formal garden and an ornamental pond. A figure sat on a bench near the pond, accompanied by statuary that depicted characters from classical mythology.

On closer inspection, the lone figure turned out to be a young man, engrossed in a book. Heidi walked by the opposite side of the pond and noticed the man raise his head from his book to study her. To her surprise he waved to her and she sheepishly waved back. As he put the book down beside him on the bench, Heidi suddenly recognised him as Dean Swift.

At first Heidi thought it would be easier to keep walking in the opposite direction. More than anything, she felt wary about engaging in conversation with anyone associated with Tsucol. Something about Dean's disarming smile made her feel comfortable about approaching him. Even so, her stomach began to churn as though she were about to face Les himself.

'Hey, long time no see,' said Dean in a tone that made Heidi feel totally at ease.

'Are you on the night shift this week?' she asked, curious whether he might have also left Tsucol.

'No, I'm kind of taking time off due to a bereavement.'

'Oh I'm sorry to hear about that,' replied Heidi as she sat down beside him. She felt awkward about asking whether it was anyone close. It seemed a stupid question really, but she had known people to take time off when their pets had died.

Not sure what to say next, Heidi picked up the book that lay beside Dean. It was a collection of the major poetical works of Lord Byron. An Oxford World Classics edition, with a portrait of the poet on its cover, dressed in a luxuriant Greek costume.

'You've come to the right place for this,' she said, holding up the book.

'Yes I often come here to get my head together,' said Dean in a way that suggested to Heidi that he was feeling as melancholy as she was.

'Yes it's very tranquil.'

'So what are you doing these days?'

Here comes the awkward question thought Heidi, 'I'm resting, as they say in the acting profession.'

'Ah yes I had a long spell of resting myself,' said Dean, perking up a little. 'I could do with a rest from Tsucol to be honest.'

'Bit stressful is it?'

'I'm always reminded these days of the scene in *Schindler's List*, where Ralph Fiennes is holding a gun to some guys head because he hasn't fulfilled his quota.'

'Oh yes I remember,' recalled Heidi, 'and it turned out that he hadn't done enough because the machine was broken down.'

It had never occurred to Heidi when she had worked at Tsucol that the operatives were anything other than extensions of the machines they worked at; she could see things more clearly now.

'My team leader phoned me up this morning to ask me when I would be back at work,' said Dean. 'I only phoned in myself yesterday to tell them my best friend had died in a fire.'

'Oh my God!' said Heidi, remembering reading about the fire in the newspaper. 'I had no idea it was you. You must be still recovering yourself, surely?'

'I'm fine; we only went in to rescue the neighbour and she wasn't even in at the time.'

'Oh my goodness that's terrible,' said Heidi, putting her hand on Dean's shoulder as tears began to run down his cheeks.

It was clear that Dean was grieving for his friend and Heidi concluded that it might be cathartic to help him release some of his emotions.

'Anyway,' he finally continued, 'my team leader phoned up and suggested that I might be better off at work than moping about at home.'

Heidi held her hands to her mouth in shock and disbelief. Dean suddenly seemed to see the ridiculousness of the situation and began laughing.

'Sounds like I'm well out of it then,' Heidi said, hardly being able to resist hearing the latest Tsucol gossip.

'Oh you'd love it there now. Do you remember when there was a ban on people reading the *Daily Sport* ?'

'I think that was me who put that ban in place. It was degrading for women to have to be confronted by that sort of filth each time they came into the canteen for a sandwich –' Heidi realised that she was getting on her high horse, 'but go on anyway.'

'Yeah well someone wrote a letter to the *Daily Sport* about the ban and it was subsequently printed. Then the most surreal thing happened. I was coming out of the factory one afternoon, on one of those rare occasions when we managed to finish on time, and there were two topless models and a photographer outside.'

'You're joking!'

'No straight up, they were inviting people to come and have their picture taken with the models.'

'Did you go up to them?' she asked in a tone of mock reproach.

'No I was too embarrassed to do anything like that. Then Les Johnson came outside to try and get them off the property and the girls just threw their arms around him. Les, being the arrogant bastard he is, couldn't help smiling and then the photographer took his picture.'

Heidi was on the edge of her seat now, pleased that she had made the effort to come out.

'The *Daily Sport* only went and printed the picture of Les and then Mal Bolge flew over from America to find out for himself what had happened.'

'Wow it has to be something big before they send in the big guns like that.'

'Yeah well I heard that Les cleared his desk and stormed out of the office after Mal Bolge sounded him out. Rumour has it he told him where to stick his job.'

Heidi was enjoying a tremendous sense of *schadenfreude* from the news she was hearing from this handsome Hermes.

'Oh yeah and I don't know whether it's true or not, but everyone is saying that Les has got Jill from the office up the stick and he's said he doesn't want anything to do with it.'

Dean observed the barely contained expression of triumph on Heidi's face and felt pleased that he had been the one to cheer her up.

'Don't suppose you fancy a tea or a coffee in the café do you?' he asked nonchalantly.

'I'm not sure I've got enough after being mugged at the gate.'

'Please allow me the pleasure of buying you the beverage of your choice,' he said as he stood up and bowed chivalrously. He removed the wide-brimmed cricket hat he wore and flourished it in the direction of the café.

The Abbey café was situated in the west wing of the old house. Dean ordered coffee and ice cream for them both and they sat outside in a shady courtyard. Several peacocks had decided to perch on the ancient wall that enclosed the courtyard and quietly groomed themselves.

A couple of American tourists were seated at a neighbouring table, evidently unimpressed by everything they had experienced during their time in England.

'At least it was better than the crumby hotel in Aarksford,' one of them droned. 'I don't know why that guy had to get so pissed, just because I didn't stand in line at reception.'

Heidi picked up the book of Byronic verse that Dean had put down, unable to concentrate with the irritating whinging sound ringing in his ear. She opened the book at a random page and began to read a stanza which seemed to sum up her year so far.

I had a dream, which was not all a dream.
The bright sun was extinguish'd, and the stars
Did wander darkling in the eternal space,
Rayless, and pathless, and icy earth
Swung blind and blackening in the moonless air;
Morn came and went-and came, and brought
no day…

For the first time in months she felt alive again and realised that the darkness that Byron's poem envisaged was finally giving way to light.

'Have you any plans now you're a free agent?' Dean asked.

Heidi sighed and gazed at the blue sky as though she had never truly seen it that colour before, 'I've spent the last 10 years focusing on being some kind of big shot business woman and Its only just occurred to me that the best years of my life have just passed me by.'

'You're still in your prime, though. Someone with your confidence and intelligence can do anything you want if you put your mind to it.'

'I'm afraid the confidence took a bit of a pounding and I don't know if I'll ever straighten it out again.'

'Oh I've fallen head first into my own sloughs of despair, but the real strength and courage comes when you pull yourself out again. You start to appreciate the light more when you've been down there,' he said, pointing towards the open page which contained Byron's 'Darkness'.

There didn't seem anything sententious about Dean's comments and Heidi sensed a kindred spirit in the boy who she had held a fascination for since their first encounter. She felt safe in his presence and realised that she had been looking in all the wrong places for happiness up until that moment.

CHAPTER FOURTEEN

Corky triumphantly rang his bell then proudly surveyed his new cage. The brass bars of his domed parrot cage shone in the sunlight, which filtered through the living room window. Since the demise of Myfanwy, Corky had been my sole companion and I decided to upgrade his accommodation. The sturdy Edwardian bricks of the house had withstood the heat of the blaze that had consumed the next house.

As Myfanwy's sole beneficiary, the ownership of the house had been bequeathed to me. It had come as a surprise that someone as unorganised as Myfanwy had found the time and inclination to make a will. The house, the *Quadrophenia* video and the boating blazer had all been handed down to me.

An inquiry concluded that the fire had been started deliberately. Speculation began about whether there had been racist motives involved. The news had reported a fire in a North London house, targeting a married couple who had been investigating the activities of the far-right group known as the British Free Corps. I recalled Myfanwy mentioning that Cuckoo Walsh had been involved in far-right political activities and with him living around the corner, his involvement seemed plausible. He had been questioned about his whereabouts on the night of the fire, but he had an airtight alibi in that he had been at Wembley that evening for the semi-final match.

Aashi had moved back in with her father on Goldsmith Street, placing her gutted home on the property market. According to the police, there was evidence that Aashi had been receiving hate mail, but due to her illiteracy she hadn't been sure of the nature of the letters. Whoever was responsible, my friend had been the tragic victim. It seemed ironic that Myfanwy had spent so much time trying to avoid Aashi and he had lost his life running headlong into her burning bedroom.

It was a Monday morning and I was on the night shift later that evening. The long weekend always looked appealing when I left work on Friday afternoon, but when I woke up on the Monday it was just an entire day waiting around for another week of nights to commence. At least I could look forward to meeting Heidi at the weekend. Since our chance meeting at Newstead Abbey, we had begun to see each other regularly. She would already be busy at work doing whatever temporary office work the employment agency had found for her.

I wandered into Myfanwy's bedroom and sat on his bed. He hadn't left much behind to show for his life. The Welsh flag still hung on the wall, along with his mod memorabilia: photos of the mod rally at Clacton; the iconic 'Maximum R & B' poster that advertised The Who's residency at the Marquee Club; and a couple of scooter club patches.

I looked inside his wardrobe, wondering how I could ever part with any of his things. His old prison issue shirt and his iridescent two-tone jacket, hung alongside his parka and a pair of Levi's jeans that he had worn in the bath to shrink down to a skin-tight fit. In the bottom of his underwear drawer I found old newsletters from a Style Council fan club called The Torch Society. An Ashes test match ticket was kept as a reminder of the day he flirted at Trent Bridge with a well-known Queen's Council and made the acquaintance of his favourite rock star. How we had ended up on a pub crawl with the one and only Tip Topley still baffled me. Only Myfanwy could have got into a situation where he began the day by hobnobbing with celebrities and ended it with a near-fatal drug overdose. That day seemed like a surreal dream to me, which the ticket failed to render credible.

I lay on his Union Jack quilt and sobbed, as I had done at the crematorium on the day we all bid him farewell. There had been a motley assortment of mourners at Myfanwy's cremation; smart mods and scruffy mods; a couple of football casuals from the Coocachoo Crew; a few Dickensian scoundrels who he had mentored as thieves. There were no family members present, apart from an elderly lady who referred to herself as his Aunty Pat. *Jump and Dance* by The Carnaby played as his already badly burned body disappeared into the flames of the furnace. Most of the mourners made their excuses and vanished before the wake, which took place at the White Hart.

I went back to my own room, not sure how long I could stay in an empty house with so many memories haunting it. I lay on my bed and prepared to doze off. I always took a nap before my first night shift, though it never adequately alleviated the desperate weariness that would come in the hours before dawn. Deprived of sleep, a nightshift worker craves sleep, in the same way that someone lost in a desert thirsts for water. I gazed at the light on the ceiling, which reflected through a gap in the curtains. The sunshine transmitted a hazy red that bounced from a car outside and made a vague impression above me. The silence outside was interrupted by the rapid, Woody Woodpecker rattle of a magpie.

A robust knock at the door startled me from my alpha brainwaves, into beta mode. I decided that it would probably be someone faking deafness, selling dish cloths and tea towels. Myfanwy had briefly done a stint going door-to-door, feigning disability and selling sundry items of household use. A second knock at the door made me sit up and speculate whether the police had returned with questions concerning the fire. On the third occasion I decided it would be a good idea to go and see who was so persistently trying to gain my attention.

The banging continued as I hastened towards the front door. A tall, skeletal looking man loomed on the doorstep. He appeared to be in his early-50s, wearing a white Lacoste polo shirt, faded jeans and a pair of Nike trainers. His head was closely shaved and he grinned at me with a set of teeth that looked as though they had been borrowed from Shane McGowan. He had the emaciated build of a junky, which belied a wiry athleticism that I guessed had taken form in prison.

'Is Myfanwy in?' he asked in an accent that sounded as though it originated in East London or maybe Essex.

'He's not in right now,' I said, hoping the stranger might go away and never return.

'Have you any idea what time he might get back?' he continued. 'I'm an old mate of his, we err—well we used to be mates in the nick. That's my name, Nick.'

I couldn't recall Myfanwy mentioning anyone of that name and didn't remember seeing him at the funeral. There was something almost pitiful in the disappointed expression Nick wore that made me decide to tell him the truth.

'Look I hate to be the bearer of bad tidings, but Myfanwy passed away recently.'

Nick looked me in the eye as though he was trying to work out whether I was just trying to get rid of him. He then began to look around at the bricks of the house, tears welling up in his eyes. He didn't look like the type of person who was given to lachrymose displays of emotion and appeared to be embarrassed about losing his composure.

'I don't suppose there's a boozer round here is there?' said Nick after taking a few deep breaths. 'This has really choked me up this has. I don't know if he ever mentioned me to you; we got really close about 10 years ago when we were banged up in Lincoln.'

'You're not Sutts are you by any chance? He was always banging on about someone of that name.'

'That's me; Nick Sutcliffe, some calls me Sutts.'

I had heard many tales about the illustrious life of Sutts, who had taken on an almost mythical status for Myfanwy. Sutts had been part of the nascent mod scene that flowered in London in the early 1960s; an androgynous, pill-popping wide boy, who had created Bank Holiday havoc at seaside resorts and then found himself a pawn in a gangland war between the Kray and Richardson factions.

I took him round to the William IV pub on Sutton Road, where we held our own wake for Myfanwy. Sutts had a wad of banknotes in his jeans and wouldn't allow me to pay for a single round. The morning sun had given way to a cloudy and humid afternoon. We vacated the stifling atmosphere of the interior of the pub for the fresher air of the beer garden. The area at the rear of the William IV held no verdant qualities and consisted of a couple of benches at the end of a large car park. It was enclosed on two sides by the backyards of the terraced houses of Harrington Street and Spencer Street; a third side was occupied by the bus garage.

Sutts was quaffing his lager with a sense of urgency that suggested he was on his way back to jail instead of celebrating new-found freedom.

'Here's to Myfanwy eh!' he said ernestly, holding his glass aloft 'A diamond geezer if ever I met one.'

'May he sup with Keith Moon in rock 'n' roll heaven for all eternity.'

'Too right mate. I couldn't have put it better. Do you reckon this fire might have been started deliberately then?' asked Sutts.

'The fire brigade and the police are investigating it as a possible racist attack.'

'I'd like to get my hands on the toe rags that killed my mate. When you said he was dead I wondered if the old AIDS had caught up with him.'

'Oh did you know about his HIV status then?' I asked. 'You could say it had caught up with him. He'd developed this non-Hodgkin lymphoma thing and his doctor hadn't given him long to live. Then he went and did his Batman routine and ended up getting himself fried for his troubles.'

'He came to visit me a few years ago when I was doing a spell in the Scrubs and told me about the HIV. You say the old girl next door wasn't even in at the time?'

'Well she wasn't really old, but yeah basically I was sat next to a fire engine with an oxygen mask on my face and she suddenly turned up in a taxi.'

'Trust that soppy bastard to end up brown bread over some bird,' said Sutts with a wry smile.

I had a presentiment that the gathering clouds were about to release a thundery torrent of rain as I felt gentle drops of warm moisture on my face. We repaired to the dryness of the saloon bar, as the raindrops quickly turned into a major downpour. We stationed ourselves on barstools and continued our convivial session. *Wannabe* by the Spice Girls was playing on the jukebox.

'What the fuck's this?' said Sutts, almost choking on his beer.

'The bastard children of Bananarama,' I replied. 'We need to put some decent music on.'

We inspected the selection of compact discs on the jukebox that was mounted on a wall, 'Oh nice one!' exclaimed Sutts with glee. 'Booker T & the MG's *Green Onions*. That one always takes me back to my days selling purple hearts at the Aquarium Ballroom in Brighton.'

'Myfanwy was always telling me about when you used to go and see The Who when they first started.'

'Yeah well the first time I saw them they were going by the name of the High Numbers. I saw them at the Railway Hotel in Wealdstone. I saw them again at the Goldhawk Social Cub in Shepherd's Bush a few months later and they'd changed their name to The Who by then.'

So is it true you were involved with the Kray twins?' I asked with growing fascination.

'Yeah well that was Charlie Richardson, when he heard I was sleeping with boys as well as girls, he decided it might be a clever idea to get me noticed by Ronnie Kray; sleeping with the enemy and all that.'

'I bet that was fun, he was supposed to be a bit of a psychopath wasn't he?'

'He was a very sensitive and tender man,' said Sutts with a touch of sarcasm. 'He always looked after me because his mum took a shine to me, and I used to make her a nice cup of tea and bring her a sticky bun sometimes.'

Thunder rumbled outside and the dark sky was intermittently illuminated with flashes of lightning.

'I think Myfanwy is trying to join the party,' I said, gesturing towards the heavens. The unmistakable introduction of *Jane Does it That Way* by the Prentice Boys interrupted the stentorian declamations of the thunder. 'Now I know it's Myfanwy stomping in heaven, he loved this one.'

'Nah bunch of poncey college boys!' Sutts said derisively. 'I've shit better; no the Pretty Things and the Downliners Sect were more my bag; not to mention the Oo' of course.'

'Funny you should say that actually, me and Myfanwy once met Tip Topley and he really was the most pretentious and narcissistic character I've ever met.'

Sutts looked sceptically at me and replied, 'When did you meet him then, pretending to be narsty and a sissy or whatever you said?'

'Oh it's a long story really.'

'One thing you learn in the nick is that there is always plenty of time to hear a good story and Myfanwy was the best at spinning a good yarn.'

We ordered more drinks and I regaled Sutts with the account of our chance meeting with Tip Topley on a riverboat, which just happened to belong to the artist who had created some of the most iconic album covers of the 1960s. Myfanwy's encounter with QC Edward Towton particularly drew the attention of my drinking partner. He claimed he had met the likes of Towton many times in the courtroom and I palpably sensed a rancorous hatred of all guardians of the judicial system.

A commotion from the tap room diverted our attention from my reminiscences. Through the passage between the two bars, I could see Cuckoo Walsh brandishing a 20-pound note as if he had won the lottery. Beside him was his young apprentice plasterer, Josh. Cuckoo was noisily demanding to be served by the pretty young barmaid, who seemed unfazed by his demanding tone.

Cuckoo was wearing an old Lonsdale sweatshirt, which was bespattered with plaster. Josh wore a faded New York Yankees baseball cap, which was similarly festooned with evidence of his trade. I had a sudden recollection of seeing Josh before somewhere, wearing the black hooded sweatshirt from which he was presently producing a packet of cigarettes.

Cuckoo spotted me looking over at him and commented acerbically, 'If looks could give you AIDS, I would be dead by now. What's your problem?'

I slowly shook my head and turned away, not wishing to aggravate the pugnacious Walsh.

'Who's that cant?' asked Sutts.

'You don't want to know,' I replied quietly, desperate to avoid a confrontation. 'Why don't we go somewhere else.'

'I haven't finished this yet,' said Sutts, eyeing Cuckoo as he downed his beer.

We left through the back door and headed along Sutton road towards the town centre.

'What was that all about?' continued Sutts, still agitated by Cuckoo's comments. 'He said something about AIDS; was he having a pop at Myfanwy or what?'

'Myfanwy told him all about his HIV status just to get him off his back a while ago. You know what Myfanwy was like; he didn't give a shit.'

'He's looking for a right good kicking if he keeps giving it bunny like that.'

'I think he's pissed off because the police questioned him about the fire,' I replied, sensing that I was in the presence of a useful ally if Cuckoo attempted any further provocation.

'What! You reckon he had something to do with torching that bird's house?'

'Myfanwy said something to me about Cuckoo being involved in some neo-Nazi group called the British Free Corps; I just happened to mention it to the police.'

'I'll cuckoo him if I get hold of him in a dark alley,' said Sutts in a genuinely menacing tone.

We reached the bottom of Sutton Road and entered the Red Lion. We sat down at a couple of tall stools near the bar and gazed at the assorted items of Americana that adorned the walls. Some pubs had taken to decorating their interiors with shelves of books, bicycles and packing cases; others furnished their rooms with themed memorabilia. The Red Lion had opted for an American diner look, complete with red faux leather seats and sepia photographs of New York. There was even a full-size canoe suspended from the ceiling. Usually whatever was in vogue in London would arrive in the provinces a few years later.

We sipped our bottles of Budweiser and Sutts ordered a hamburger and fries. His repast seemed to settle his mood once more and we recommenced our reminiscences of Myfanwy.

'He was always telling me how you looked after him in jail when some heavies started on him.'

'It was the other way round really,' Sutts reflected. 'I'd got someone on the outside, bringing in heroin that I was dealing. There was this big spade called Joel Watts who was the top boy in Lincoln for the drug game. I got Myfanwy to help me shift this stuff, because he knew all the faces in there when I arrived. Joel got wind that Myfanwy was selling brown on his patch and sent a couple of his crew to give him a slap for dealing on his watch. He was already getting a pasting when I got there but I managed to get them off him and then a couple of screws came by and split us up. He never told them who he was getting the shit from and he saved me from a proper seeing to.'

It was getting close to four o'clock and I realised that I needed to get home and take a couple of hours sleep before my night shift. Sutts and I parted like old friends and he said he would call round again sometime. I made my way back home along

Bancroft Lane in order to avoid incurring the wrath of Cuckoo once again. With my mind still focused on the incident in the William IV, I suddenly remembered where I had last seen Josh.

I had the vivid recollection of climbing off the coach, on the night we arrived back home from the Italian trip. The realisation that I was back in the gloomy heart of Mansfield had registered when I had seen Josh in the bus station. He was sat on the backrest of a bench, his head shrouded in the hood of his black sweatshirt. Could it be that he had been sent by Cuckoo to start the fire that night. He could quite easily have made it back from Harrington Street to the Rosemary Street bus station in a few minutes. The more I speculated whether Josh had been responsible for Myfanwy's death, the more his presence at the bus station seemed to be a complete coincidence. It was a Saturday evening and he could have been waiting for a bus after watching England play Germany. Josh just didn't seem like the kind of person who would get involved in anything like that.

After I arrived home I went straight to bed and fell into a deep, alcohol-induced sleep. I was rudely awakened by more thumping on the front door. I felt dehydrated and groggy after my slumber and resentfully went downstairs to greet the persistent visitor. I opened the door and was confronted by the sight of Sutts leaning against the wall, with blood pouring down his face.

'Any chance I can come in for a bit?' he asked, quite politely under the circumstances.

I led him into the living room and told him to sit down while I found something to hold against his wound, to stem the flow of blood. I found a tea towel in the kitchen and ran some water over it.

'Here put this over the wound,' I said, offering him the towel. 'I think I might have some Germoline somewhere.'

I had no First Aid training and had little idea how to react in such situations. The gaping wound on his forehead looked as though it needed stitches.

'Do you think we ought to get you to the casualty department?' I asked.

'No I'll be just fine here for now,' replied Sutts, wincing as he pressed the towel to his head. 'I bumped into your mate Cuckoo again after you left. He came into that boozer with all the American stuff. I was having a game of pool with some old geezer and Cuckoo comes over and starts giving it the big 'un.'

'Shit, it looks like he gave you a proper good hiding.'

'No I started it to be fair,' Sutts blithely confessed. 'I smashed a pool cue over his back. I had the best off it for a while, then he got me round the neck and slammed me head into the bar. Someone behind the bar said the old bill were on the way and everyone had it on their toes. I can't risk going down the hospital and getting picked up by the law; I'm on probation at the moment and I'll be straight back inside if they get hold of me for this.'

I figured that it would be for the best if Sutts stayed with me that night and to keep a low profile until the following morning. I knew that Myfanwy would have done the same and I had grown quite fond of Sutts in the brief time that we had spent together. I still couldn't risk leaving him alone in the house while I went out to work so I decided to take the night off.

CHAPTER FIFTEEN

'There you go lads,' said John Freeman as he looked through his rear-view mirror, 'Princess Diana is available again. Get yoursens for'ard, you never know your luck.'

Josh was staring vacantly out of the window, sat in the rear of the car. The radio news announcement about the formal divorce of the Prince and Princess of Wales had no impact on him at all.

'Imagine munching on that after Charlie has been there,' marvelled Sammy from the passenger seat, 'it's mind blowing.'

'He probably had someone else to do all that for him,' said John.

'What like a servant or something?' replied Sammy, taking the bait.

'Yeah didn't you know that?' asked John, shaking his head incredulously.

'I'm in the wrong job lads,' said Sammy, settling back in his seat and retreating into his own world of sexual fantasy.

In the backseat, Josh had other things to worry about other than the cunnilingus arrangements of royalty. The police had questioned him about the fire on Harrington Street and he also fitted the description of the Islington arsonist. He was left to sweat awhile in an interview room, before he was questioned again by two gentlemen from MI5. They were more interested in his involvement with the British Free Corps and more specifically with the organisation's major players.

The truth was that the police didn't have enough evidence to convict Josh of any offence. The British Security Service wanted to use Josh to gather information that might lead to the prosecution of leading members of the BFC, which included Cuckoo Walsh.

After finishing the Heanor job, Cuckoo had casually informed Josh that he didn't need him anymore. He was aware that Josh had been questioned by the police and was clearly distancing himself from the young man who was becoming something of a liability.

'Just be careful you don't end up face down in the river like Nappy Andrews,' were Cuckoo's final chilling words to Josh.

It had come as a blessing in disguise to be fired by Walsh. Josh found employment as a material handler at Tsucol and became reacquainted with his old friends, Sammy and John. He had to confess that he had been afraid of Walsh and hadn't really understood the whole neo-Nazi thing.

More than anything, Josh regretted causing the fire that had been responsible for someone's death. When he had torched the house in North London, he knew that the house had been left empty by its owners, while they attended an Anti-Racist Alliance march in Bethnal Green. Nothing could change the fact that Josh's actions had killed someone and his sleep was plagued with nightmarish visions of his victim. His stomach churned constantly and he lived in constant fear of the BFC permanently silencing him.

As the car sped down Hermitage Lane, they passed Dean Swift on his bicycle. Josh felt afraid every time Dean looked at him. He was certain that Myfanwy's best friend knew he had been involved in the arson attack since the encounter in the William IV pub.

He bought a hot chocolate at the drinks machine and then went outside to the smoking area for a cigarette before the shift began.

'Here's Dolly the sheep!' called out Feggy Edwards. Josh was mystified why Edwards had taken to calling him by that name. He had decided on a whim that Josh had a face like a sheep and had named him Dolly, after he had heard the news about the cloned sheep that went by that name. *First I'm a dog, now I'm a fucking sheep,* thought Josh.

'Fuck off chicken catcher,' retorted Josh, who had retaliated by naming Feggy after his former position at a chicken farm.

The witty badinage was suspended when it was time to begin the day's work. Everyone got into position to do the mandatory exercises, which were aimed at alleviating repetitive strain injury. Josh went through the motions with the same degree of apathy displayed by most of the other participants in the exercises. A special tape that announced each exercise had been recorded by Les Johnson before he had been fired. He had always boasted about his days as a disc jockey at the Woodpecker in Mansfield Woodhouse and had been keen to display his mixing skills. It had come as a surprise to many that the recording hadn't been changed since Les had left Tsucol in ignominy. He cheerfully announced each exercise while *Disco 2000* by Pulp played in the background.

'And now we do the Rigsby position,' said Les, trying to adopt a Jane Fonda-type speech register, 'Put your hands on the small of your back and gently lean backwards.'

'My God. Miss fucking Jones!' someone called out sardonically.

Once the exercise program was complete, everyone made their way to their work areas, where they were briefed on the day's targets and any ongoing issues that needed to be highlighted. It frustrated Josh how much time was wasted at the beginning of each shift, which would inevitably lead to mandatory overtime at the end of the day.

Josh had been assigned to John Freeman's cell when he had completed his training. He had expected things to go well, working under his old friend, but John transformed into a totally different human being as soon as he took charge of his team.

'Just watch your thread ends guys,' John reproached everyone. 'We're getting a lot of complaints from the QA people, so just be aware of this issue folks.'

Since joining John's team, Josh had been removed from the sewing machines due to his ineptitude and transferred to the position of material handler. He located a trolley of work, fresh from the cutting machine, and began to distribute it on the shelves behind each machine.

'Watch your thread ends everybody!' called out Sammy in his best Popeye voice.

Josh creased up laughing every time he heard his old friend's impersonations. He found it reassuring to be working alongside Sammy. His only regret was that Spike no longer worked at Tsucol. In his first week there, Josh had seen Spike a couple times before he had arrested for the murder of Nappy Andrews. He was currently serving time on remand at Nottingham prison while he awaited his trial.

Josh couldn't believe that Spike could be responsible for the brutal killing of Nappy. Since Cuckoo had warned Josh about encountering a similar fate if he didn't keep his mouth shut, he was certain that Walsh and his BFC associates were responsible for the murder. Spike had been charged for killing Nappy after a blood-smeared blackthorn stick had been found amongst some trees near the site of the murder. The stick had belonged to Spike, who said he had left it lying outside the office where he had been on duty. Spike claimed that he had left the stick several days earlier and forgotten all about it.

A motive had been established when it transpired that Spike's grandfather had been burgled during a spate of robberies that had been attributed to Nappy. Nappy's father had given information that Spike had been heard making threats of reprisals at the Three Lions pub in Meden Vale. Spike had admitted to the police that he had partly blamed the break in for the rapid deterioration in his grandfather's health.

During the 20-minute dinner break, Josh bought a cheese and ham roll from the food dispenser and once again settled himself outside. He perched himself on the back-rest of a chair, resting his feet on the metal seat. The habit of sitting in this manner originated when it was discovered that a family of rats had taken residence in a dustbin near to the *al fresco* dining area. Feggy Edwards had aimed a drinks can at the bin one night and a pack of gargantuan rodents had emerged and scurried away.

A couple of people sat in the adjacent seats, who Josh didn't know, were discussing the carminative effects of Aldi baked beans. They gave Josh a withering glance that suggested he had broken some kind of unspoken code, which forbade him to sit at their table. Josh glanced around and saw Dean Swift sitting alone on a bench, meditatively watching smoke spiralling from his cigarette. He spotted Josh looking in his direction and nodded acknowledgement. Feeling the urge to atone somehow for his crime, Josh walked over to attempt to converse with Dean.

'How's it going mate?' he asked, feeling as though he had 'MURDERER!' tattooed on his forehead.

'Have you got a relation named Mike Hunt?' Dean asked.

'Oh yeah, my cunt, very funny, never heard that one before,' said Josh, sensing that the conversation was getting off to a jovial start.

'So how does this job compare with working for the infamous Cuckoo Walsh?'

'It's steady enough,' replied Josh, not wishing to commit too much information about his former employee.

'You seemed thick as thieves with him the last time I saw you together in the pub.'

'We'd just finished a job up Heanor way and he was getting the drinks in to celebrate. You can't turn down free ale can you?'

'I don't know, it depends who's buying.'

Josh adroitly rolled himself a cigarette and then offered his pouch of tobacco to Dean.

'No thanks,' Dean said curtly, 'I'm rubbish at rolling fags. My mate Myfanwy, now he could roll a fag in his pocket, he was that tight when it came to crashing.'

'No way!' replied Josh gullibly.

'Not really, but he learned how to roll in prison; like matchsticks they were, they roll them really thin to conserve their tobacco rations.'

Josh stared at the floor and spat out a piece of tobacco. He looked around to see if anyone was getting up and returning to their cells yet. Normally he was the first in the canteen and one of the last back.

'So what did you reckon to Euro 96 then Josh?' asked Dean.

Josh shrugged his shoulders, wondering where this conversation was leading, 'We seem to get wanked every time we get into a penalty shoot-out with the Germans.'

'Yeah I still remember that night in 1990 when we were *this* close to being in the World Cup Final,' said Dean, holding his thumb and forefinger 10 millimetres or so apart. 'I didn't have the pleasure of going through all that stress again this time round; I was on my way back from my holidays that night.'

'Did you go anywhere nice?'

'Italy, yeah very nice, you should try it some time.'

'I don't really like foreign food,' said Josh as he tossed his cigarette butt away and hastened to follow his colleagues who were returning to work.

Dean hurried on past Josh and held the door to the canteen open for him, 'Actually I think I saw you the night we came back from the holiday, you were sat in the bus station; been watching the game in town I expect.'

Josh smiled and nodded his head and quickly turned into the toilets while Dean continued ahead of him towards the production floor.

Emptying the contents of his bladder, Josh emitted a sigh of relief, feeling as though he had just been put through some kind of subtle cross-examination.

'Wow, you look as though you're ready for that,' said Dean, approaching the next urinal.

'Yeah, don't know what's wrong with me today,' said Josh, hastily shaking off the remaining drops of urine and zipping up his jeans.

'Where did you end up watching the game?' called out Dean as Josh hastened to the door.

'Oh Café Imperial I think, can't remember,' said Josh as he held open the door, eager to get away from Dean's incessant questioning.

'Oh right, Feggy Edwards was in there as well, did you see him? He says there was glass flying everywhere after the game ended.'

'I can't say I remember seeing him. I didn't really know him before I started working here.'

'You were probably too pissed to remember much about it,' said Dean as he slapped Josh on the back and followed him onto the production floor.

They walked silently through the rows of buzzing sewing machines. Josh quickened his pace.

'So, do you still hang about with Cuckoo since he laid you off?' Dean asked.

'No I'm giving him a wide birth nowadays.'

'Very wise,' said Dean. 'You might get into a lot of trouble hanging about with shady characters like Mister Walsh.'

Josh made a left turn towards his own cell and Dean returned to his machine, welcomed by the puerile banter of Feggy Edwards. Josh quickened his pace as he saw John Freeman and Bill Green walking towards him. He began to scroll through his mental list of excuses for returning late from his break. He had already received a verbal warning for his poor time keeping.

'Josh, we've been looking everywhere for you,' said Bill Green. 'What have you been up to you naughty boy? The police are waiting at reception, they want to have a chat with you, youth.'

CHAPTER SIXTEEN

A member of the public had come forward with information after reading in the local newspaper about the fire. A man who had been walking along Sutton Road approximately half an hour before the fire was reported remembered seeing a young man walk out of the yard of the bus garage. The description given matched the one made by a neighbour, who had reported seeing a man fleeing from the house in Islington moments before it was engulfed in flames.

Caving in under the pressure of guilt and robust questioning, Josh confessed to both incidents. The two officers from the British Security Service subjected Josh to further cross-examination about the activities of the British Free Corps. He continued to remain silent about his role within the BFC but was reminded that assisting the police with their enquiries might have relevance on the outcome of his sentencing.

After being formally charged, Josh was placed in custody, on remand at Whippletree Prison. The Category B prison was located on the outskirts of Nottingham. It was the first time Josh had ever been into Nottingham, let alone the interior of a prison. Whippletree was one of the new privately managed prisons, contracted to Gogal Custodial Services. The late-Victorian penal institution looked like everything Josh had ever imagined a prison to be as he approached the large blue gate and the begrimed red brick wall.

On his first day of confinement, Josh found some solace when he came face to face with Spike, who was also on remand.

'What are you doing here, daft-lad?' enquired Spike as he approached Josh from behind.

Josh spun around in trepidation and breathed a sigh of relief as he set eyes on Spike, 'Am I glad to see you.'

Josh confessed his entire relationship with Cuckoo Walsh and the BFC, and how one thing had led to another.

'And you were daft enough to start setting fire to houses, because that daft bastard told you to?' said Spike contemptuously.

'Okay!' replied Josh, resisting the urge to cry. 'No need to rub it in, I feel bad enough as it is.'

'Alright, chill out, we'll sort it out together. You need to keep it together right now or there are people in here who'll eat you alive.'

As the first days turned to weeks, Josh began to fall into the routine of prison life. Spike was ambivalent to his own confinement, claiming that it was no worse than being in the army. Josh noticed that Spike appeared to be resigned to his fate and didn't exhibit any of the old recalcitrant spirit of his punk days.

One day, the two of them leaned over the railing that overlooked a huge safety net. Beneath the netting, they could see the other prisoners trying to occupy themselves, to make the time pass by a little quicker. They were standing on the landing outside Spike's cell and Josh futilely tried to imagine that they were on a hotel balcony, checking out bikini-clad women on a sandy beach.

'Sometimes I wish that netting wasn't there,' Spike suddenly confessed, 'I would jump if I had half the chance.'

Steady on mate, that's not like you,' said Josh, amazed by this sudden revelation.

'I lie awake at night thinking about shit that I saw when I was in the Gulf,' Spike continued. 'You don't know what it's like not being able to sleep in a place like this. It's the only time you're ever really free here.'

'You'll be all right mate,' said Josh. 'They'll find out who killed Nappy and you'll be back drinking cider on Wood Hill again, like in the old days.'

'You know, I don't even care anymore whether I get out or not. The worse part about it is I can't even remember what happened that night. I remember going to sleep but what if I did kill him? I said to myself I'd put him six feet under for robbing grandad.'

'Yeah but that was just talk; we all say things like that sometimes. I once said that I wanted to kill Sammy, when he fucked off with all my punk records and sold them. You'd know if you'd done something like that.'

'No you don't get it,' replied Spike, massaging his temples, 'I saw some really fucked up shit in Iraq and it's messing with my head. I keep seeing this guy who I was mates with holding his guts in his hand. He's just stood there with his guts hanging out and holding them out to me as if to say, 'What am I supposed to do with these Spike?' I don't know what the fuck's happening to me anymore.'

Josh left Spike alone, wondering how he would ever manage if his hero couldn't even cope himself. He sat near the pool table and watched a couple of the inmates playing a game. As he watched the coloured balls glide across the green baize, he was transported back to the Blue Boar in Mansfield. He could almost see every piece of graffiti that was scratched into the wooden benches; the sound of the old rock 'n' roll records that he always hated, but now recollected with fondness; the vinegary snakebites and arguments about which rules of pool they were playing by.

'Do you fancy a game?' asked one of the players after his opponent had left the table.

Without another word, Josh racked up the balls and watched while the other man played the break shot. Josh watched the balls scatter, as the white ball smashed into them. He studied the subsequent position of the balls and potted one that sat waiting on the edge of a corner pocket. His opponent was a small, stocky man in his mid-40s. His dark hair was fashioned in a brush-like rockabilly flattop. Josh looked at the tattoos on the man's arms as he prepared to take his shot. On the left forearm there was an image of Elvis Presley, a Confederate flag adorned the right arm.

As the game progressed, Josh became uncomfortably aware that he was being scrutinised. A tall black man with greying dreadlocks flowing from his head like Medusa's snakes grimaced at Josh. He had the build of someone who worked out regularly and looked as though he could break Josh in two, along with his pool cue if he dared to defend himself with it. It suddenly occurred to Josh that this man might know about his involvement with the British Free Corps and was preparing to inflict some kind of reprisal.

The rockabilly cleared the table as Josh's attention to the game deteriorated. He potted the final ball, placed his cue on the table and silently walked away. The dreadlocked assassin was heading towards Josh and he desperately searched for assistance from Spike. The area had suddenly cleared, leaving the pair of them alone.

'Fancy a game then kid?' he asked Josh in a broad Black Country accent.

Over the next few weeks, Josh became acquainted with this man, who introduced himself as Isaac Perry. Josh managed to beat Isaac at pool on several occasions and then began to learn chess from him.

'Pool's okay but chess is the game of kings,' said Isaac.

At first Josh found chess far too complex a game for him to master. Isaac patiently corrected him when he couldn't remember whether a piece was meant to move diagonally or in a straight line. After a few weeks, Josh had learned the rudiments of the game and was beginning to spend more time playing out strategies in his head.

The prison library was the last place Josh had imagined himself visiting during his confinement, but he found a book about chess there which Isaac had suggested he read. The last book he could recollect reading had been *Cider with Rosie*, which he had reluctantly read at school. He assiduously digested the contents of the book, reading and then re-reading the secrets it held. Isaac looked astonished one day when the two of them were engrossed in a game and Josh executed the *en passant* move to capture one of his opponent's pawns.

Most of the warders remained aloof around the prisoners but Josh found an exception in Mister Balfour. This amiable prison warder from Dumfries took a shine to Josh and showed him how to make use of his time. He encouraged Josh's passion for chess and found him a place in a workshop, packing emergency supplies, which were to be sent to civilians affected by the war in the former Yugoslavia. The work was repetitive and unrewarding but passed the time and earned Josh enough to buy tobacco.

The daily routine became easier after Josh had been detained on remand for several months. He still felt remorse for his crimes and found it difficult to live with the fact that his acts had caused someone to die horribly. He began to seek succour by visiting the chapel and talking to the prison chaplain. Josh had never held any religious beliefs but the chaplain's advice that he should seek atonement for his crime began to take root in his mind. He finally made up his mind that he must tell the police everything he knew about the activities of the British Free Corps. He knew that this would be difficult, as he was part of a cell, of which only Cuckoo knew the identities of its participants. He had taken his orders from Walsh and so it was Walsh who he would implicate.

The barrister who was put in charge of defending Josh prepared a case which suggested that he had been in the thrall of Walsh. He argued that Josh had been a lonely and vulnerable youth when he had been indoctrinated into the evil world of a neo-Nazi organisation. Though in reality Josh had been malleable enough to obey Walsh's orders, his barrister argued that he had been put under unbearable pressure and intimidation in order to commit multiple acts of arson.

The trial began at Nottingham Crown Court and Josh sat in the dock and listened to the prosecution present its evidence. Here Josh came face to face with Cuckoo for the first time in many months. Walsh gave evidence, in which he told a story of how he had merely offered Josh the chance of learning a trade, with only philanthropical motives in his heart. It had been Josh, he claimed, who had formerly been part of a gang and wore clothes characteristic of the skinhead youth-subculture. It had been Josh who had introduced Mister Walsh to the music of Screwdriver, a Rock band alleged to be associated with neo-Nazi organisations.

When questioned about his past criminal charges during his time as a football hooligan, Cuckoo explained that he had turned over a new leaf and was committed to running his business as a plasterer. Since Josh's departure, Cuckoo had replaced him with a Pakistani youth named Bilal Ali, who he claimed was a most efficient and trustworthy employee.

When it was Josh's turn to give evidence, Cuckoo was not present, but his friend Doberman listened with interest from the public gallery. Josh was cross-examined by his barrister about every detail of his relationship with Cuckoo, since the day they had met. Doberman left the court after the morning session had been concluded. He had heard all he needed to hear from Josh and decided that it was time to make several phone calls.

Josh returned to Whippletree Prison and resumed life there during the weekend, before his case resumed again on the following Monday. He went over everything that he had said in court and was confident that his defence barrister would get him a lighter sentence.

He played a game of chess with Isaac on Saturday morning and then spent some time talking about his trial with Spike. Josh noted a clear improvement in Spike's mood since the time he had confessed to harbouring suicidal thoughts. He had begun counselling sessions and was diagnosed with combat-related, post-traumatic stress disorder. The headaches, fatigue and bouts of insomnia were attributed to something that the media were calling Gulf War Syndrome.

Josh left Spike alone in his cell, writing a letter to John. He walked along the landing towards his own cell, with the intention of resuming a new book that Isaac had given him called *The Two Knights' Defence*. It was deserted on the landing, apart from a man who was leaning on the railing near Josh's cell, rolling a cigarette. He wore his long hair in a ponytail and had a platted beard. Josh recalled playing pool with the man and remarking on the elaborate oriental tattoos on his arms. Spike had mentioned that he was a member of the Restless Travellers' Motorcycle Club and had been sent down for attacking a Hells Angel with a meat cleaver.

Josh walked into his cell and knelt to pick up the book which was lying on his bed. He didn't hear the bearded biker silently walk up behind him brandishing an improvised blade. Josh turned around in time to see the blade heading towards his right kidney. Suddenly Spike appeared as if from nowhere and swiftly grabbed the attacker around the neck with one arm and bent the man's other arm around his back with the other. The blade fell harmlessly to the floor and Spike dragged his prisoner out of the cell.

Unsure what to do with the blade, Josh hid it inside the pages of his book.

'I only came in to see if you had a pen!' said Spike with a wry smile. 'I knew all that army training had to pay off sooner or later.'

'The bastards are trying to kill me Spike!' exclaimed Josh in a panic. 'I'm not safe in here anymore, what am I going to do?'

Spike considered Josh's options for a moment and then replied, 'You've got two choices really, either keep your back to the wall all the time—'

'Or what?' Josh implored.

'You're going to have to escape.'

CHAPTER SEVENTEEN

The gas canister was empty and the caravan was becoming very cold. Josh parted the curtains and rubbed away the moisture from the window so he could see outside. It would be a couple of days before John would return with gas for the fire, tobacco and food. The dog ends in the ashtray had been stripped of every strand of tobacco and Josh was dying for a smoke. He had three Pot Noodles left and a couple of packets of savoury rice, which he was leaving till last. He couldn't alleviate his nicotine cravings by comfort eating any longer, now he was down to his last rations.

It had been a miserable and lonely Christmas for Josh, alone on the Oasis caravan park in Ingoldmells. He had to console himself with the fact that he was free from danger, from the BFC assassins who stalked him. He had successfully escaped from prison to end up a virtual prisoner in the isolation of a cold, static caravan. The only memories of holidays he had were the weeks he had spent with his parents in Mablethorpe when he was a small child. His parents had been happy then and he had felt secure and shared their happiness. He was sure the sun had shined every day back then, and when he had built sand castles his father had bought a packet of flags, which he mounted on his fragile battlements.

On the Monday that his trial was scheduled to recommence, there had been an adjournment when an important witness had failed to show up at court. Josh was taken back into custody and went back to work to take his mind off the trial. He kept the knife which he had retained after the attack, in the hope that it might prove useful in the event of any future confrontation. Mister Balfour was on duty that day and he talked to Josh about the days when the tartan army of Scottish football fans used to converge on Wembley stadium for the home international fixture with 'The Auld Enemy'.

Spike was working with Josh that day and they fitted together a large triple-walled, cardboard box. They then proceeded to pack the waist-high box with blankets and coats, destined for the Balkans. It was Spike who conceived the idea of packing Josh into a box and transporting him far from the interior of the prison. At an appointed time, Spike told Josh to climb under the contents of the box, which they had almost finished packing. Spike had already observed that a lorry would arrive at the same time each day to pick up the boxes.

Mister Balfour was inspecting all the completed boxes to ensure that no one attempted to stow away. Another guard had phoned in sick and Balfour was working a double-shift. The warders constantly bewailed the understaffing in the prison. Gogal Custodial Services kept their personnel down to a minimum, in order to manage their business more cost-effectively; as a consequence, the staff in Whippletree were under constant pressure.

Once the boxes were given the all-clear, they were wrapped with cling film and taken to the despatch area. Mister Balfour's colleague that day was a guard who, Spike had also observed, liked to pass the time of day with the lorry drivers. Mister Birch was a warder who always remained taciturn amongst the prisoners, but more than made up for his uncommunicativeness when he had a spare moment with his colleagues.

After Mister Balfour had checked their work, Josh quickly dived into the box and burrowed under the sea of blankets and coats. Spike swiftly wrapped the cardboard vessel and then wheeled it to the despatch area, where the work was already being loaded onto the wagon.

The improvised escape plan miraculously worked and Josh soon heard the sound of the lorry's engine announce his departure. Half-an-hour later, he was sure he must have passed the gates of the prison and be on the way to some far off location. He began to fear he might suffocate in his new environment and commenced struggling to escape the confines of the box.

It was fortunate that he still had the knife concealed in his trouser pocket and he started stabbing holes in the cardboard. He managed to perforate the walls of the box, before the blade became embedded in the cardboard and its improvised handle came away in his hand. He then started kicking at the lid of the box, until he finally freed it from the clingfilm wrapping.

Shortly after freeing himself, Josh heard the lorry reversing and readied himself to disembark. He hid behind one of the boxes and waited for the wagon doors to open. He could hear the voice of the driver outside and grew impatient, as he listened to a conversation about the chances of a labour landslide in the next election.

Realising that he might attract attention, wearing only his prison issue sweatshirt, Josh found a coat inside the box he had occupied. It suddenly occurred to him that he might be forced to endure cold weather for the foreseeable future and he decided that it might be wise to take one of the blankets.

The wagon doors were finally opened and Josh peered from his hiding place. He could dimly see the inside of a warehouse, and a forklift truck was parked nearby. The warehouse appeared to be deserted and Josh took the opportunity to proceed. He walked to the end of an aisle of racking, which contained similar boxes to the ones he had packed. He turned right and passed several more aisles before coming to a door. He peered through the door and, after establishing that it was deserted, cautiously continued into an empty corridor. Several lockers lined the walls of the corridor and a clocking-in machine signalled that he must be near an exit.

He continued along the corridor and was about to open another door straight ahead, when a door to his left suddenly swung open. A bespectacled man with curly grey hair, wearing a high-visibility jacket, emerged from an office, where a radio could be heard.

'Alright mate, you look lost?' said the man amiably.

'Have you got the paperwork for the Nottingham delivery?' enquired Josh. 'We can't leave until we get a signature.'

The man looked puzzled for a moment and then said angrily, 'I thought that twat said he'd sorted this!'

He then turned around and returned to the office. Josh quickly walked through the door he had been about to open and found himself in a reception area with a settee and a large pot plant. He opened the glass doors that led to a staff car park, then walked up a grass bank and onto an industrial estate.

Estimating that he had been in the back of the lorry for roughly an hour, Josh came to the conclusion that he couldn't have travelled very far from Nottingham. He realised that his absence must have been reported and that the police would already be searching for him. He decided that it would be a good idea to get away from the roads as quickly as possible. A cyclist passed him by and rode onto a footpath which ran beside a builder's yard and a railway line.

He walked for half-an-hour along the path, which took him through a housing estate, before emerging onto a busy main road. He crossed the road and climbed over a fence, into a field. He walked along the hedgerows of several fields, aware that he needed to get as far away as possible from the warehouse where the police would soon start searching for him.

He continued until it grew dark and found himself near to some allotments, which bordered a village. He explored the usual assortment of sheds that occupy such places in search of shelter for the night. After trying several doors, he found a shed, which was secured by a cheap padlock, and broke open the door with a piece of wood.

It was bitterly cold that night, even with the coat and blanket to protect him from the worst of the weather. Josh hadn't eaten since breakfast and had been too nervous about his trial to have much of an appetite. He was exhausted, hungry and far too cold and anxious to get much sleep. He eventually succeeded to fall into a troubled sleep, which was quickly disturbed by random sounds which he feared might be a police search party.

With no idea how long he had spent in the shed, Josh decided to keep moving, in the hope that he might find some food and establish his location. He continued his journey under the cover of hedgerows and dark paths. The sound of church bells marked the hour, informing him that it was only four o'clock in the morning. The December sun wouldn't trouble him for another four hours so he pushed on in the cover of darkness.

He eventually found himself in another village and decided to see if he could find something to eat. Passing along a quiet lane, he recognised the unmistakable sound of a milk float. Josh was soon in possession of a bottle of milk, which he drank down in one long pull, and another which he stored in his coat.

It soon became evident to Josh that his journey in the lorry had taken him as far as Northamptonshire. He stumbled into an old man who was walking his dog and told him that his car had broken down nearby and he had no idea where he was. The old man had been very happy to help Josh and enlightened him as to his location. Josh also managed to get 20 pence in order to phone for help. He had every intention of finding a phone box and calling for help, but he needed to weigh up who might respond to his call without turning him in to the police.

The decision was made all the easier when Josh realised that he could only remember John Freeman's telephone number by heart. He was fortunate when he rang the number that John picked up the receiver straight away. Josh had lost track of which shift John was working on and wasn't sure of the time when he dialled.

It had been a gamble that had paid off when John arrived in his car and agreed to help Josh. After Josh had explained his predicament, John implored him to turn himself in and seek protection from the British Security Service. Josh was adamant that his life would be in peril if he returned to custody and he told John to stop the car and let him out if he didn't want to help.

John owned a key to his father's caravan in Ingoldmells and, being certain that it would be unoccupied in December, drove Josh to the bolthole on the Lincolnshire coast. There he had remained for over a month, keeping himself occupied with a portable television and a pocket-sized chess board.

During John's last visit, Josh learned that Spike had been found not guilty of the murder of Nappy Andrews, due to lack of evidence. He had also managed to avoid prosecution for any involvement in Josh's abscondment when several prisoners had testified that Spike had been working in another area at the time of the escape.

It was out of the question attempting to venture out into the caravan park when there were still several people who resided there on a permanent basis. Josh's confinement was becoming more unbearable than it had been in prison, where he had at least enjoyed the company of fellow inmates. He sat in front of the television watching a *Vicar of Dibley* Christmas special, and his spirits reached a new low point.

Without the consolation of tobacco and a scarcity of food, Josh's only option was to go to bed and masturbate. John had been kind enough to supply him with a pile of old Danish pornographic magazines that had once belonged to his father. He settled down with a vintage copy of *Rodox* and studied a series of photos which involved two men and two women. The women wore outfits in the style of 1920s flappers, while the men wore striped blazers and straw boaters. The group where soon in a state of undress and the phrase 'a place for everything and everything in its place' took on a new meaning.

Josh was becoming engrossed in the pictures, imagining himself to be sandwiched between the two ladies, minus the vile bodies of the bright young gentlemen. Josh was about to come to the conclusion of the story when the sound of a car outside startled him. He was sure it couldn't be John visiting at such a late hour.

Pulling on his tracksuit bottoms, Josh ran over to the window near the sink and peered through the curtains. He quickly stepped away when he saw a man and a woman inside a red Mini Cooper. Josh could only conclude that either the police had found him or assassins of the BFC had come to deliver retribution. He ran back into the bedroom and tried to open the window as a means of escape, but he was unable to budge it an inch. As Josh heard the door to the caravan opening, he dived under the bed.

He could hear footsteps clumsily stumbling around in the dark and braced himself for the moment when the light switch was located. He could hear the footsteps approaching and expected the bedroom light to come on at any moment. A woman's voice could be heard whispering and then giggling.

The door opened, but instead of seeing the lights come on, Josh heard the bedsprings squeak as the couple fell onto the bed in total darkness. The sound of kissing and clothes being hurriedly removed informed Josh that his visitors were neither officers of the law nor assassins bent on revenge.

'Oh my God you're big!' the woman exclaimed with a degree of trepidation.

Josh's relief that he wasn't in danger quickly evaporated as he was forced to be a captive audience for this pornographic show. The erection he had clutched a few minutes earlier had wilted to a stump.

'Do it properly or don't do it at all!' berated the woman. 'I don't care if you've been locked up inside!'

'Oh come on, you didn't seem to mind last time,' a voice replied, which sounded familiar to Josh.

The bickering continued until the couple settled on a mutually agreeable sexual technique and Josh began to feel the rhythmic bouncing of the mattress above his head. A sudden scream from the woman led Josh to assume that she had either been murdered or she had reached an orgasm. There was a brief fidgeting and then the sound of someone breaking wind.

'Oh you're a real charmer you are,' the woman hissed.

'But it was alright when you did it when I was going down on you?'

Josh was sure he recognised the voice of Spike and it occurred to him that he must have obtained a key to the caravan without John knowing. He continued to lie still under the bed, in case Spike's woman decided to call the police.

It grew quiet for half an hour and Josh began to consider creeping out while the pair were asleep. He was about to crawl across the floor when a pair of feet came over the side of the bed and the woman felt her way out of the bedroom. Josh listened to a tinkling sound, which was followed by the toilet flushing.

Spike took the opportunity to break wind again while he was alone. The woman returned and demanded another good seeing-to. The more Josh listened to her voice, the more he thought that he recognised its owner. It was a voice he hadn't heard for many years, but he recalled hearing it at a friend's house.

'I bet Alex doesn't get you wet like that,' Spike boasted.

Josh was shocked to discover that it was John's mother, Maggie, doing the dirty on her husband.

The second bout of love-making was more successful than its predecessor and Josh thought that it would never end. Fearful that the bed might collapse on top of him, he decided that he would make a run for it. He was about to crawl from his hiding place, when he discerned a figure peering through the interstice of the open door. Josh tried to make out who the voyeur in the darkness might be. The face that peeped through the narrow gap, accidently pushed the door slightly, revealing to Josh the unmistakable silhouette of male genitalia. It was now apparent to Josh that someone was masturbating in the doorway with his trousers around his ankles.

Realising that his situation was completely out of his control, Josh shrank back as far as he could. The odours that accompany the heat of carnal passion began to envelop the bedroom. Maggie's exhortations were growing more obstreperous in their tone, as though she were possessed by demons.

Suddenly the figure in the doorway pulled up his trousers and stormed into the room.

'What the fuck do you think you're doing with my wife?' cried out a voice that Josh recognised as Alex Freeman.

'I'm with a real man,' said the panting Maggie. 'Stick around and you might learn a thing or two.'

'Bollocks to this!' said Spike, as Alex's trousers dropped to the floor for a second time. 'I thought I'd seen some fucked up shit in the army, but this takes the piss.'

Spike leapt from the bed and grabbed his clothes, then rushed from the bedroom.

'I told you he wouldn't be up for it,' said Alex. 'I feel like a right pervert now.'

'Oh shut the fuck up!' Maggie snapped. 'I'll go after him and try and persuade him to come back.'

Josh watched Maggie's feet emerge from the bed and hastily pull on her knickers and dress. The cuckold followed the lover out of the bedroom and Josh prepared to make his escape as the farce came to an end.

As the Freeman's went off in hot pursuit of Spike, Josh grabbed his coat and made a run for it. He breathed in the chilly fresh air as he crouched behind a caravan to take stock of his situation. It felt good to be outdoors again and Josh made his way towards the sound of waves lapping on the beach.

Josh soon found himself on the sandy beach and fell on his knees, staring out onto the moonlit sea. He had the sudden urge to run straight into the inviting waves and allow himself to be enveloped in the cold and cathartic water. He had finally returned to the only place where he had ever felt true happiness. The soothing sound of the tide receding in the distance brought a calmness to Josh that he hadn't experienced in years.

The serenity of the beach was brought to an end by the sound of discordant singing:

'We are the nutters, the nutters from Notts!'

Josh looked round and saw two figures coming towards him, arm in arm.

'Yeah but didn't you experiment when you were a teenager?' said one drunkenly to the other.

'I think everyone goes through that phase don't they?' replied the other. 'Playing with each other; it's a healthy part of growing up innit?'

The conversation ceased as the two promenaders came face to face with Josh.

'Dog!' exclaimed Sammy.

'Sammy?' replied Josh, unable to believe his eyes.

'I feel sick,' said Luke.

CHAPTER EIGHTEEN

'I just wanted to wish you a Happy New Year Uncle Andy, before the party starts,' said Luke, 'and thanks for the new phone, it's brilliant.'

'Don't get too bladdered,' chuckled Cuckoo Walsh.

'No, I'll stay sober all night,' said Luke, who had no intention of touching alcohol, while he had a bag of ecstasy tablets in his pocket.

'Yeah I bet,' said Cuckoo. 'What's this thing you're going to?'

'It's a Vibealite all-nighter at Fantasy Island, called Pleasuredome.'

'What, like *Welcome to the Pleasuredome* by Frankie Goes to Hollywood?'

'You know I'm not into all that grandad music you listen to Uncle Andy.'

'Cheeky bastard,' said Cuckoo. 'So, who are you going to this Pleasuredome with? Any fanny going?'

'Plenty of fanny, it's me and Sammy and his mate Dog.'

'Dog? Who the fuck is Dog?'

'You know him, that youth who used to do a bit of labouring for you. They call him Dog for some reason.'

'Okay Luke, well have a good night and Happy New Year,' said Cuckoo and then abruptly terminated the call.

Cuckoo was sitting on the settee, at the home of his girlfriend, Dawn Townroe. Dawn's teenage twin daughters Mel and Bev were playing on their new Playstation. Cuckoo stared distractedly at the television screen as a pair of futuristic racing cars sped through the air. Dawn thought that Cuckoo looked mesmerised by the bright colours and the Chemical Brothers' soundtrack of the game, which was called *Wipeout*. He was lost in thought, working out his next move, now that he had found the location of Josh.

Since Josh had escaped from prison, Cuckoo had been told by his superiors in the British Free Corps that it was down to him to clear up the mess. He was angry that he had been blamed for Josh's whistleblowing and the failure to silence him. It had been decided that Josh's escape should be viewed as a victory for the BFC, against the system that sought to bring them down. The word got around that Josh was a hero of the BFC, who had cunningly evaded the clutches of the British Security Service that was trying to set him up as a scapegoat. It was imperative that Josh never returned from his exile and betray his brethren.

Dawn cuddled up to Cuckoo and watched her daughters, enthralled by the games console that Cuckoo had bought them for Christmas. It had been the first time in years that she spent the holiday with a man – since she had given her adulterous husband the boot when the twins had still been toddlers. She remembered Cuckoo from his days as a hooligan and used to think of him as a bit of a knobhead when Colin had hung around with him, when he had fancied himself as a football casual. She had always said that if Colin had been able to fight with his cock, he might have had a better chance of standing his ground alongside hardened street fighters like Cuckoo.

'Go and get ready girls,' said Dawn, 'your dad will be here to pick you up any time now.'

Mel and Bev reluctantly turned off the games console and trudged out of the living room.

'You're not worried about that kid blaming you for that fire again are you?' Dawn asked Cuckoo. 'He's long gone now; he knew he was going down for a long time. I still can't believe he had the cheek to try to blame you, just because you laid him off work.'

'No, I'm not worried about that,' replied Cuckoo. 'Listen, that was my nephew on the phone; he's at some all-night rave at Ingoldmells and he wants me to pick him up in the morning, because his mate who has given him a lift there has left him in the shit and gone off with some lass.'

Dawn sat up, somewhat disappointed on hearing this news, 'Well okay, I was looking forward to us seeing in the New Year together.'

'Oh don't worry, that's in the bank. It just means I won't be able to drink that much tonight.'

Dawn perked up at this news and rubbed a hand up Cuckoo's thigh, 'I wasn't planning on spending all night drinking anyway.'

'I'll only be gone a few hours, I should be back in time for that roast beef you're cooking and then a bit of football.'

Cuckoo had certainly got his feet under the table since meeting Dawn. Her semi-detached house on Chesterfield Road was a vast improvement on his old terraced dwelling on Spencer Street. He couldn't believe how gullibly she had fallen for all his bullshit, about turning over a new leaf since his Coocachoo Crew days and wanting to settle down. He had been wary of committing to a relationship since his wife had run away with another woman.

The doorbell chimed, and Dawn reluctantly dragged herself from her lover's arms, 'That will be Wonderboy and his bimbo,' she said rolling her eyes.

Dawn's antagonism towards Colin's new girlfriend hadn't gone unnoticed by Cuckoo. He attributed this to Jeanette's slim body and pretty face, which galled Dawn. He had to confess that Colin had done well for himself with that one, while some might view Dawn as a bit of a pig.

Colin Townroe sheepishly shuffled into the living room and nodded acknowledgement to Cuckoo. His girlfriend greeted Cuckoo with more enthusiasm and came over to give him a New Year kiss. Dawn pushed past Colin, giving his girlfriend a look of withering contempt. Colin stood next to the Christmas Tree and distracted himself by staring into the fish tank. Jeanette leapt up from beside Cuckoo and rushed over to Dawn and Colin's wedding photo.

'Oh Dawn I like your wedding dress, I bet you wish you could still get into that.'

'Cheeky cow,' muttered Dawn.

'We're going to have a big wedding aren't we duck?' remarked Jeanette enthusiastically.

Colin turned and silently raised an eyebrow as if to suggest that it was the first that he had heard about it.

You're welcome to him duck, thought Dawn.

'I hope you're going to pick me for your best man,' said Cuckoo, registering Colin's discomfort.

'Hey Dawn we could have a double wedding,' Jeanette suggested.

Cuckoo scrutinised Colin to establish whether he might be suitable material for the BFC. He recollected the last time he had relied on the services of the timorous Townroe and concluded that he would sing like a bird if he was detained by the police. Cuckoo had viewed Colin as a good prospect for the Coocachoo Crew in the golden years of hooliganism. He had proved that he could talk the talk but would run faster than Linford Christie when it came to the push. Colin had kept his distance from Cuckoo after leaving him in the lurch during a crucial battle with Chesterfield's Khmer Blues outside the Sherwood Rooms.

Mel and Bev appeared, and Colin embraced them with all the enthusiasm of a part-time dad who would have preferred to be somewhere else.

'What are you going to see?' asked Dawn.

'*Jingle All The Way*,' Mel answered, 'Arnold Schwarzenegger.'

'Come on then girls,' said Colin, pushing the twins through the door, 'we'll miss the beginning if we don't get a move on.'

'Oh isn't he masterful?' said Jeanette.

'Oh he's a regular He-Man that one,' Dawn replied caustically.

As soon as the front door closed, Dawn straddled herself across Cuckoo and put her arms around him, 'Well if you're going to leave me here all alone in the morning, we'd better make the most of having the place to ourselves while dickhead has got the kids.'

Several minute later, Cuckoo was holding Dawn's ankles, her naked legs pointed in the air in a 'V' shape. The headboard was banging against the wall, which Cuckoo remedied by stuffing a pillow behind it. Dawn held her breasts to stop them from bouncing up and down but Cuckoo grabbed her by the wrists to expose them. He pushed himself against her legs to support them and pinned her wrists to the bed. Dawn pulled her hands free and took Cuckoo's hands, entwining her fingers between his in an attempt to adopt a more romantic posture.

Cuckoo's robust style of lovemaking contrasted with that of the more sensitive Dean Swift. She sometime missed the attentiveness of Dean and wished that her new lover would display some sign of emotion, as he grunted and thrusted himself into her. She was pleased that Dean had found someone else nearer to his own age. Although Dawn was only 10 years older, she had felt insecure about the age difference. She felt that Dean would make a good father one day and she had no intention of giving birth to any more children. She had feared that he would one day resent her when he wanted to have children of his own.

Dawn felt guilty about the manner in which she had ended her dalliance with Dean. Cuckoo had arrived on the scene and she had been forced to make a choice. A hastily written note arrived through Dean's letterbox one morning which said:

'I can't be with you any more when I'm in love with someone else. You need to get on with your life, without me in it.'

The afternoon's carnal delights ended abruptly as Cuckoo won his race and came first. Dawn failed to come second, until her lover turned over and quickly began snoring. She surreptitiously brought herself off, while Cuckoo slept peacefully beside her. As she rotated a fingertip gently over her clitoris, she visualised Dean's tongue deftly pleasuring her.

★ ★ ★ ★

The architect responsible for the creation of Fantasy Island had created an environment that looked like a cross between Bedrock and the Aztec Zone in *The Crystal Maze*. A huge pyramid-shaped roof topped the structure, which now dominated the skyline of Ingoldmells.

It had been Sammy's idea to come to the all-nighter dressed as the Joker. The plan had changed when Josh had appeared, and the costume gave the fugitive the perfect opportunity to avoid recognition. In the nearby Burger King, Josh ravenously tucked into a quarter-pound hamburger and fries. Rather than deflecting attention, his disguise gave him a singular appearance that couldn't be ignored. With his hair dyed green, red and white face makeup, green waistcoat and burgundy suit, Josh looked every bit the nemesis of the caped crusader.

'Woah!' said Luke as he watched Josh fall to his feast. 'Anyone would think you haven't eaten for a month.'

'He's a proper gannet this one,' said Sammy, who didn't wish to disturb Luke's ignorance of Josh's situation. 'You ought to have something to eat yoursen youth.'

'No mate, I'm gonna get off me tits tonight and the only food I want is these Mitsubishis,' said Luke, producing his bag of ecstasy tablets.

Later that night, the rave was only just warming up whilst elsewhere the strains of *Auld Lang Syne* were being sung. Whistles were being blown and light sticks were waved about like Bonfire Night sparklers. A laser show endlessly lit up the dance floor, while Breeze and Styles provided the hardcore sounds.

For the first time in months, Josh felt completely free, as he moved to the rapid beat of the music. His Joker costume was proving to be a major success with the girls and he felt popular for the first time in his life. He watched Luke and Sammy dance with the fervour of whirling dervishes, fuelled by illegal chemicals. Josh enjoyed the euphoria produced by the tablet he had swallowed a couple of hours earlier. He found the natural high of feeling like a caged bird set free much sweeter.

When things finally began to wind down, as the first light of the new year prepared to make its entrance, Josh returned to the beach. He was accompanied by a girl from Grantham, who had begun to grow paranoid and experienced a panic attack after her fifth pill. Josh had been dancing with her for an hour, when all of a sudden her serene expression changed to one of anxiety and confusion. He had suggested that she might benefit from some fresh air and had walked with her as far as the beach.

They sat together and listened to the calming sound of the North Sea. The girl, whose name was Angie, closed her eyes and took some deep breaths. Josh silently sat beside her and suddenly thought how surreal his situation was. He was an escaped convict, dressed like a clown, playing the role of responsible adult with a girl who was freaking out on drugs.

Angie pulled the hood on her sweatshirt over her head for warmth and produced a packet of cigarettes. Josh accepted a proffered smoke; he couldn't remember the last time he had smoked so much and he hadn't a penny to buy his own.

'Wow that got really scary back there,' said Angie as she inhaled deeply, illuminating her face.

Josh gazed in admiration at her pretty pointed nose and full lips, 'It's enough to send anyone a bit nuts listening to that music all night.'

'Thanks for looking after me anyway, this probably wasn't how you were expecting the night to turn out.'

'I'm sitting on a beach with a pretty girl and I can think of far worse places to be right now.'

'I bet you say that to all the girls.'

'To be honest there haven't been that many of those, I never really cracked that one.'

'I must look a right mess,' said Angie, as she wiped her cheeks where her eye make-up had run, when she had started crying during her panic attack.

'That makes two of us then.'

The cold, North Sea wind forced them to abandon their position and they decided to make their way back to Fantasy Island. Unbeknown to Josh, Cuckoo Walsh had arrived in Ingoldmells and sat in his car watching people emerge from the rave. He saw a girl in a black hooded sweatshirt walking by, accompanied by a man dressed as the Joker. He watched as the pair crossed the road towards a group of revellers, who had just emerged from the Pleasuredome.

Cuckoo scrutinised everyone he saw but was oblivious to the presence of Josh in his disguise.

Inside the glove compartment of Cuckoo's van, was a 9mm pistol, a silencer and 20 rounds of ammunition. He nervously opened the glove compartment and took out the weapon and its accessories. A police car cruised past, its occupants more interested in the refugees from the rave. Cuckoo hastily stuffed the gun back into its hiding place until he was satisfied that the patrol car wasn't going to return.

Slipping the gun in his pocket, Cuckoo decided that it was time to extend his search for Josh. He began by taking a walk down to the beach, where he had seen several of the ravers heading. He felt self-conscious with the pistol in his pocket, even though it was adequately concealed. He was confident about using the weapon but had never fired at anyone in cold blood before. At the annual British Free Corps firearms training sessions in the Peak District, he had always proved to be an exemplary shot.

After finding the beach deserted, he began walking back towards Fantasy Island. He concluded that Josh had to be lurking around somewhere but would be keeping a low profile. As he made his way up Sea Lane, Cuckoo was surprised how much Ingoldmells had changed since the last time he had visited the seaside village.

As he passed near to Fantasy Island once again, he recognised his nephew amongst a group of people. Not wishing to be recognised, Cuckoo ducked back into a doorway. Luke had his arms around the man in the Joker outfit and appeared to be drunkenly ranting. As Cuckoo watched Luke making a fool of himself, it suddenly occurred to him that the idiot in the fancy dress outfit fitted the same height and build as Josh. It made complete sense that Josh wouldn't want his identity uncovered. Cuckoo had to admire the audacity of the youth for parading around in front of hundreds of people when he was wanted by the police and the BFC.

Whilst distracted by the revelation that Josh was standing before him, Cuckoo hadn't noticed Luke rolling around on the floor. He watched as his nephew threw himself around in a dying fly dance routine. The expressions of concern on the onlookers' faces alerted Cuckoo to the fact that Luke was in distress. Unwilling to reveal his presence to Josh, Cuckoo watched helplessly from his vantage point. He had never had children of his own and Luke was the nearest he had had to a son.

He almost came running from his hiding place as he watched Josh begin to search the pockets of Luke's jeans. Josh pulled out Luke's mobile phone and frantically tried to work out how to make a call on the new-fangled device. From where Cuckoo was standing, it looked as though Luke was experiencing a seizure; he couldn't recollect his nephew being prone to epileptic fits.

After Josh had made a call on the phone, he entreated the crowd that had formed around Luke to move away. As the fit began to subside, he put his jacket under Luke's head and asked if anyone had a bottle of water. Someone handed Josh a bottle and he encouraged Luke to take sips of water to alleviate any dehydration.

An ambulance arrived shortly after Josh's call and most of the bystanders dispersed, unwilling to face any drug-related questioning. Only Sammy stayed with Josh, while the paramedics loaded Luke into the ambulance. A short discussion took place between Luke's companions and Sammy suggested that he should go to the hospital with Luke, while it would be wise for Josh to make himself scarce. Before he left, Sammy gave Josh the keys to the caravan where he and Luke had been staying.

As the ambulance pulled away, Cuckoo watched Josh walk away in the direction of the seafront. Conflicting emotions began to take hold of Cuckoo, which forced him to abandon his mission to execute Josh. He returned to his van and made his mind up to at least grant the traitor a stay of execution until he had visited Luke in hospital. He drove away towards the general hospital in Skegness; recalling its location after he had once spent an afternoon there one Bank Holiday Monday with a broken nose.

CHAPTER NINETEEN

When John Freeman received a phone call from Sammy informing him that he had seen Cuckoo Walsh at the Skegness General Hospital, he knew he had to get to Josh at once. He had a splitting headache after drinking heavily the night before. He and Sally had seen the New Year in at the Mansfield Woodhouse Ex-Servicemen's Club. A duo had churned out everything from the Drifters to Take That. Sally and John had capered to *Hi Ho Silver Lining* and been one number away from winning the bingo flyer.

A gang of women had come into the concert room for a drink, on their rounds of the local drinking establishments. While they stood near the bar with their drink, one of them began to improvise an embarrassing Mick Jagger routine, while the duo sang *Satisfaction*. She strutted with her hands on her back, lips protruding and thrusting her head back and forth like a chicken. Freddie Starr would have cringed at such a performance.

Sally found the whole thing hilarious and John shook his head in disbelief. The impressionist took umbrage when she caught sight of Sally's sniggering. She looked at the couple and felt a moment of spiteful jealousy at the uxorious attention Sally received from her husband.

'Hey Sexy!' she called across to John. 'Remember these cock sucking lips?'

Sally turned a bright shade of red and gave her a venomous look.

'What are you fucking staring at, you ugly bitch?' snapped Mick Jagger.

The gang of women thought the entire scene was hilarious and turned their backs on Sally without another thought. They finished their drinks and prepared to leave and move on to the Angel. Sally patiently watched them file out and make a right turn, down the corridor that led to the toilets. John went to the bar to get the next round of drinks. As soon as he joined the queue, she got up and headed towards the ladies' lavatories. She marched straight through the door and saw the ersatz-Jagger applying make-up in front of the mirror. Sally tapped her on the back and then administered a swift head-butt to Jagger's nose. She then grabbed her by the hair and dragged her into one of the cubicles, where she proceeded to shove her head down the toilet bowl and pulled the chain.

'Anyone else got a problem?' asked Sally, as she casually strolled past the rest of the gang, who stood open-mouthed in disbelief.

When John finally returned from the busy bar, Sally was sat waiting, gazing at John with maritorious pride.

John's mum was minding Kevin while they enjoyed their evening out. Whilst crossing the football pitch next to the club, Sally suggested that they make love under the stars, like they had done when they had first been together. They had scarcely managed to pull down their jeans, when a drunken reveller tripped right over them, dampening their ardour.

The second surprise of the evening came when they returned home. They opened the living room door and found Spike entertaining John's mum with a Black Mamba dildo. Sally found the situation highly amusing, but John was left in a serious state of shock. His mother was sent home in ignominy, while Spike, who claimed he had been seduced, managed to secure the settee for the night.

When John prepared to leave for Ingoldmells the following morning, he decided that having Spike around might be a good idea, in case Cuckoo Walsh turned up with some of his BFC thugs. As they drove through the rural landscape of Lincolnshire, John was still refusing to speak to Spike. Stretched out in the back seat, Spike snored loudly and John glanced through his rear-view mirror, observing him as he turned over like a baby in his cot.

John had already made one visit to the caravan park earlier in the week and found that Josh had disappeared. He had feared that either the police or the BFC had caught up with Josh, or he had simply decided to chance it alone somewhere else. It wasn't until Sammy had called that John had been apprised of the situation.

The aspirin tablets John had taken before he had left the house began to alleviate his headache. He sipped a can of Tizer and switched on the radio. The Christmas number one, *2 Become 1* by the Spice Girls, was playing and John quickly turned off the radio again as the song brought back traumatic visions of what he had witnessed in his living room a few hours earlier.

The sound of the radio had awakened Spike, whose head suddenly appeared next to the driver's seat like a curious dog.

'Where are we?' he asked groggily.

John ignored Spike and took another pull on the can of Tizer.

'Oh give us a swag of that mate,' pleaded Spike. 'I'm spitting feathers here.'

John shook the can to ascertain how much Tizer was left, took another long drink and then handed the can to Spike.

'Oh cheers pal,' said Spike, as he discovered that the can only contained a few tantalizing drops of liquid.

'You do realise, I'm going to have to get some kind of counselling after what I saw last night,' said John morosely.

'Oh get over yourself! She's an attractive woman with needs; get off your fucking high horse.'

'My little lad was upstairs, what if he'd come down?'

'Yeah okay, I'm sorry.'

'How do you think me dad's going to feel when he finds out about you two carrying on; he's already had one nervous breakdown after she fucked off, when he was still grieving for one of his sons.'

'Yeah well, you needn't worry about that,' said Spike sheepishly.

'What's that supposed to mean?'

'He kind of knows; they've got this sort of arrangement.'

'I'm going to be a stretcher case by the time I'm done today!' said John incredulously.

As John muttered to himself, occasionally shaking his head, Spike slipped back onto the back seat and resumed his sleep.

When Spike awoke again, he looked out of the window and recognised the railway station of Skegness. They drove along the deserted high street towards Lumley Road and the diminutive landmark of the Clock Tower. On the seafront they drove past the deserted Pleasure Beach Fairground and the pier, until they came as far as the seal sanctuary.

'Where the fuck is the hospital anyway?' asked John, finally breaking the silence.

'I don't know but I know the cop shop is up here somewhere.'

'There isn't a soul around to ask for directions,' remarked John disconsolately, 'it's like a ghost town.'

'What did you expect in January?' replied Spike. 'Kiss Me Quick hats and the Radio One Roadshow.'

Eventually they pulled up beside an elderly dog walker, who gave them directions. When the train station came into view for a second time, Spike was tempted to get out and hang around for a train. After realising that they had taken a wrong turn, they soon found themselves outside the hospital.

It had never occurred to John that Skegness was like any other town, with its own population going about their business throughout the year. It had always seemed a magical place, where people came to spend the summer as bingo callers and Butlins Redcoats and then went home again during the winter. One big illusion, set up for the holidaymakers and day trippers, without a life of its own.

After finding a place to park, they headed towards the main entrance. Sammy was sitting on a bench outside, smoking a cigarette and sipping a can of shandy. Spike grabbed the can and gulped down the fizzy liquid until there was none left.

'You can finish that if you want,' Sammy said dejectedly, as he watched Spike crush the can under his foot.

'Right so where's Josh then?' asked John impatiently.

'I'm guessing he's back at the caravan.' replied Sammy. 'Probably shagging that lass he was sniffing around all night.'

'Oh great!' said John sardonically, 'At least one of us is having a good time then.'

'So where's Walsh then?' asked Spike.

'He's in there with Luke, I'm staying right out of his way; he thinks it was me who gave Luke the pill. He won't have it that his nephew deals drugs in his spare time.'

'Right, well, we'd better get down to Jinglebells and make sure Dog is alright,' said Spike.

'I wonder if the outdoor market will be on today?' remarked Sammy 20 minutes later, as the pyramidal roof of Fantasy Island hove into view.

'We're not here on a fucking shopping excursion,' replied John, who was becoming exasperated by the lack of urgency his companions were displaying.

Until that morning, Spike had been ignorant of Josh's whereabouts since his escape and was filling in the blanks one step at a time. He had been under the impression that Josh had been hiding out with Sammy and Luke and was surprised when he discovered that he had been using Alex Freeman's caravan.

'So when did he last stay in Alex's van?' he asked, recalling his bedroom farce there a few nights earlier.

'I don't know,' replied John, 'he wasn't there when I came round a couple of days ago. When did he bump into you two?'

'Night before New Year's Eve,' said Sammy, 'he was just sat there on the beach.'

'I reckon them BFC nutters must have come looking for him and he did a runner,' remarked Spike innocently.

'I don't know,' said Sammy, 'he didn't say anything about that, but something seemed to have put the shits up him and he wouldn't say.'

As the car drove up a narrow road between rows of empty caravans, a pair of men appeared. They crossed the road from between one row of caravans and disappeared into the adjacent row.

'That little fat bloke reminds me of him that used to be on that *Sergeant Bilko* programme late at night.'

'Doberman?' replied John.

'I didn't see any dogs' said Sammy.

'No, the character was called Doberman,' replied John in exasperation.

'He always reminded me of Benny in *Top Cat*,' said Spike.

John pulled to a stop and climbed out of the car, 'Come on Top Cat I don't like the look of these two cunts!'

'Who's Benny?' said Sammy.

'Hey John!' remarked Spike. 'Sammy is like Choo-Choo; remember the gay one in *Top Cat* ?'

'Will you shut the fuck up about *Top Cat!*' John hissed.

After almost losing sight of the two men, John halted by the side of a caravan as he caught sight of them moving stealthily along the next row. Doberman was accompanied by none other than Cuckoo's faithful lieutenant from the Coocachoo Crew, Strachan.

'That's the Scottish arsehole who me and Keats had a row with in the Masons,' whispered John.

'Well if Dog is back in our caravan, they're getting very warm,' said Sammy, 'because it's on the end of the row they're searching.'

They continued to surreptitiously pursue the pair. As Doberman and Strachan passed each caravan, they peered through any curtains that might be open and leaned against doors, listening for any sign of movement. By the time they had reached the caravan which Sammy indicated, John had motioned to Spike and Sammy to swiftly move across to the front of a neighbouring caravan.

They watched as Doberman indicated to Strachan that he could hear noise from within. Strachan reached into a pocket in his leather trench coat and pulled out a handgun with a silencer attached to its barrel.

'Sammy!' hissed John, 'Run like fuck past your caravan and make sure they see you.'

Sammy looked at John in disbelief and then comprehending his role as a distraction, began running past Doberman and Strachan. He still wore the whistle he had taken to the rave, attached to a piece of string around his neck. As he ran past his caravan he stuck the whistle in his mouth and blew like a deranged football referee.

Strachan's first instinct was to kneel down and throw the gun underneath the caravan, certain that the police had arrived. Spike suddenly marched out from his hiding place towards Doberman and Strachan.

'Wait till I get my hands on that cheating bitch!' he called out, and then walked straight into the caravan and slammed the door.

John remained hidden where he wouldn't be recognised by Strachan, waiting to reinforce Spike if the situation became desperate. He watched as Doberman silently shook his head towards Strachan and gestured to move on to the next caravan. Strachan retrieved his gun and the pair cautiously proceeded in their search.

Once inside the caravan, Spike was greeted by the sound of vigorous sexual activity. A moment later he was joined by John and then Sammy finally arrived.

'I'll fetch the car and we'll get him somewhere safe,' said John.

'Seems a shame to disturb these two lovebirds,' remarked Spike as the rhythmic banging of a headboard emanated from the bedroom.

After bringing Josh home with him, John was aware that the arrangement would have to be a temporary one. Now he had witnessed with his own eyes the mortal danger Josh was in, it was crucial to move him as far away as possible. During a phone conversation with Ray Keaton, John summarised Josh's situation. Ray had been introduced to the British Free Corps on several occasions during poetry readings, where he had been accosted by the organisation. He had been accused by the BFC of spreading Republican propaganda with his poetry. His latest collection of poetry was underpinned with sentiments about a peaceful solution to the troubles in Northern Ireland, and lamentation of the casualties incurred on both sides of the divide.

Ray had once been a fugitive himself, when he and his wife had fled from a Dublin Gangster called Tamburlaine Doyce. The couple had found themselves in Belgium, hiding from Doyce, who was bent on revenge after Ray had eloped with his former lover. The couple had eventually settled in London with their children. Doyce had finally traced them to their Kilburn home after years of searching.

Fortunately for the Keaton's, Doyce had also been pursued and was subsequently executed by Republican assassins, after he had turned supergrass.

Ray agreed to harbour Josh in a small cottage in Connemara which he had bought as a place to write. He agreed to look after Josh, if John could get him safely across the Irish Sea by whichever means he could. John's problem was whether he could obtain a false passport or find someone who owned a boat. In the meantime, he was paranoid that his home might be under surveillance by either the police or the BFC.

John's previous anxieties about work and anti-social behaviour in his neighbourhood had evaporated, only to be replaced by the stress of harbouring an escaped felon. He was worried about the danger he was placing his family in, especially now that Sally was carrying their second child.

The neighbourhood had resumed into a state of calm since Sean Cain had led teenagers in his reign of terror over residents. A local man called Mark Daft had put an end to Cain's mischievous spree. Daft was in his late-20s, had learning difficulties and lived with his mother. He would go out to the allotments every day with his pellet gun, where he had been given permission to shoot rats. One day he set out along Vale Road, passing under the railway bridge that led to the allotments. Cain and his friends were hanging around on the bridge and decided to throw stone chippings from the railway line at passers-by. They had been throwing the stones at various dog walkers and gardeners, with well-aimed throws, intended to land near enough to infuriate their targets without actually hitting them.

Cain had grown bored with the game and become bolder, when Mark Daft had come shuffling around the corner from Brown Avenue. As his target emerged under the other side of the bridge, he threw a medium-sized stone that hit Mark Daft squarely in the middle of his back. Seized by rage, Daft had climbed up onto the bridge, taking out his pellet gun and loading it as he made his way up the slope. Cain stood triumphantly waiting, with his followers behind him. After being shot in his left eye with Daft's gun, Cain was taken in an ambulance to the Queen's Medical Centre in Nottingham. Nobody saw Sean Cain again after the incident and his friends ceased their mischief, after learning the hard way that not all adults play by the same rules.

Life at Tsucol also grew easier for John after a year in the position of team leader. He was transferred to a new cell, which consisted of a more experienced team, who were consistently reaching production targets. John had to confess to himself that the new team ran itself, yet he still received praise from his superiors.

Amongst the members of John's new team was Dean Swift, who became an unlikely ally in the quest to keep Josh one step ahead of his pursuers. Since the meeting at the poetry reading, John had remained on friendly terms with Dean and the two had found time to discuss their mutual passion for literature. John began to give Dean a regular lift to and from work, when they began working together.

One evening Dean had stayed behind with John to finish some rework and John suggested dropping by the Sir John Cockle for a pint on the way home. The subject of the fire came up and John was surprised to find that Dean didn't hold any animosity towards Josh.

'So have they done anything with that house next door to you since the fire?' John asked.

'Yeah they've gutted it and done it up. I think they are going to turn it into flats.'

'I never thought I'd hear of that lad getting involved with anything like that,' said John morosely, 'He used to be a bit of a daft lad when he used to knock around with me and Spike but he wouldn't have hurt a fly back then.'

'It all depends on the company you keep,' said Dean. 'Some people are very manipulative; they can find someone impressionable like Josh was and get them to do anything.'

John remembered when he had first met Sally, when she was living on the streets of London, after running away from a controlling and psychotic boyfriend.

'Do you reckon they'll catch up with him then?' asked John, trying to gauge Dean's opinion of Josh.

'Well he's no Ronnie Biggs is he,' chuckled Dean. 'I just hope those BFC thugs don't get hold of him; I hear they're trying to do him in, so he doesn't start naming names.'

'Where did you hear that?' John asked inquisitively.

'Sammy reckons he's seen Josh and he's lying low because the BFC are searching for him. He should hand himself in to the police if you ask me and blow the whistle on the whole bunch of them. There must be some kind of witness protection program he can go on.'

'That's all well and good in films like *Goodfellas* but it doesn't work out like that in reality,' replied John gravely. 'The whole reason he did a runner was because the BFC tried to kill him while he was inside.'

John didn't speak about Josh for several days but he began to sense that he could trust Dean. He finally broached the subject one evening when they had stopped for a quick drink at the pub. John intimated that he knew the whereabouts of Josh without directly disclosing his own role. The more Dean learned about the attempt on Josh's life and the plan to transport him to Ireland, the more he grew enchanted by the romance of the situation.

'It's just like a Robert Louis Stevenson novel,' said Dean enthusiastically . 'We've got to get hold of a false passport somehow. I know a bloke who might be able to help but I haven't seen him around for ages.'

'Do you think you might be able to put Josh up for a few nights then?'

'I'll need to sort it out with Heidi but I'm sure she'll go along with it.'

They drank to Josh's freedom and Dean thought that it was like being in an episode from *Secret Army*.

CHAPTER TWENTY

Amidst the maze of buildings of Mansfield's King's Mill Hospital nestled the Millbrook Mental Health Unit. Heidi and I arrived on time, for the commencement of the evening visiting sessions. Heidi's father, Tony, would already have bought himself a meal in the cafeteria, before his second visit of the day. He would stay by his wife's side for the duration of the allotted visiting time, as he did each afternoon and evening. Heidi's mother had been admitted for observation, after she had begun to have difficulty standing up, without falling over again.

Heidi had moved in with me shortly after Christmas and we walked together each day, the short distance from my house to the hospital. We found Tony in the day room, trying to tempt Elaine with one of her favourite Jaffa cakes. Elaine seemed to have taken a shine to me and Tony eagerly informed her of my presence. I think she probably thought I was a younger version of her husband, who she recollected with more clarity than the people who surrounded her in the present day.

'Do you know where we are?' an elderly man asked me as I sat down.

I shook my head and said, 'We'll soon be going home mate, don't worry.'

Another man with dementia began to wail and curse, as his relatives desperately tried to calm him down. As soon as he fell asleep, they left, eager to get back to their own lives.

I held Elaine's hands and she attempted to stand up, thinking that she needed to be somewhere. She quickly sat down again, only to start the process of getting up again. I guessed that there might be some kind of cardiovascular benefit from her actions if nothing else.

Heidi had brought her mother a stuffed monkey that she had owned since she had been a little girl. We had discovered that Elaine found comfort in clutching teddy bears and the one she had previously been in possession of had been stolen by another patient. She fumbled with the monkey for some time, before taking Tony's hand and giving it to him.

Heidi and her father told Elaine various pieces of gossip; the latest storyline in *Coronation Street*; the goings-on at the Baptist church; Jeanette's new boyfriend. It was hard to tell if any of the information was registered by Elaine but it was better than sitting in silence. It had been over a year since Elaine had lost the ability to communicate vocally. She would occasionally utter a disconnected word or point and mumble something incoherent. Now she was heavily medicated, Elaine spent most of her time asleep. This latest development had made life for Tony more peaceful than the days when she had been disruptive. The downside was that he was no longer eligible for the monthly respite that had been a lifeline for so long.

After spending an hour with Heidi's parents, we left the nurses to bath Elaine and put her to bed. We drove along Sutton Road and stopped at the new pub that had been built next to the bus garage. The Bold Forester had been fashioned with stout oak beams, wainscoting and an equally stout, Dickensian landlord, to give it an olde-worlde charm. The quaint furnishing was contrasted with several television screens that showed all the latest football matches. The overall effect produced was a cross between the bar in *Cheers* and the Maypole Inn in *Barnaby Rudge*. The pub's greatest attraction was its wide range of cask ales. The portly landlord had already gained a reputation as a real ale alchemist at his former pub, The Plough on Nottingham Road.

I ordered a pint of Bartholomew's Fair porter and an orange juice for Heidi. She was already sitting down at a table with her friend Jeanette and her boyfriend, Colin. It was quiz night at the Bold Forester and Heidi had invited her friend to help us win a gallon of beer. As I paid for my drinks, Colin joined me at the bar and ordered a bottle of Hooch for Jeanette and a pint of Fosters for himself.

'It's dead in here,' said Colin, surveying the half-empty pub.

'It will get busier later on,' I replied. 'They take their quizzes seriously in this place.'

'So what do we get if we win then?'

'Gallon of ale; works out at about two pints each.'

'Well that's a bag of wank between four of us,' said Colin disappointedly.

'I doubt whether we'll win against that lot anyway,' I said, nodding my head towards where half a dozen people were assembling at the corner of the bar. 'They usually win every week.'

Once we had settled down at our table, we discussed what we should name our team. Heidi eagerly held her pen over her quiz sheet, waiting for us to decide.

'Let's call ourselves the lovers,' said Jeanette.

Colin rolled his eyes, 'Fuck that, let's call ourselves the A Team.'

'What do you think we should call ourselves Dean?' asked Heidi, who had noted my ambivalence towards the subject.

'I don't know; Dave Dee, Dozy, Beaky, Mick and Titch.'

Colin chuckled at my suggestion but Jeanette re-joined, 'Don't be silly Dean, there are only four of us not six.'

'Oh yeah silly me,' I replied, sarcastically.

'There were five in Dave Dee, Dozy, Beaky, Mick and Titch, not six,' said Colin.

'No,' said Jeanette, counting on her fingers, 'Dave, Dee, Dozy, Beaky, Mick and Titch, there look, six,' she said, triumphantly holding up six fingers.

'There were seven actually,' I said sardonically, 'you forgot 'And'.'

Jeanette gave me a puzzled look and Colin said, 'Yeah you forgot And, his name was Andrew but they shortened it to And because it took too long to say the name of the band otherwise.'

Jeanette looked from Colin, to me and then to Heidi for conformation. Colin and I grinned mischievously at each other.

'Ooh you pair are tricking me!' said Jeanette, slapping Colin on the arm. 'Heidi, tell your boyfriend to behave.'

Heidi was already writing down the team name she had decided on, 'Right then that's settled, we're called the Antic Dispositions.'

The quiz commenced, and my eyes soon began to glaze over, during a round on current affairs. My attention became focused on the assorted pictures that decorated the walls. There were a couple of sepia photos of Victorian life in Mansfield; strange charts from bygone days, with diagrams of various vegetables. A portrait of Thomas Wyatt, the poet credited for bringing the sonnet to England in the 16th century, seemed strangely out of place amongst the other pictures.

'Colin, who is the leader of the Labour Party?' asked Jeanette.

'I'm not sure,' He replied, drawing a blank, 'isn't Neil Kinnock still the Labour Leader?'

'There Heidi!' Jeanette said triumphantly, 'I'm not the only one who doesn't know who it is.'

'I thought everyone knew it was Tony Blair,' said Heidi.

'Oh yeah, that's right,' replied Colin, 'his Missis is the daughter of Tony Booth, who used to be in *Till Death Us Do Part*.'

'You stupid scouse git!' I said, doing a poor impression of Alf Garnett, which Colin appeared to enjoy.

'You know the Monkees did a song called *Randy Scouse Git* after Micky Dolenz heard Alf Garnett say it.'

'I love monkeys,' interrupted Jeanette. 'I love anything on the telly with animals; I wanted to go and see *Reservoir Dogs* when it came out but I was up to my neck in nappies at the time.'

I was warming to Colin's knowledge of pop music, when I received a tap on the shoulder. I looked around and saw none other than Sutts, grinning down at me like death personified.

'Fancy seeing you here,' I remarked. 'I thought you'd fallen off the edge of the earth.'

'No mate, I've just done a six-month stretch in the Scrubs for affray,' Sutts explained in a blasé tone.

'So what are you doing back in this godforsaken place then?' I asked.

'Well I've taken quite a liking to it up here. I've got a little drum on Moor Street, handy for this place.'

'Do you play the drums then?' asked Jeanette.

'Drum and bass, place,' Sutts explained.

Jeanette looked puzzled and resumed her conversation with Heidi about not being able to receive Channel 5 on her television.

I joined Sutts at the bar during an interval in the quiz. While queuing for drinks I watched an old cricket match on one of the televisions. The satellite sports channel was showing recorded highlights of an old Ashes test match at Old Trafford. Shane Warne, with his trademark bleached blond hair and lips and nose smeared with zinc sun reflector, prepared to bowl a delivery to the perpetually hirsute Mike Gatting. Warne caused the ball to spin so much in the air that it drifted sideways, wide of Gatting's leg stump. It landed in a rough patch where it turned and lifted in the opposite direction, removing the batsman's off stump. Gatting walked away in a state of disbelief, while Umpire Dickie Bird looked on in astonishment.

'How do you fancy going down to Trent Bridge one day?' said Sutts. 'Have a few beers and relive that day you were telling me about, when you and Myfanwy met that Topley geezer.'

I was keen on the idea of watching some cricket with Sutts. Since my first experience of test cricket, I had gradually learned to love the game. We were discussing possible dates for visiting Trent Bridge in the forthcoming season, when Cuckoo Walsh came strutting through the doors. He was accompanied by Dawn Townroe, who smiled and waved when she saw me.

Sutts didn't immediately recognise Cuckoo when he saw me wave to Dawn and I didn't intend to encourage further confrontation between the two. When the quiz recommenced, I noticed Cuckoo putting coins into a fruit machine, while Dawn playfully ran her hand over his posterior.

'Ere that's the cant that started a barney when we was in that Yankee boozer!' observed Sutts.

'Oh that's all I need!' said Colin. 'Cuckoo and my ex.'

'Don't be silly Colin,' said Jeanette, waving to Dawn and gesturing for her to join them, 'Andy is just a pussycat really.'

As the couple approached the group, Cuckoo hesitated, as he recognised the man he had brawled with at the Red Lion, 'Look mate I don't want any trouble,' he said with uncharacteristic contriteness. Sutts shrugged his shoulders as if to suggest that he didn't mind, one way or the other. Heidi, Colin and I, completed the remainder of the quiz, while Jeanette talked at Dawn about her wedding plans. Sutts and Walsh ended up arm in arm, like two lovers making up.

I was keen to have a quiet word with Sutts about the possibility of him being able to arrange a false passport for Josh. Heidi had been reluctant to take in an escaped convict but agreed to having Josh under our roof if he could be moved as quickly as possible. With Walsh hanging around, there was a palpable sense of danger. His incongruous amiability was making me paranoid that he might have an inkling that Heidi and I were hiding Josh. It was fortunate that Heidi was unaware of Walsh's involvement in the plot to kill Josh, or she would have been hysterical.

When the answers to the quiz questions were read out, we discovered that we had scored 20 out of 30. The team who usually won took the gallon of beer after correctly answering 29 questions. Jeanette, who hadn't contributed anything to our score, was genuinely disappointed that we hadn't won.

Cuckoo was still clinging to Sutts, impressed by his stories about his time with the Krays. Cuckoo's phone began playing a Mozart melody; he looked at the caller identity and then quickly rejected the call. I observed how his face had suddenly turned pale, as though the devil himself had just tried to call. The ringtone began again and this time Cuckoo rushed towards the toilets to answer the persistent caller. I grabbed the opportunity to have a word with Sutts alone.

'Sutts, can I speak to you outside a minute?' I asked.

'Ooh sounds a bit naughty!' he replied.

We stepped outside and sat on the grass bank at the front of the pub, which overlooked the A38 and the playing fields of the Moor Lane school.

'Would you know how to go on about obtaining a false passport?' I asked.

'Sounds a bit dodgy,' replied Sutts with an apprehensive expression. 'Are you in some kind of trouble?'

'Noo! I'm writing a crime novel and I just want to get some genuine ideas,' I explained, using a pretext I had already conceived and rehearsed.

'Well I know a couple of forgers who could do you a handsome passport, but it don't come cheap.'

Cuckoo suddenly emerged, looking for his new friend.

'I'll come round and speak to you about it tomorrow,' said Sutts, sensing the urgency of my request.

Heidi and I were back home half-an-hour later, after I stopped at the An Lushan Chinese Takeaway on Padley Hill. With Josh in the house, I needed to buy extra provisions, so I ordered an extra portion of Singapore rice and special curry. The waiting area of the takeaway was deserted and I amused myself by gazing at the fish that swam gracefully around a large aquarium. A television set mounted on the wall was showing the end of *Newsnight*. Jeremy Paxman was interviewing Freddy Nordville-Best, who had recently attained the title of 14th Marquess of Straffield. The second son of the 13th Marquess of Straffield had risen in status since his father and elder brother, Lionel, had both been killed in a plane crash. Allegations of drug use and sex with underage boys had created a certain amount of media interest in Freddie's title and he was giving Paxman an exclusive interview in his quest to defend his honour.

The food arrived just in time, as the triumphant quiz team noisily entered the An Lushan. When I arrived home, I took a plate of Chinese food up to Josh's room. We had installed him in the small bedroom at the rear of the house. He was contentedly engrossed in playing *Populous II: Trials of the Olympian Gods* on my Sega Mega Drive. I had installed a portable colour television and the games console in his room, to keep him occupied and he had spent all his time playing my considerable collection of games. I placed the plate next to where he sat cross-legged on the floor. He was frenziedly tapping the controller, alternately flattening or raising land, for his little people to cultivate and build on. The towering figure of Poseidon suddenly emerged from the sea and proceeded to march across the land, destroying all in his path.

'Bollocks!' he muttered, switching off the console in disgust. 'Oh cheers mate,' he said as he grabbed his plate and ravenously shovelled rice and curry into his mouth.

I had only just picked up my own food, when a knock at the door interrupted my repast. Heidi looked at me in trepidation, fearing that the police had discovered

Josh's bolthole. I opened the door and found Sutts waiting outside. On the pavement, Cuckoo Walsh and Dawn were loitering.

'Blimey you look like you've seen a ghost mate,' said Sutts, slurring after overindulging on fine ales. 'Sorry to disturb you but do you mind if I use your Khazi? We've just been down to the chinky and Tommy Turtle is sticking his head out here mate, I'm not kidding.'

Before I had the chance to direct Sutts to the outside toilet, he was already bounding up the stairs. The front door was wide open and I went over and shut it. I saw Cuckoo trying to look innocent, as he stood beside the house where someone had died thanks to his hatred. Dawn looked rather embarrassed as she stared up at the bedroom where she and I had made love. Cuckoo was still unaware that I had been the lover who she had rejected in favour of him. I stood leaning against the door, trying to rationalise why Cuckoo was standing outside the house, where the man he was intent on killing was hidden. *They're just here because Sutts was desperate for the toilet,* I tried to convince myself.

Sutts appeared in the hallway several minutes later, looking refreshed, 'Fack me, that's a weight of my mind!' he exclaimed in a relieved tone, wiping his forehead. 'I'll come round tomorrow night and discuss that bit of business you mentioned earlier.'

I watched him walk away down Harrington Street with his new friend. When I closed the door and returned inside, Heidi was waiting, looking pensive.

'So that's the famous jailbird is it?' she asked.

'He's just an old friend of Myfanwy's,' I said, shrugging my shoulders. 'He's not a bad bloke really, bit of a loveable rogue that's all.'

'Well I don't feel comfortable with him swanning in and out of here at all hours!' she retorted angrily. 'As if it isn't bad enough we've got an escaped convict lodging here!'

'Keep it down,' I hissed, 'the neighbours can hear everything through these walls.'

'Well excuse me Dean but I'm going to go back to Dad's if you don't get rid of these people soon. I should be helping him more with Mum anyway.'

'Just give me a couple of days and I'll get rid of both of them,' I pleaded. 'Please don't leave me, I love you so much.'

CHAPTER TWENTY-ONE

When Sutts left Dean Swift's house, he unwittingly gave the game away, 'I just went upstairs for a pony and I saw that geezer who I saw you with a few months back at that boozer round the corner.'

Cuckoo shrugged his shoulders, 'I can't remember, when was this?'

'When you started giving it some bunny, before we kicked off at the Red Lion,' Sutts explained, 'There was a young lad stood at the bar with you.'

'Oh he was just some kid I had labouring for me,' said Cuckoo as it dawned on him who Sutts was alluding to. 'He lives with your mate does he?' he asked disinterestedly.

'Looks like it dunnit; I could hear this funny music coming from this bedroom, so I stuck me loaf in there and he's sat there playing some soppy computer game.'

Cuckoo now found himself in a dilemma. He had already failed to finish off Josh and had told Doberman that he couldn't go through with the killing, nor would he have any further involvement with the British Free Corps. This sudden change of heart had not been acceptable to Cuckoo's comrades, who began to suspect another traitor in their midst.

Family life with Dawn and her daughters was growing on Cuckoo. He was also spending more time with his nephew, who had made a full recovery since the night in Ingoldmells. The Pakistani labourer who Cuckoo had employed to improve his image in front of a jury, had also won the heart of his employer. The BFC had been an antidote to his disillusionment with football hooliganism. His racism had been a bitter reaction to his wife eloping with a woman of Afro-Caribbean origin, who also happened to be a Labour councillor for the ward of Clifton North. In short, he had renounced his allegiance to a cause that espoused racial and political hatred.

The morning after the quiz at the Bold Forester, Cuckoo sat at the breakfast table with Dawn. First one, then the other twin, appeared in the kitchen after 10 minutes of noisy preparation for school. Dawn was watching *The Big Breakfast* on a colour portable television that was perched on a shelf that Cuckoo had assembled.

'This programme has gone downhill since Chris Evans left,' Dawn reflected.

'Ginger twat,' grumbled Cuckoo, 'can't stand him.'

'Andy!' Dawn chided, slapping him on the arm. The twins both giggled at Cuckoo's coarse language.

'Well, he is,' argued Cuckoo, 'and that scouse knobhead who used to be on that music programme for kids, what's his name?'

'Keith Chegwin,' replied Bev.

'It was called *Cheggers Plays Pop*,' said Dawn.

'Should be Cheggers drinks pop, now he's off the booze,' retorted Cuckoo.

'His sister is Janice Long,' remarked Dawn as she spread butter on her toast.

'Who?' said Cuckoo.

'Keith Chegwin.'

'I thought he was related to that Maggie Philbin?' said Cuckoo, growing more confused.

Looking at the time that was displayed on *The Big Breakfast*, Cuckoo decided it was time to stop talking about Keith Chegwin's family tree and get a move on.

'Right then, you pair need to get a move on if you want a lift to school,' he announced authoritatively, which was ignored by the twins, who were engrossed in the antics of Zig and Zag.

Once he had coaxed the girls into the passenger seat of his van, Cuckoo made his way to the Brunts secondary school. The van was soon vibrating to the sound of *Barbie Girl* by Aqua. Cuckoo normally favoured the Russ 'n' Jono show on Virgin Radio, but the radio had been swiftly tuned to GEM AM the moment the twins climbed into the vehicle. A commercial for double glazing came on after Aqua and Bev grew impatient for more music. She switched from the radio to the cassette player and *White Power* by Screwdriver began to play. Cuckoo swiftly ejected the cassette and then threw it out of the window.

'That's enough of that,' he said and then switched the radio back on.

As the van drove up Carr Bank, Cuckoo felt a sudden queasiness in his stomach after hearing the snatch of music on the cassette. The girls thought he was quite cool, arbitrarily throwing things out of the window. He felt guilty that he was exposing them to something evil that might infect their minds with hatred. He crossed Woodhouse Road and arrived at the school. As he sat and watched the twins mingle with their friends as they passed through the school gates, he thought about the call he had received the night before. He hadn't recognised the voice that had spoken to him, but he had fully comprehended the gravity of the message. 'We know where you're living now,' a deep unfamiliar voice with a West Country burr had threatened.

The problem for the British Free Corps was that Cuckoo knew too much. Now that he had decided to renounce his loyalty to the cause, he had become a thorn in its side. He had been involved in the BFC since it had been a fledgling organisation, that had sprung up as a faction of the British National Party. In 1988, Cuckoo had travelled to West Germany to support England in the European Football Championships. He had participated in running battles on the streets of Dusseldorf, between rival groups of English, Dutch and German football hooligans. During that time, he became acquainted with two brothers from Fulham, Brian and Tommy Stevens. The brothers shared Cuckoo's sense of disenchantment with hooliganism since English football clubs had been banned from Europe in 1985. As the younger element of the casual firms were seduced by 'The Second Summer of Love', the violence in Germany seemed like a swansong for veterans like Cuckoo and the Stevens brothers. Whilst fraternising with German and Dutch hooligans, the three of them made their first contact with members of several European neo-Nazi organisations. The seed was sown that would lead to the formation of the British Free Corps. A network of contacts was built up, consisting of the core membership of the BFC and associate organisations in Northern Ireland, Europe and the United States. Cuckoo knew the names of all those involved; lists of names and addresses of potential political and racial targets; previous criminal activities and names of arms dealers. To become a renegade from the British Free Corps, with so much information, carried the stiffest penalty and yet Cuckoo was sceptical that his erstwhile associates had the bottle to take him down.

Doubling back in the direction he had taken towards the school, Cuckoo headed towards Rosemary Street. Waiting beside the road near the Rosemary Shopping Centre stood a young Asian youth wearing a black and white Newcastle United shirt. Cuckoo defiantly pulled up alongside the curb on the double yellow lines. The young Pakistani labourer named Bilal Ali jumped enthusiastically into the passenger seat.

'Allreet boss!' he said cheerfully.

'Come on you Toon wanker,' said Cuckoo playfully, 'we've got a lot on today.'

'Bring it on!'

'How do you reckon Newcastle will get on now Keegan has resigned Billy?' asked Cuckoo, who always referred to Bilal as Billy; more often than not he called him Billy Bullshit, due to his tall but entertaining stories.

'It's shite man!' replied Billy, shaking his head morosely. 'I thought he was gonna take us all the way after signing Shearer. It's bollocks man!'

Cuckoo had detested Billy when he had originally employed him. The idea of taking on a Pakistani had been suggested to him by Doberman, who argued that it would camouflage his image as a racist in the eyes of a jury. Despite Cuckoo's constant undermining attitude and open hostility, Bilal Ali had continued to turn up every day and worked diligently. Cuckoo couldn't help but warm to the amiability and alacrity of the 19-year-old Geordie. Billy's parents had settled in Newcastle after fleeing from Uganda when its president, Idi Amin, ordered the expulsion of the country's Asian minority. The worst thing that Cuckoo could call Billy now was Mackem, the nickname Geordies used for their local rivals in Sunderland.

Billy amused himself with his Tamagotchi, while Cuckoo mused over his predicament. They were heading towards a new job at Lowdham. A new Category B prison was being built near the village and Cuckoo had secured the contract as plasterer on the building project. Lowdham was situated in a rural area of Nottinghamshire, near to Southwell. The peaceful countryside brought a serenity to Cuckoo each day that he travelled to work.

As they travelled through Lowdham, Cuckoo noted the Magna Carta public house.

'I reckon we ought to call in there tonight Billy Boy.'

Billy was figuring out what to do next with his virtual pet, 'I think Mushy needs a vet,' he said morosely.

'Who the fuck is Mushy?' asked Cuckoo.

'It's me Tamagotchi,' explained Billy, 'I don't know whether to give it an injection or just pet it.'

'Well if it's poorly, you need to give it the injection obviously?' said Cuckoo, amazed that he was even having this conversation.

'Ah bollocks!' said Billy vehemently as his virtual cat grew wings and descended to heaven. 'It's fucking killed him like.'

'Well you'll have to get another one then!' said Cuckoo.

'No I'll just have to start again with this one now.'

Cuckoo drove on in silence, reminiscing about the days when he owned a rabbit. His father came home with a Staffordshire Bull Terrier and the dog had savaged the rabbit to death. His father had belted him for crying about the rabbit and that had been the end of it. Now people were getting emotional about plastic animals that you could bring back to life with the press of a button.

'What were you saying about going to the pub?' asked Billy, who had been pestering Cuckoo to take him to the Magna Carta since they had begun the job at Lowdham.

'I thought your lot didn't reckon to drink?' replied Cuckoo.

'What Geordies? Nah man, wah can drink you Notts pussies under the table any time.'

'Cheeky bastard!' said Cuckoo, smiling at the boy's audacity.

The work routine of Cuckoo and Billy was cut short later that morning by a telephone call from a police officer. Dawn was in hospital, suffering from lacerations to her face after a vicious attack with a carpet knife. Cuckoo later learned that shortly after he had left for work, a man in blue overalls had knocked at Dawn's front door. She had come to the door still wearing her dressing gown and had assumed that the man had come to read the electric meter. He was a red-haired man in his early-30s of medium height and average weight. He had smiled and said good morning quite amiably and then produce a carpet knife from a pocket in his overalls and proceeded to slash at both sides of Dawn's face as she recoiled in shock. He had then casually walked away, leaving Dawn sitting on the doorstep with her face covered in blood. The postman came calling a few minutes later and phoned for assistance from the police and ambulance service.

While her physical wounds were healing in hospital, mental lesions began to tear at her mind. The scars left by the knife attack would leave her disfigured for years. Each day that Andy Walsh visited her in hospital, she became convinced that the attack had been the result of something he had been involved in. She knew he had played a major part in the violent world of football hooliganism. She had supported him and been convinced of his innocence when he had been accused of playing a part in racist attacks. He had wept like a child before her and begged her to believe him when he told her he had nothing to do with the arson attack that had left a young man dead.

He finally broke down and confessed to her in hospital that he had been threatened by the BFC and had attempted to sever his ties with the organisation. Dawn's maternal instinct was more concerned with the welfare of her daughters than her own safety. She told Andy to pack his belongings and never come near her or her family ever again.

Cuckoo spent several nights sleeping in his van and trying to figure out his next move. After one particularly sleepless night, he picked up Bilal Ali at the usual place and decided that he was the only person in the world who he could now confide in. After finishing early that afternoon, he took Billy to the Magna Carta and bought him a bottle of Newcastle Brown Ale.

'You have to drink it out of a half-pint glass and pour the rest in when you're finished,' explained Billy.

'Why don't you drink it straight from the bottle?' replied Cuckoo. 'What is it with the youth of today?'

The Magna Carta was empty, apart from Cuckoo and Billy. A fruit machine flashed invitingly in a corner.

'I bet that bandit is ready to drop,' said Billy expectantly. 'Lend us a quid and I bet I can win it straight back. I've got a system with bandits see.'

'Mug's game,' said Cuckoo. 'My old man used to throw away all his money on nags, that's why we never had owt when I was a kid.'

After reluctantly parting with a pound coin, Cuckoo watched Billy race across to the bandit like a child at an amusement arcade. He watched as Billy popped the coin into the slot and the machine lit up and began to sing in gratitude for the offering. After a couple of futile attempts, Billy studied the machine as he was offered the option of holding several of the reels. He bent down and tried to get a better view of the fruit that waited out of sight. He slammed a couple of buttons and then the sound of a lone coin dropping into the tray informed Cuckoo that Billy had won back his original stake. Before getting the chance to reclaim the pound, Billy had picked it up and put it back into the slot. A photo of Nicky Campbell grinned from the slot machine and a digital approximation of the *Wheel of Fortune* theme tune added a sense of fun to the experience of losing money.

'That machine's rigged man!' said Billy as he returned empty handed.

Cuckoo sat with a pensive expression on his face, 'I'll give you the quid back as soon as I get paid,' said Billy, fearful that he'd offended his boss.

'Forget it,' said Cuckoo dismissively, 'I'm just tired that's all. I haven't been sleeping very well lately.'

'Is that because you're sleeping in the back of the van like?' asked Billy.

'How did you know I've been sleeping in the van?'

'Because you've got all your stuff in there, your toothbrush and all that.'

'Yeah well me missus kicked me out and it suits me to keep my options open regarding digs at the moment.'

'You can always come and stay with us; me Ma makes a top lamb Balti.'

'Cheers kid, that sounds very tempting but I've got some very dangerous people on my back at the moment and I wouldn't want them to come knocking on your door.'

The two sat in silence for a few minutes until Billy plucked up the courage to continue the discussion, 'Is it the same people who did those bad things to your missus?'

'I've done some pretty bad things myself kid; you wouldn't want to know me if you knew half the stuff I've done.'

'One of my mates says you used to be the top boy of the Mansfield football hooligan firm. Did you ever have any battles with Toon fans?'

'No,' laughed Cuckoo, 'we were never in the same league as your lot, on or off the pitch. The nearest I ever came to feightin' with Geordies was against a bunch of Hartlepool lads.'

'We call them monkey hangers, because they once hung a monkey as a French spy.'

'Yeah we've heard about that down here as well,' chuckled Cuckoo. 'No, I'm not proud of some of the things I did back then; especially when it involved people who had just turned up to watch a game of football.'

Cuckoo bought Billy another bottle of Newcastle Brown and a packet of scampi fries, 'I'm starving man,' said Billy as he devoured the malodorous snacks.

'They stink,' said Cuckoo, screwing up his face. 'I had an auntie who smelled just like that on a hot day.'

'Do you reckon they'll ever catch that lad who set fire to that house?' asked Billy, with a mouthful of scampi fries.'

Cuckoo shrugged his shoulders and stared into his glass of orange juice.

'Someone told me that everyone says you had something to do with all that and I said they were talking shite,' continued Billy.

'What if I told you it was true?'

Billy looked at Cuckoo as though he must be joking, then seeing a tear run down his face, he replied, 'You can't change what you've done boss, but you can make a start by putting things right. You're a good man, it's just taken you a long time to realise that.'

CHAPTER TWENTY-TWO

The stifling routine of Tsucol led me to seek employment elsewhere. I briefly found work at a factory in Kirkby in Ashfield called Claremont, where ladies underwear was manufactured. I was transported from the latest paradigm of manufacturing methods to a more anachronistic environment. A union shop steward informed me on my first day that I needed to join the union. Each week a raffle took place, which I won on my first day. The canteen sold hot food, a luxury I hadn't experienced for many years. The atmosphere at Claremont reminded me of the factory in *Coronation Street*, where shrewish, militant women ate cream buns and considered themselves artists at their trade.

Unlike Tsucol, I had the luxury of sitting down at my machine all day. I was trained on various types of machine from the lockstitch to the overlocker. I enjoyed a spell of working on a twin-needle machine, which sewed elastic onto the waists of knickers; a task which only required sewing a straight line, which was a blessing after the serpentine seams of car seat covers.

I was one of only three men who worked at Claremont in a workforce of 200. One of them, a youth called Ryan, started at the same time as me. He had spent a few weeks doing basic training with the Royal Navy before Claremont. He had clearly found the going tough, but constantly regaled me with stories about, 'when I was in the navy,' like an old seadog. The other male machine operator was a young Bangladeshi man called Shakib, who was by far the most skilled machinist in the factory. He worked furiously to make his piece rate pay but still found time to help me when I ran into trouble with my own machine.

After only a month, I was laid off from Claremont and sought work with an employment agency. After a short interview at an office on White Hart Street, I was offered work at a factory near Grantham, which manufactured chips. I was told to wait outside the Rosemary Shopping Centre the following morning at 4:30. I joined a bleary-eyed collection of individuals and climbed onto a mini bus, which picked up further passengers between Rainworth and Newark.

The tasks assigned to agency workers at the chip factory were generally easy. Most of the time, I stood watching a conveyer belt full of chips, picking out any black or green specimens. Woollen liners were provided, to be worn underneath rubber gloves, to keep out the cold when handling the frozen chips. In another section of the factory, whole potatoes were flushed through pipes of hot water. The slimy tubers came steaming onto a belt, where we would chop off green chunks with a knife. It was far more desirable to work in the cold area, checking frozen chips, to the hot and malodorous section where unmutilated potatoes emerged.

Apart from the long journey and early start, the work at the chip factory was totally stress-free. Some would have found watching a belt filled with chips all day highly tedious. For a daydreamer like myself, it was a pleasant interlude after the stressful environment of Tsucol. Working a regular eight-hour day shift was also more gratifying for my mental health than the instability of shift work. The most annoying aspect of the job was when one of the supervisors omitted to add your name from the list of daily agency workers and the weekly pay would be a day short. Helmets with ear defenders attached were obligatory wear. The constant rumbling of potato products being vibrated along belts created a thunderous noise. The veteran full-time workers could all converse by lip reading. The helmets were indispensable in an environment where pipes criss-crossed everywhere overhead. The entire environment was like the engine room of a huge ship. The floor would always be constantly wet, where teams of cleaners had hosed down each area.

My colleagues who travelled with me into Lincolnshire each day were a motley assortment of characters from all walks of life. Some people turned to agency work to tide them over till they found full-time employment, after being made redundant. Others like myself sought work from the agency after leaving a job in dubious circumstances and had no references from former employees. The agencies asked few questions and were more interested in providing their clients with their quota of labour.

I quickly made friends with a man in his mid-50s, who, after finishing his shift with us, would spend another five hours packing razors at a factory in Forest Town. He had once owned his own business, but had found himself in massive debt, which he now tried to whittle away on a Sisyphean treadmill. Despite his dire straits, he always remained cheerful and courteous. He looked forward to his evening job, where he would meet his paramour, to whom he wrote sonnets.

A former Mansfield Brewery worker would arrive each morning, still half-cut, and sleep blissfully during the drive to work. He would rock sideways, waking up his neighbour and himself, and then settle down to sleep again immediately. A lively youth from Mozambique was the only passenger on the bus who had any energy at such an ungodly hour, and he would constantly pester people for cigarettes.

It was the day of the general election and I was visiting Heidi, who had moved into her parents' house. I had arrived in time to accompany her and her parents to the polling station. The agency had informed us that we were on a four-day week at the chip factory until further notice. Some of the workers were disgruntled about losing money but I looked forward to enjoying a few long weekends. I had already placed my vote for Mansfield's long-standing Member of Parliament, Alan Meale, in the hope that he would retain his seat. I voted at the polling station, situated at the Ladybrook Community Centre, and was now heading to the Manor Comprehensive School in Mansfield Woodhouse, where Heidi and her father would vote.

With the help of Sutts, Josh had been successfully despatched across the Irish Sea to safety. Unfortunately, Heidi had grown tired of my involvement in the affair and moved out. I continued to visit her as often as possible and help with the care of her mother in any way I could.

Elaine was now completely reliant on round-the-clock care. Nurses visited her four times a day, to help with baths and putting her to bed with the aid of a harness. She could no longer get up from her armchair, let alone manage to walk up and down stairs. The task of lifting her up to go to the toilet and other fundamental daily activities had become too burdensome for Tony. He now devoted all his time to trying to spoon-feed his wife. Coaxing her to open her mouth and masticate a morsel of food was a long-drawn-out process. Sometimes Elaine would refuse to part her lips to allow entry of food into her mouth and Tony fretted that she would starve herself to death.

The weather was set fair as we strolled towards the school. I pushed Elaine's wheelchair, while Tony fretted that she might get cold if her blanket kept slipping down. The fresh air and change of scenery seemed to agree with Elaine, who serenely watched the world go by.

'In the 19th century, philanthropists started encouraging the working-classes to improve themselves with education instead of spending their precious free time drinking alcohol,' I explained to Heidi, who wanted to learn more about socialism. 'Then the labouring classes began to get organised as soon as they started reading books. Then in the 1970s and 80s, Thatcher got wise to all this and started stamping out the influence of the unions. Now people just close their curtains and ignore the world outside while they watch Sky Sports and drink super strength lager.'

'But what's that got to do with socialism?' asked Heidi, still puzzled by the whole concept.

'What I'm trying to get at is that New Labour isn't about socialism. It's just Tories with red ties.'

'So how are you supposed to know who to vote for then?'

'Well that's what I'm railing at,' I continued. 'The whole idea of our political system, is to have two opposing parties with views that are antithetical to each other, and that way they continually hold each other in check.'

'But surely John Major is totally different from Tony Blair?'

'Ostensibly yes, but beneath Major's most agreeable periphrasis and Blair's demagoguery, there is little difference; oligarchy disguised as democracy. When they ousted Thatcher, it was a revolution more profound than anything that has happened since William III arrived in Brixham Harbour.'

'Plato didn't seem too impressed with democracy,' interjected Tony. 'Have you read *The Republic* Dean?'

'That's enough politics now you boys,' said Heidi, in a gently reproving tone, 'You'll be discussing Rousseau next and we'll never hear the end of it.'

As we walked along Park Hall Road towards the school, I became distracted by several cars that where obstructing the pavement.

'Oh don't worry about us pedestrians,' I grumbled. 'The pavement is just an extended car park these days.'

I spun Elaine's wheelchair and backed onto the road to pass the cars. It was hazardous stepping out behind the cars on the busy road. I spun the wheelchair round a second time to remount the curb. Elaine sat impassively as she rotated one way and then the other. I was reminded of the opening sequence of *Joe 90,* as I watched her spin around.

Inside the polling station, Heidi and her father joined the queue of voters. Whilst I waited with Elaine, I was surprised to be greeted by the beaming face of Sarah Figg. Sarah was volunteering as a poll clerk and informed me that she was also teaching foreign languages at the Manor School. I learned that she was now married, with two children and had lived in a small village near Rouen for four years.

Sarah and I had been involved in a brief, adolescent relationship, which ended when she enrolled at Warwick University, My heart rate quickened as I recalled the day when Sarah and I had made love in a field near Cuckney. I savoured the memory while I waited for Heidi and her father to place their votes. I surreptitiously glanced at Sarah as I waited near the door with Elaine. Sarah was busy checking the papers of several new arrivals and appeared to be oblivious to my presence.

We adjourned to the Park Hall Tavern for refreshment and Tony handed me a 20-pound note to purchase drinks. While Heidi and her parents made themselves comfortable at a bench outside, I went in search of drinks. The games room was full of noisy regulars, preparing for a darts and dominoes night. A strong smell of cheese and onion sandwiches brought back memories of childhood teatime.

I continued onwards to the more salubrious surroundings of the saloon bar. The room appeared to be deserted. Some simpering giggling from a corner of the room informed me that I was not alone. I glanced around and saw Colin Townroe engaged in some heavy petting with a woman who might have been his mother. Colin pulled a wandering hand from beneath the table where they sat and sheepishly waved at me. His companion continued to coquettishly titter, amused by Colin's discomfort.

I leaned on the copper bar top and surveyed the prints of hunting scenes that decorated the walls. A flamboyant gay queen known as Fancy Pants appeared behind the bar. He wore a sparkling gold shirt and brown leather trousers. His neatly cropped hair was freshly dyed blond to conceal the grey that betrayed his advancing years. Despite his over-the-top, camp affectations, it was wise not to mock this tall and robust man, who had been known to throw people through pub windows.

As I ordered drinks, Colin sidled up beside me and, tapping his finger against his nose, said, 'Yow ain't seen me alroight!'

'I haven't seen anything,' I replied. 'Not sure about Heidi, though, she's waiting outside.'

'Don't you watch *The Fast Show*?' he asked, disappointed that I hadn't responded to his impression.

'No,' I replied curtly.

'I'm just having a catch up with me auntie,' he continued, trying to play the innocent.

'Oh, you're a very demonstrative family aren't you?' I said contemptuously. 'Are you giving gynaecological examinations for a living now then?'

'Look just don't say anything to Jeanette,' he pleaded, 'just keeping my options open youth, know what I mean?'

'I'm not remotely interested mate,' I replied. When Heidi and I returned early from taking Jeanette's kids to the cinema, it had appeared that she was also keeping her options open when I saw a man sneaking up her garden path with his clothes in a state of disarray.

I left Colin at the bar ordering a double Bailey's for his girlfriend.

'Ooh, last of the big spenders!' Fancy Pants remarked with a withering glance.

I joined the others outside and watched a Morris dancing side perform in the car park. The Mansfield Morris men were doing a tour of local pubs, which they embarked on each year in the month of May. A little man who resembled Professor Yaffle was playing a tune called *Glorishers* on an old Jeffries concertina. The Morris side performed a leapfrog routine to the tune with surprising adroitness, considering the advanced age of the majority of their ranks.

'A Little Trite Music,' said Tony sceptically.

'I think it's nice!' interjected Heidi. 'You like it don't you Mum?'

Elaine did indeed display signs of lucidity, as the reeds of the Anglo concertina echoed against the brick walls of the car park.

'I could just see you and Dad all dressed in white, jangling your bells and waving your hankies around.'

'I can never find a blessed handkerchief, so it would be a miracle,' replied Tony with a wry smile.

I spent the evening with Heidi and her father, waiting for the first results of the election to come in. Heidi tried to help her father to give Elaine her bottle of Ribena, after he had spent a futile hour trying to coax her to take a drink. He constantly criticised Heidi for not holding the towel properly underneath her mother's chin. His belittling attitude began to irritate me, as Heidi tried her best to help him. It didn't seem important to me whether or not a few drops of the cordial ran down Elaine's chin. Since retiring, caring for Elaine had become his *raison d'etre* and he criticised nurses and family alike for their ineptitude in administering to his wife's needs.

A Dimbleby buzzed in my ear all night and my only distraction was an episode of *Blackadder the Third*, all about electing a Member of Parliament for a rotten borough. Edward Towton was appearing as a political pundit on the election special; offering his expert opinion on the latest statistics, which were presented on Manhattan charts and huge maps of the United Kingdom.

I stayed the night with Heidi, creeping into bed with her from the spare room which I had been assigned. She spent half the night watching the election results on a portable television, and I gave up and fell asleep long before she finally succumbed to sleep. She woke me in the morning to inform me that Labour had won a landslide victory and the domination of the Tories had finally come to an end. The Labour Party had adopted *Things Can Only Get Better* by D:Ream as their anthem. Tony Blair and his supporters were singing the song as they celebrated their victory. I had voted for the first time in 1987 in the hope that Neil Kinnock would replace Margaret Thatcher and had been disappointed when the Tory leader had secured a third term in office. As I listened to the strains of *Things Can Only Get Better*, I had to ask myself how things could possibly get any worse for the people of Mansfield.

CHAPTER TWENTY-THREE

On the Saturday morning after the election, I set off for Nottingham with Sutts. Since suggesting to Sutts that he might enjoy a day at Trent Bridge, he had frequently reminded me to take him there. Since my first taste of test cricket, my aversion to the game had finally ended with a Damascene conversion. When the West Indians had toured England in 1991, I had somehow grown fond of cricket, during a summer in which I had the opportunity to spend copious amounts of time reading Jack Kerouac novels and discovering the simple pleasure of listening to *Test Match Special*.

Something finally clicked during that season, as I watched England's batsmen dig in to earn a series draw against the fearsome pace bowling of Curtly Ambrose and Courtney Walsh. During the rain breaks I caught up on some of cricket's most illustrious moments, watching the BBC's extensive archive of test match footage. I swapped my Kerouac for Cardus, Crusoe and Swanton. Diogenes predated Kerouac by 2,000 years, as the founder of the beat generation anyway. I was eventually baptised as a Notts member on a rainy day at Trent Bridge.

Sutts came knocking at my door much earlier than the time we had agreed on. He was keen to make the most of his day of cricket and was already cracking open a can of beer as he passed through my front door. Notts were playing Warwickshire on the second of a four-day Championship match. It had taken some time to get Sutts to understand the concept of turning up for a day of cricket and not necessarily watching the game from start to finish.

'I either watch the whole game or not at all,' he had said indignantly, when I had first discussed catching a day of cricket.

We made our way to the train station, where the new Robin Hood Line was taking passengers between Mansfield Woodhouse and Nottingham. We bought our tickets in the building which had originally been built in the 1870s. When Doctor

Richard Beeching had pruned back the branches of Britain's railways, Mansfield had felt the secateurs. The building had once been a trendy bar called Brunel's in the 1980s and had then been renovated for the Robin Hood Line.

Once outside, we passed through the subway that crossed underneath the railway lines. I felt a thrill as I recalled the evening when Dawn and I had fondled each other there, when the site was still under construction. Waiting on the platform for the Nottingham train, a crowd of people were gathered, all excited about the novelty of travelling by train. Gangs of middle-aged women cackled nervously, eager to spend all their money shopping. Parents struggled to control their excitable children as they looked forward to a day of sightseeing. A number of ageing gentlemen wearing sunhats carried bags full of newspapers, flasks, umbrellas and cricket almanacs; standard provisions for seasoned county cricket spectators. A couple of train enthusiasts waited anxiously for the arrival of the train with cameras. One of them passed the time taking photos of the railway lines.

'Did you and Myfanwy go down to the cricket on the train when you met up with that Towton geezer?'

'No, I told you,' I explained, growing tired of Sutts' constant cross-examining about my first visit to Trent Bridge, 'Myfanwy came out of prison that day and ended up stealing someone's test match ticket. I didn't know he was there till I bumped into him by chance later on. I didn't even know I was going until my dad woke me up and asked me if I fancied a day of boozing in Nottingham.'

The train eventually rolled into the station and everyone darted towards the doors, with all the urgency of refugees. I sat looking out of the window of the carriage, as the train sped through Sutton in Ashfield, Kirkby, Newstead, Hucknall and Bullwell. The yards of industrial units passed by, occasionally interrupted with an interlude of verdant pastures, sylvan groves and gothic churches.

I overheard a couple of people discussing the future extension of the Robin Hood Line, reaching Shirebrook, Creswell and finally Worksop. I thought about visiting Creswell Crags when the trains began to travel in that direction. In the limestone gorge of Creswell Crags, our ancestors once sheltered in caves, as far back as the palaeolithic age. There was evidence that the caves had been used for shelter since the time of the Neanderthals until medieval times. During the Ice Age, people had settled there, when they followed the movements of deer and other prey across the landmass called Doggerland, which had once connected Britain with Europe. It fascinated me to imagine prehistoric people, treading the same land where I lived. They were the true pioneers of the human race, living short and brutal lives. From the moment they were born, their lives were fraught with danger until the day they died, amidst the natural world that they were an integral part of.

'Is this Nottingham then?' asked Sutts, like an impatient child on his first visit to the seaside.

'No,' I replied, 'this is Hucknall, only one more stop after this.'

'So is the cricket ground near the station then or what?'

'It's about 15 minutes' walk through the Meadows estate.'

'Walk!' he whined. 'I hope there are a couple of descent boozers on the way down there.'

Sutts was starting to irritate me with his irascibility. I was beginning to regret inviting him into my life when he first showed up at my house. I had pitied him when I had first met him, and we had grieved together over the loss of Myfanwy. I blamed him for Heidi's move back to her parent's house. I blamed myself for getting involved in the business with Josh but concluded that things might have been more awkward if Sutts hadn't been on the scene to supply us with the fake passport.

Once we had stopped at Bullwell, it was only a short journey to Nottingham. Familiar landmarks presented themselves; the star-shaped clock on the Shipstone's Brewery building; the Nottingham Canal; Nottingham Castle, like an acropolis and stronghold of both royalists and parliamentarians during the Civil War. The modern architecture of the Inland Revenue Centre was the final reminder that we were approaching the station.

As everyone disembarked from the train, I saw a woman wearing large dark glasses and a wide-brimmed straw hat. The brim of the hat was pulled down, concealing her face, and she walked with her head bowed. Either side of her, two identical looking teenage girls with strawberry blonde hair, walked arm in arm with her. Her body language told me she wasn't confident amidst so many people and the girls clung to her reassuringly.

I lost sight of her when I visited the gents but came face to face with her while I waited outside the toilets for Sutts. Our eyes met and I saw deep lines of scarification on either side of her face. I smiled and tried to conceal the shock of seeing the extent of her injuries. I was reminded of the bronze heads of the queens of Benin, which featured ritual facial scars.

'I've missed you at work,' I said, feebly trying to avoid the subject of her attack.

'Are you going anywhere nice?' asked Dawn nervously. Her eyes darted from left to right as she watched every movement of passers-by, in trepidation of being attacked again.

Dawn's confidence was clearly shattered, and she didn't look ready to face the busy streets of Nottingham. Her daughters suddenly appeared after buying refreshment at the café. They scrutinised me and clung defensively to Dawn. Sutts lurched out of the gents and belched robustly. I made a hasty farewell to Dawn and made my way from the platform, before Sutts created any more anxiety.

It was a mild day but dark clouds were threatening us with showers. Sutts paid for his ticket and I knew he wouldn't be happy if bad weather suspended play and he discovered that he wasn't entitled to a refund. I acquired a member's guest pass for him so that he could visit the members' pavilion and partake of refreshment in the Long Room bar if it rained.

There were probably around 500 people scattered around Trent Bridge that day. The numbers were boosted by a few dozen Nottingham Forest supporters, who were biding their time until they went across the road to see their team take on Wimbledon in a desperate bid to avoid relegation. I had already watched Forest lose an FA Cup fifth-round match against Chesterfield at Saltergate. The Second Division Spireites went all the way to the semi-finals and took Middlesbrough to a replay before bowing out of the tournament.

We sat in the upper tier of the Radcliffe Road Stand. The most ardent connoisseurs of cricket were concentrated here, in the seats that overlooked the wicket. At the end of the season, the old Radcliffe Road Stand was being torn down and replaced with a new stand, with media centre and hospitality areas. The latest construction would complement the recently built Hound Road Stand which had its own banqueting suite and turret-like towers. Some of the regulars had christened the new Hound Road Stand 'Pippin Fort'.

Trent Bridge still retained some of its picturesque appeal, with the old pavilion and Parr Stand. The William Clark Stand had been built in front of the Trent Bridge Inn courtyard and had become an enclosure to coral gangs of drunken louts. The big scoreboard rivalled the one at the Adelaide Oval but was dwarfed by the concrete monstrosity that was Trent Bridge House; a council building that loomed over the cricket ground like a tower block. The Fox Road side of the ground lay bare apart from the car park and a few spectators in deck chairs. The residents who resided on Fox Road could enjoy an unrestricted view of play if they so desired.

Out in the middle, Notts captain Paul Johnson and Tim Robinson were doggedly constructing an innings. The South African pace bowler Allan Donald was steaming in belligerently at the Radcliffe Road End and delivering explosive, short pitched balls, which threatened to take the heads from the Notts batsmen. They both wore the full panoply of protective guards and headgear that had become standard kit for any batsman who valued his safety. After each delivery, Donald glared at his prey and muttered expletives in Afrikaans as he marched back to his mark.

Bowling at a more economic pace at the Pavilion End was the former England fast-medium bowler Gladstone Small. He obtained the breakthrough for Warwickshire by delivering an outswinging ball, which Paul Johnson couldn't resist parrying with a cover drive. The ball clipped the edge of his bat and flew invitingly into the greedy hands of a slip fielder. As the weather grew increasingly gloomy, the umpires decided that Donald's hostile bowling might prove a danger to the batsmen and play was suspended for bad light.

We adjourned to the Long Room, where Sutts once again seemed preoccupied with the events that took place there 12 years earlier.

'So was Myfanwy pals with this Boz character before this big fall out?'

'I was under the impression that Boz had tried to rape Myfanwy in borstal and had been stabbed in the eye with a biro for his efforts, so no I don't think they were on each other's Christmas card list.'

'Alright sarky bleeder,' interjected Sutts. 'But it seems a bit of a coincidence that Myfanwy was down here on the same day that Boz and his mate were hanging around.'

I attempted to end the conversation by picking up a copy of *The Daily Mail* that was lying on a table. In an exclusive interview, Edward Towton was scurrilously criticising the Blair administration. Accompanying the article was a black-and-white photograph of Towton when he was National Chairman of the Young Conservatives in 1964.

'What's that nonce doing in the papers!' Sutts snapped as he abruptly snatched the paper from me.

Several members, representing both teams, raised their eyebrows at the sound of coarse language. Sutts trembled as he held the paper tightly in his hands.

'What's the matter?' I asked.

Without answering, Sutts screwed the newspaper up and threw it on the floor. He stood up, knocking over his chair as he fled from the Long Room.

'I didn't think Notts were playing that badly?' said an elderly gentleman in a green and yellow striped blazer.

I rushed after Sutts, and as I left the pavilion I saw him barge past a steward who was posted at the Dixon gates. I caught up with him as he made his way in the direction of the River Trent. I persuaded him to stop and have a drink in the Trent Bridge Inn. I couldn't understand what had rattled him about the newspaper article.

The interior of the Trent Bridge Inn had deteriorated over the years. It was no longer furnished with the pictures and memorabilia that reminded visitors of the significance of the pub, and its role in the history of cricket. There was a brisk trade that lunchtime, as early arrivals for the football match and the cricket fans sought refreshment. A couple of Warwickshire supporters were lamenting the demise of the Trent Bridge Inn since they had last visited Nottingham. They both spoke with broad, Black Country accents and wore cricket pullovers bearing the Warwickshire badge, with its distinct bear and ragged staff design.

Sutts nursed his pint of lager and glared at the Warwickshire supporters, whose pedantic discussion of cricket statistics was beginning to irritate him.

'Did that bloke in the paper send you down or something?' I asked, concluding that Sutts had met Edward Towton in court at some stage in the course of his illustrious career as a villain.

'When you told me about Myfanwy and this Towton fella,' he explained, 'I had no idea who he was. I just thought it was some old beak, same as all the rest. I never even made the connection when I read in the paper about that business in the hotel. When I saw that picture today, it was like seeing a ghost from the past.'

Before continuing his explanation, Sutts drained his glass and headed to the bar, in search of a refill. When he returned, he lit a cigarette and continued:

'I told you about when I was involved with the Krays for a bit; well it was not long before everything started to fall apart for them when I met Edward Towton for the first time. The twins were looking into managing a pop group and they started sniffing around that geezer you're always on about, Tip Topley and Toy Mistress. They originally wanted to manage one of Joe Meeks' bands called the Tornadoes. They sent me down there to sweeten things with Meek but he wasn't having any of it. He was so paranoid and blocked up on pills that he couldn't get a hard on when I got his cock out. A few weeks later he shot himself and his landlady. I was supposed to go down there that day and try and get him going again, but when I got to his place in Islington there was coppers and an ambulance outside. If I'd been a bit earlier, I might have been brown bread as well.

'So Ronnie starts looking into managing Toy Mistress and promises to help them out when they get busted for drugs. Towton was already known to Ronnie, seeing as they both liked young boys. He decides to kill two birds with one stone, by getting Towton involved in the drugs trial and compromising him into doing them a few favours when it suited them. He was a rising star in politics at the time and the twins liked the idea of getting a Member of Parliament in their camp.

'Ronnie arranges to have a party with all these old poofs and a few of the boys, myself included. I got introduced to Towton, though I didn't have a clue who he was. He referred to himself as Lord Gaveston, so I thought he was nobility.'

'I bet he didn't act like nobility when he got you alone,' I said, remembering what I'd read in the papers about Towton's peccadillos.

'He was a fucking animal!' said Sutts vehemently. 'He had this other bloke with him who held me down while Towton did the business; I blacked out at one point. I was bleeding for weeks after. You couldn't just go down to the hospital for something like that in those days.'

Dredging up the traumatic memory of the incident with Towton was clearly devastating to Sutts. Tears began to run down his face in an uncharacteristically lachrymose display of emotion.

'I read in the papers that when they found the body of that youth in the hotel, there was internal damage,' I said. 'It makes you wonder what he's been getting away with for all these years and he's on the telly all the time, having a ball of it.'

For the second time that day, Sutts made a hasty exit, leaving another drink half finished. I followed him onto the street and chased after him as he ran past the traffic on Radcliffe Road. The rain was falling heavier and there seemed little chance of a resumption of play at Trent Bridge. We had burned our bridges as far as returning to the cricket anyway, after leaving without a pass to get back in again.

I caught up with Sutts as he rushed across the bridge that gave the cricket ground its name, 'Where are you going!' I called out to him.

'I don't know!' he screamed in despair.

I continued to follow him at a safe distance, afraid that he might lash out at me in the erratic state he was in.

I followed him onto the London Road and persuaded him to stop and have another drink. We crossed a bridge, over the canal towards Meadow Lane. We went inside a pub called the Navigation Inn, which sat between the canal and the Meadow Lane football ground. Forest fans were already making their way up the road to the Forest Ground in their red shirts, bearing the tree logo. It was a different story outside Meadow Lane. Notts County were playing their final game away and were already lamenting finishing the season at the bottom of Division Two.

Inside the Navigation Inn, Mambo Lambert held court with Doberman and some of the hardcore Notts County hooligans. A few veterans from the Coocachoo Crew had been invited to join Lambert for a last hurrah against the Wimbledon firm, which was supposed to be turning up in large numbers for the Forest game.

I recognised a few of the faces from Mansfield as I waited at the bar to order drinks. Obstreperous shouting and laughter emanated from the adjoining room. Sutts was in a completely subdued frame of mind now and I decided that it might be a good idea to simply abandon the outing and get a train back to Mansfield. The barmaid was busy serving customers at the other side of the bar and I was about to suggest leaving when the landlord appeared from the cellar and began pouring our pints.

I recognised the scarred face of the Scot Strachan, who had been instrumental in starting the trouble in the Masons Arms on the evening of the Ray Keaton poetry reading. He was accompanied by several illustrious names from Mansfield's football casual culture. Pluto Lockwood had been one of the leading members of the Coocachoo Crew in the 1980s. In the spirit of Thatcher's Britain, Pluto had got on his bike and sought his fortune in various private enterprise ventures. His entrepreneurial spirit had taken him away from the world of football hooliganism in favour of the sunshine of the Algarve region of Portugal. He successfully ran a bar in the holiday resort of Alvor, where British tourists could enjoy televised live football and full English breakfasts. Each year, he enjoyed a reunion with his old friends from the Coocachoo Crew and was occasionally persuaded to make a cameo appearance in a confrontation with a rival firm.

'Swifty me old knacker, what are you doing here?' a voice from behind me called out and slapped me on the back.

Feggy Edwards had just walked into the pub. He was wearing his Inspiral Carpets 'cool as fuck' t-shirt and a floppy fishing hat.

'You look like you're going for a night out at the Hacienda mate,' I said.

'Yeah top mate, mad for it,' he replied, doing a little Liam Gallagher-type shuffle from side to side. 'No mate I'm just having a bit of a reunion with a few of the football lads and I thought I'd get my baggy gear out for old times' sake.'

'I thought you'd finished with all that lark.'

'I haven't seen any of the lads for a while and Pluto asked me to come along, so I thought I'd come down for a catch-up.'

Suddenly we were surrounded by Pluto and the rest of the Mansfield contingent, who had come over to greet Feggy.

'Someone get him a pair of maracas, it's Bez,' said Pluto, grabbing Feggy's hat and tossing it to Strachan.

Strachan tossed the hat across the room to where Doberman was drinking with the Notts County crew, as Feggy futilely attempted to grab it. Doberman donned the hat and Feggy decided to forget about it rather than approach the intimidating looking FUH contingent.

I was beginning to regret choosing the Navigation Inn as the next port of call. Sutts was becoming visibly irritated by the rambunctious group, who had interrupted our session. I was anxious that he might be capable of anything in his current frame of mind. Strachan was standing in front of Sutts, with his back to him.

'Go and fetch his hat back, you rotten sod,' Pluto asked Strachan, playfully pushing the Scotsman who lost his balance and fell backwards, spilling Sutts's beer.

'Watch it you fucking clumsy, sweaty sock!' growled Sutts.

'Yeah farking leave it out you Scotch cant!' said Pluto, trying to mimic Sutts.

I was now surrounded by vicious thugs, a deranged criminal my only ally. My eyes darted to the nearest exit, but I was penned in by bodies. Feggy was still grinning moronically as though the whole situation was one big joke. I gave him an imploring look which he answered with a wink, which was intended to reassure me but had failed the mark, miserably.

Strachan was holding his ground, toe-to-toe with Sutts. The two leaned into each other, gently butting their heads together like stags.

'I still want to hear an apology from you, you Scotch prick!' Sutts reminded Strachan.

'Are you one of thae Wimbledon cunts?' replied Strachan, looking at Pluto Lockwood for backup. 'I reckon you've strayed into the wrong pub.'

'Fucking Wimbledon!' bellowed Sutts. 'Do I sound like one of those West London ponces, you donkey?'

'Tell the truth, all you southern numpties sound the same to me,' replied Strachan.

'Ayup lads!' Pluto called to Doberman and his crew, 'I think we've got one of the Wimbledon lads here, fancies himself against all us lot.'

The landlord began taking notice of the fracas and called from behind the bar, 'Right that's enough. I think you'd better leave before things get out of control,' he said, nodding towards Sutts.

My trepidation was slightly alleviated by the landlord's intervention. I was ready to flee through the door and run as fast as I could from the Navigation Inn.

'I'm not going fucking anywhere till I've finished my pint!' announced Sutts. 'Football 'ooligans; I've shit 'em!'

There was a sudden moment of eerie silence as everyone watched Sutts leisurely drink his beer. I began to squeeze through the bodies that barred my way, all focused on Sutts.

'Right then lads,' said Doberman in a tone of composed authority, 'looks like we'll have to help him find the way to the door if he doesn't want to leave here quietly.'

I had my hand on the door, ready to make my retreat. There was nothing more I could do to help Sutts, and the phrase, 'every man for himself' was screaming from within my mind. I looked around one last time, as the host of hooligans began to converge around Sutts.

'Okay I'm calling the police!' the landlord called out, holding up his mobile phone to demonstrate that he was serious.

He was universally ignored by everyone but myself. Sutts continued to drain the last dregs from his pint glass in an exaggerated display of bravado.

'Now back right off!' he ordered, pulling a pocket-sized Beretta Bobcat pistol from the pocket of his anorak. The entire assemblage that confronted Sutts, took a step back en masse.

'Dean!' Sutts called out without looking at me. 'Don't go running off without me, we're nearly all done here.'

For the first time during the entire incident, everyone looked round at me.

Strachan was sceptical about whether Sutts was capable of using the handgun and, stepping forward, said, 'Put that fucking popgun away before you do yourself an injury, you're nae Clint Eastwood big man.'

In an instant, Sutts grabbed Strachan by the hair and shoved the barrel of his gun into the Scotsman's mouth and said, 'Alright then, have any more of you ladies got anything to say?' his question was met by silence. 'Right then, everyone walk slowly back over to where you was all having a nice little tea party when we came in. You behind the bar, put that phone down and empty the till.'

The landlord compliantly did as he was told and then handed the cash from the till over to Sutts. I was now the unwilling participant in an armed robbery. I had only gone out with the intention of watching a day of cricket. Sutts took the gun from Strachan's mouth and placed it behind his head. With his free hand he grabbed Strachan's hair once more and shoved him roughly against the bar. He then began to stuff the bank notes from the till into his anorak pockets.

Dragging Strachan around by the hair, he pushed him towards the door, where I was still standing, too petrified to move. I stepped to one side as Sutts shoved Strachan through the door. I had the choice between staying behind with the angry hooligans or following an armed man outside as his accomplice. I was so desperate to get out into the fresh air, that I chose the latter option. I watched Sutts push

Strachan as far as the edge of the canal. Strachan was made to stand at the edge of the water, while Sutts stood behind him with the gun pointing at the back of his head.

'Don't do it Sutts!' I pleaded, as I helplessly witnessed what looked like a cold-blooded execution.

Strachan was standing with his eyes closed, his lips were moving as though he were saying his final prayers. Sutts lifted up a foot shod in a desert boot and kicked Strachan hard in the backside. Strachan fell with a splash into the murky water of the canal.

I heard the splash and for a moment my ears deceived me into thinking I had heard the sound of a gun. Strachan began struggling amongst the weeds and detritus, convincing me that he hadn't been mortally wounded. Sutts put his gun away in his coat, nodded to me and then began running at full pelt along the towpath, back in the direction of the River Trent. Eager to be free of Sutts, I made haste along the towpath in the direction of the city centre, before Strachan emerged from the canal and his comrades from the Navigation Inn came to his aid.

I followed the path alongside the canal, until I emerged near the railway station. I was fortunate to arrive on the railway platform, in time to catch the train back to Mansfield. My journey home was fraught with anxiety about being apprehended by the police as an accessory to a robbery and witness to someone being held at gunpoint. I had viewed Sutts as a likeable, petty villain, in much the same mould as Myfanwy. I was now convinced that he was completely unstable and a dangerous individual who I must avoid at all costs.

CHAPTER TWENTY-FOUR

The following day Dean was apprised of the events of Saturday afternoon by an excitable Feggy Edwards. Dean was watching a Toy Mistress Tribute band at the Bold Forester when Feggy arrived to give his version of events. The band was called Toy Mister and featured a Tip Topley lookalike whose claim to fame was that he had been a runner-up on *Stars in Their Eyes*

It turned out that after Strachan had returned to the pub, soaking wet, everyone bar the landlord had enjoyed a good laugh about the gun incident and the ducking. The police had been duly informed of the situation and it was agreed by all that it would be advisable to evacuate the premises. Doberman was particularly keen to avoid any involvement with gun crime, at a time when his activities with the BFC were in danger of becoming compromised.

The allied contingents of the Coocachoo Crew and FUH emerged into the street as the sun appeared from behind stubborn rainclouds. As they shielded their eyes from the brightness, they were greeted by a hoard of West London hooligans, who suddenly appeared from Iremonger Road. From London Road came a group of 30 youths representing Nottingham Forest. A vanload of police officers headed down Meadow Lane, in response to the call from the landlord of the Navigation Inn. After assessing the situation and concluding that they were hopelessly outnumbered, they called for backup and remained at a safe distance from the scene of the battle.

Feggy found himself being pushed back towards the canal by the momentum of the attack by the Londoners. Like the Romans at Lake Trasimene, those who were at the rear of the offensive were forced into the canal. Feggy was one of the unfortunate number who suffered the same fate as Strachan.

The situation worsened when several mounted policemen arrived and began to ride into the melee. The only sensible thing for Feggy to do at that point was to swim to safety on the other side of the canal. Finding a suitable spot to drag himself from the water, he climbed from the canal at a safe distance from the disturbances. He discovered that he had lost his hat during the confusion of battle. He was inconsolable about the loss of the floppy hat, which he had worn when he had watched the Stone Roses at Spike Island.

A triumvirate had been formed between three of the top boys from Wimbledon, Chelsea and Fulham, with the intention of wreaking havoc in the vicinity of Nottingham's two football teams. The reinforcements from the Notts County and Mansfield firms had been arranged to counter the rumoured strike by the triumvirate.

The landlord of the Navigation Inn soon forgot about the earlier incident involving Sutts, when scores of hooligans rushed through the doors, bent on rapine destruction. Part of the plan was to seize the Navigation Inn and the Trent Bridge Inn, as reprisals for breaches made upon London pubs by Notts hooligans.

Amongst the host of London thugs involved in the affray were the Stevens brothers from Fulham. Since the disappearance of Josh Hunt and Cuckoo Walsh, the British Free Corps had fragmented. Paranoia and mistrust began to infect the core members, who started to turn on each other. Doberman accused the brothers of selling him out to the British Security Service, after he was questioned about an incident which, as far as he was concerned, only he and the brothers knew about.

Cuckoo Walsh had bided his time and watched his back since the day that Dawn had been brutally cut up. After finishing the contract for the prison at Lowdham, he and Bilal Ali had spent a few months working on a new housing estate in Western Super Mare. He had finally returned to Nottinghamshire at the beginning of May, after having several months to work out his next move with the BFC.

Cuckoo made his mind up that he would end up with a knife in his back if he turned himself in to the police and was held in custody for any length of time. The fate of Josh Hunt had been in Cuckoo's hands and he was aware that someone else might not show the same mercy when his turn came.

He felt terrible remorse for ruining the life of Dawn Townroe. There was nothing he could do to turn back the clock and heal the physical and mental wounds that she would carry for the rest of her life. Each day he made a mental note of each member of the British Free Corps and tried to work out which individual had come to Dawn's house. Apart from himself, the Stevens brothers and Doberman had made up the infrastructure of command in the organisation. All decisions were agreed by the four of them before any action was taken, therefore the other three must have discussed the attack on Dawn.

Cuckoo decided that the only way he could get his erstwhile comrades off his back and avenge Dawn, was to permanently take out Doberman and the brothers. As to the identity of the actual perpetrator of the knife attack, he had a good idea who he was looking for. He recalled a red-haired man who fitted the description of Dawn's attacker. During an unofficial rally of the British Free Corps, he had briefly met a man who was reputed to have attacked a policeman with a carpet knife and boasted that he had got away with the crime. He had been one of the Fulham firm who was close to the Stevens brothers and was known by the soubriquet of 'Sharpey', due to his fondness for blades.

When Feggy emerged from the canal, soaking wet, the last person he had expected to see was Cuckoo Walsh. He had waddled across London Road in his sodden clothes, stared at by genuine football fans who were now making their way to the Forest Ground in their droves. Cuckoo came out from behind the trees that created a natural boundary between London Road and the Meadows estate. He hopped over the low, stone wall which had once held iron railings, until they had been sawn off in the 1940s in aid of the war effort

'Just the man I was looking for!' said Cuckoo, grabbing Feggy by the shoulder.

It had been a number of years since Feggy had encountered the erstwhile general of the Coocachoo Crew. After an abortive attempt to ambush Pol Potter and his Khmer Blues firm some years earlier, Feggy had considered it wise to give Cuckoo a wide berth. He had been persuaded by Pluto Lockwood to journey to Nottingham, for what he had been led to believe was going to be a peaceful reunion. The violent aspects of hooliganism had never really appealed to Feggy, who preferred the designer gear and the machismo of being associated with the football casual culture.

Unbeknown to all the belligerents who were joined in battle that day, Cuckoo had used his many contacts to instigate the battle royal that was taking place near the Navigation Inn. In an elaborate game of Chinese whispers, Cuckoo had succeeded in stirring up a hornet's nest which would bring together his three intended targets.

Feggy found himself surrounded by a group of a dozen burly looking thugs who accompanied Cuckoo. He had called in a few favours with some of his old associates from his days as a nightclub doorman. Gladstone Roberts had agreed to join Cuckoo and had also persuaded the notorious pub brawlers, the Letts brothers, to come along. Gladstone's brother Andy was a professional footballer, who had begun his career at Chesterfield and had then been signed by Bristol City. Andy had been targeted by the British Free Corps, who subjected him and his wife to a series of hate-filled phone calls. The BFC considered the marriage of a black footballer and a white woman an act worthy of retribution.

Also present was a brawny ex-miner called John Wayland. His involvement with the Trotskyist, Worker's Revolutionary and Communist League had drawn the attention of the BFC. Several of Wayland's comrades were attacked by BFC members, who were bent on destroying any far-left political groups in the United Kingdom.

Michael Lenehan managed an Irish club in Mansfield called The Lady Athenry. The peaceful social club for Irish ex-patriots, was firebombed by the BFC, who viewed the establishment as a den of Fenian sympathisers. Lenehan brought with him his brothers, Owen and Matthew, all experts in the pugilistic arts.

The crew that accompanied Cuckoo had been briefed on the plan to annihilate the central figures in the BFC. Cuckoo underplayed his own role within the organisation, representing himself as an ignorant thug who had resisted being drawn into the nefarious activities of what he had innocently perceived as a national football hooligan firm.

They crossed the London Road and ran straight into the struggle that was taking place on the stone bridge that led towards the Navigation Inn. Until they could clear the bridge, Cuckoo's plan couldn't progress any further. He could see Brian Stevens laying into some of the FUH boys on the bridge. Like Constantine at the Battle of Milvian Bridge, Cuckoo pushed his way forward towards Brian Stevens, who barred his way like Maxentius.

Feggy was searching desperately for a means of escape, but was pushed forward before Cuckoo and his crew. The new reinforcements pushed past the bruised and battered ranks, who were held on the bridge. Recognising Cuckoo, Brian Stevens renewed the energy of his offensive. Feggy was punched in the nose by a Turk in a tracksuit. Blinded by the blow, he stumbled backwards and was pushed forward by someone behind him, who was desperate to get involved in the fight. The momentum of Cuckoo and his mercenaries cleared them of the bridge and brought them into the midst of their foes. Feggy was about to climb to his feet and make a run for it, when Owen Lenehan grabbed him and dragged him forward once more.

Brian Stevens was battling with Cuckoo, who began wielding his old telescopic baton. Stevens defended the blows with his arms, but was continually pushed back in the direction of the Navigation Inn. Tommy Stevens was now visible to Cuckoo, on his right; always the weaker of the two brothers, he was deflecting blows from

Doberman, who was flailing his huge arms in cartoon fashion and wearing Tommy down.

The mounted policemen had been initially repelled by a barrage of missiles, thrown by belligerents from both sides. Reinforcements were making a second attempt at restoring order. A police helicopter hovered overhead, monitoring the movements of the opposing hooligan armies. Feggy dodged between battling bodies, desperately evading blows and seeking an escape route. He could see on his right, the uniforms of policemen, who he was ready to give himself up to. While the generals and their lieutenants continued irresistibly along Meadow Lane, some of the foot soldiers began to retreat in the face of the police intervention. Feggy found his chance to escape and joined the fleeing herd. Dodging the traffic on the London Road, he ran away through the trees from which Cuckoo had emerged earlier.

The carnage in the Navigation Inn was finally coming to an end as the sound of police sirens outside called time on the party. The pub landlord emerged timorously from his hiding place in the cellar and surveyed the damage with a heavy heart. Sunlight shone through broken windows and illuminated a room filled with broken glass and shattered chairs and tables. Behind the bar, everything had been removed apart from a jar of maraschino cherries and a couple of bottles of tonic water. The fruit machine had been tipped over in a failed attempt to remove its contents. The pool table, the landlord's pride and joy, was stripped of its red baize. The cash register, which had already been emptied, lay smashed near the entrance door.

The landlord tried to console himself that at least he hadn't been injured during the incident. He had always dreamed of completing a university degree and embarking on a career in zoology. He was leaning on the bar, contemplating his next move, when he heard footsteps crunching on broken glass. He looked up in expectation of finally seeing an officer of the law. His heart sank when Tommy Stevens came staggering through the door, followed by Doberman. The sound of more angry voices from beyond the door informed him that it was time to take shelter in the cellar once again.

Doberman knocked Tommy to the floor and began kicking him. Brian Stevens then appeared and briefly surveyed the empty pub. He had been expecting his troops to have held the pub and had allowed Cuckoo to push him backwards in a tactical retreat, cumulating with an ambush by those concealed inside the pub. He had meticulously reconnoitred the area and chosen the Navigation Inn as a Hougoumont farmhouse on his field of Waterloo. Then Cuckoo had appeared at the 11th hour like Blücher and his Prussians.

Cuckoo then arrived and pulled out the gun he had been given to execute Josh Hunt, 'I think this belongs to you, you fat cunt,' he said, pointing the pistol at Doberman.

'You haven't got the bottle,' said Doberman in a tremulous tone.

The report of the gun in Cuckoo's hand answered the doubts of all assembled. Doberman dropped to the ground with a hole in his forehead. He lay with his eyes staring at the ceiling; the sneer that he had directed at Cuckoo still on his face. He lay amongst the debris, at rest in the place that was dearest to his heart.

'Nice one Cuckoo,' said Tommy Stevens, who still lay on the floor. 'We knew that fat cunt had turned grass on us; you've saved us a job.'

Cuckoo looked down at where Tommy lay with his head resting against the bar, nodded his head in acknowledgement of the praise and then shot him three times in the chest.

'Right you've had your fun, now drop the gun on the floor!' ordered Brian Stevens, who had produced a gun of his own while Cuckoo had been busy with Tommy.

'Can't do that,' replied Cuckoo, swinging his gun in the direction of Brian, before he had time to react.

'You know I'm going to have to kill you now you've wasted my brother?' said Brian, whose physiognomy exhibited no sign of solace for the loss of his sibling.

'All this because I wouldn't kill that kid!' answered Cuckoo fervidly, 'I would never have betrayed the BFC, but you had to go and start cutting people up; you should have had a go at me, not my family!'

'You know we couldn't take that risk' replied Brian, 'it's not just us now we've got the Yanks and the Ulster mob to keep sweet. We've got to keep things airtight now and you were becoming too much of a risk.'

Brian saw Cuckoo's left eye twitch as his mind vacillated for a moment. Stevens noted the hesitation and fired his weapon. Cuckoo fell backwards against the wall, dropping his gun. He clutched his right arm where a bullet had struck. Brian cursed his poor marksmanship and aimed his gun at his target once more. He was about to shoot when an armed policeman suddenly appeared at the entrance door. A Smith & Wesson revolver was pointed at the side of the head of Brian Stevens. A second police marksman then appeared from behind the bar.

'Slowly place the firearm on the floor Brian,' ordered Mambo Lambert, as he resolutely emerged from his hiding place behind the door of the ladies' toilets.

Ian Randall, a.k.a. 'Mambo Lambert', had infiltrated the hooligan firm that called itself the Fucked Up Humbug four years earlier. At a time when veteran hooligans such as Doberman where beginning to take a back seat, Lambert was sent undercover with the FUH and gained a reputation that brought him to prominence within the firm. He had been seeking evidence of links between certain prominent football hooligans with far-right organisations. His suspicions that Doberman was involved in the BFC were growing stronger, but he still had little evidence to connect him with criminal activities within that organisation. During a football match between Chesterfield and Notts County at Saltergate a year earlier, he had witnessed a clandestine meeting between Doberman and Cuckoo Walsh. He had later seen them both before an international game at Wembley in conversation with the Stevens brothers. He hadn't found any concrete evidence to suggest that the four formed the nucleus of the British Free Corps. Lambert's presence was hardly registered when he came into the pub at the same time as Doberman. In his desperation to urinate, Lambert had rushed to the toilet and concealed himself there when he heard the first gunshot. From behind the toilet door, he realised that he had discovered the motherlode, as he listened to the revelations of Brian Stevens and Walsh.

'Mambo!' croaked Cuckoo, ignorant of Lambert's motives for his presence. 'Get out before you get hurt; this isn't a game anymore.'

'Sorry Cuckoo, it's Detective Sergeant Randall from this point on; you've left us a bit of a mess to clear up here haven't you?'

'I might have known you northern mugs would be stupid enough to let the law walk around under our nose,' said Stevens, aiming his gun at Cuckoo once more. 'You know I always had you down for Old Bill, but that whale you just shot reckoned even you were too clever to be a copper.'

'Put the weapon down Stevens, or you'll be joining your brother,' said Randall.

'I should kill you first, you rat!' replied Stevens vociferously, as he span round with the intention of shooting the Randall.

Gunfire from both police marksmen took Brian Stevens down before he got the chance to take aim at his target. Cuckoo watched with satisfaction as the last of the unholy alliance that plagued him fell dead to the floor.

CHAPTER TWENTY-FIVE

In August, John Freeman returned refreshed from a holiday in the west of Ireland with Sally and Kevin. They spent a pleasant week in a remote cottage in the company of Ray Keaton and Josh Hunt. The fresh air and open spaces of the Atlantic coast suited Josh. In the neighbouring fishing village of Cleggan, the inhabitants had taken a shine to him and he had found work with the fishermen who brave the tempestuous waves of the Atlantic to make a meagre living.

Josh introduced John and Sally to his new girlfriend, Martha Gallagher, the eldest daughter of the landlord of the Steampacket public house. Josh was a regular at the Steampacket, where he could be seen playing chess with old Dick Dignam. Ray Keaton was learning the rudiments of chess from Josh, who in turn was discovering the delights of the art of poesy.

On his return to Mansfield, John drove to his family's new home in Sutton in Ashfield. The new house was a vast improvement on the council property they had rented in Mansfield Woodhouse. The open spaces of Sutton Lawns were situated right behind the house; perfect for children but still a source of anxiety for him, when the annual Ashfield Show took place on the Lawns.

John was deeply tanned, but he hadn't gained his bronze complexion during the Irish visit. Before Tsucol closed for its annual summer holiday, he had spent several weeks in South Africa on a work-related trip. He volunteered, with a dozen other Tsucol employees, to visit a new plant in Port Elizabeth. The visit was designed to show the operatives at the new site the process involved in the manufacture of car seat covers, integrating the experienced visitors with the neophytes and proselytising the Tsucol paradigm like capitalist missionaries.

While John's colleagues were merrily jumping into the hotel swimming pool and into bed with each other in their spare time, John inadvertently learned some unsettling facts about the Port Elizabeth factory. One afternoon, a cricket match between the English visitors and the management of the Port Elizabeth factory was arranged. After the match, the South African manager, Burton Gibbs, invited everyone to a barbecue at his house. After a few bottles of Castle Lager, John found himself in need of the toilet. Someone gave him vague directions, which led him into the labyrinthine interior of the manager's home. He passed a room where an overheated conversation between Gibbs and his wife instantly distracted him from his quest to empty his bladder.

'Well all I can say is that you're morally bankrupt,' came the voice of Gibbs's wife, Annette. 'You're playing the big magnanimous boss with these people and they don't know that you're taking their livelihood from them.'

'That's the nature of global industry now,' replied Gibbs bluntly. 'We can do the job for a third of the cost of the Mansfield factory, so Tsucol come to us. What about the opportunities for the unemployed of Port Elizabeth?'

'You know that's not what I'm getting at. I thought when these people turned up, they knew what the situation was. You've got them playing cricket and going on safaris and they don't even know that they'll be out of a job by the end of the year.'

'I don't want to discuss this now,' said Gibbs adamantly, 'This is business, so just keep your mouth shut and enjoy the lifestyle I've worked hard for; and don't drink any more of those springboks.'

John returned from the South African trip without saying anything to his colleagues. They had all enjoyed the sunshine and parties of Port Elizabeth, and he didn't have the heart to share the news he had inadvertently learned from eavesdropping on Burton Gibbs. On returning to Mansfield, he found a new manager in charge at Tsucol. After a fortnight without any news about redundancies, John was beginning to wonder when the bombshell would actually be dropped about the closure.

The new manager was a taciturn German called Max Seeler; a sepulchral figure who was the antithesis of his fervently enthusiastic predecessor. He appeared beside John one afternoon, as he wrote down his production figures for the day. He silently observed John like a spectre, until he noted something which didn't seem to tally.

'What is this?' he said, pointing at the figures written in one of the columns.

'That's downtime,' replied John wearily. 'We've had the mechanics working on two of the machines for this amount of time, that's why we're behind target.'

'But surely this is incorrect,' queried Seeler. 'I have been watching from the mezzanine and I only saw the sewing mechanic make adjustments to the machine for a fraction of this time.'

John was beginning to feel as though he was being cross-examined by a Gestapo officer. He knew that Seeler was correct and that he had been caught in the act of falsifying his paperwork. He regularly exaggerated the downtime figures to justify any deficits in the daily production targets. It had been a long day; several people had phoned in sick, while several others were operating their mouths more efficiently than their machines. Seeler was beginning to make John's flesh creep and he finally snapped:

'Look mate I'm doing my best here,' he said indignantly . 'Just get off my back will you!'

Several heads popped up from behind their machines, as John's raised voice was heard.'

'You are being silly,' said Seeler impassively, 'I merely noted a discrepancy in your calculations.'

'Well if you want to sack me, that will be one less to get rid of,' John replied calmly. 'There are 500 people working here though, so you're going to have to crack on a bit if you want to get rid of everyone this way.'

'I understand how the Tsucol work ethic can be stressful for anyone,' said Seeler, trying to affect a more amiable tone. 'I myself had to spend some time off work with what the Americans call burnout.'

'I don't know how you people sleep at night,' hissed John. 'I know that you're only here to supervise the changeover with Port Elizabeth. When were you intending to tell everyone that the place is closing down?'

The knowledge that John had discreetly withheld from his colleagues was shared with no one else. Seeler seduced John into keeping his mouth shut by offering him a place on the management team at the Nottingham site where Tsucol produced pharmaceutical supplies. John's 30 pieces of silver ensured that the mortgage for the new house was paid and the Mansfield closure would go ahead smoothly.

John's conscience tormented him as he remorsefully considered his betrayal of his fellow workers. He tried to console himself with the knowledge that the closure would still take place, despite his decision to remain silent. He still felt bitter about the cynical manner in which companies like Tsucol exploited economically hard-hit communities; devouring resources like locusts and then recommencing the process elsewhere.

Once home from their holiday, John bathed and put Kevin to bed while Sally took a bath. After reading a soporific bedtime story, he joined his wife in the living room. Sally was watching *Crimewatch* impassively in a pale blue nightshirt. John judged, by Sally's weary countenance, that she would shortly be going to bed. He went into the kitchen to make a cup of tea and find something to eat. He poured water into the kettle, gazing into the darkness of the back garden. He was pleased that they had gone away during the weekend that the Ashfield Show took place. He saw his reflection in the window and admired the goatee beard he was cultivating. He spread some butter on a slice of bread after failing to find anything more appetizing for his supper. As he poured hot water onto a tea bag that lay inside his Manchester United mug, Sally called to him from the living room

'They're talking about that murder in Mansfield!' she explained excitedly as John walked through the door.

Sally was wide-awake now, perched on the edge of the settee. Jill Dando summarised the facts about the murder of Nappy Andrews, followed by a reconstruction of the crime.

'Ha! Look at the daft twat they've got to play Spike,' John sniggered. 'He looks like Bernard Bresslaw.'

'I'm sure I saw him in an episode of *The Bill* recently,' said Sally.

The gruesome killing was reconstructed in all its gruesome detail. As there was no identifiable suspect, the reconstruction showed a blurred image of a dark figure committing the murder. Jill Dando and the police officer in charge of the investigation made an appeal to the public for any information pertaining to the incident, and a hotline was set up.

'They'll never find out who did that now,' remarked John. 'They still don't know who killed that Bosworth fella all those years back.

'Well they will have to look for the culprit without me tonight,' said Sally, stretching and yawning. 'I won't take much rocking tonight.'

Sally kissed John on the head and went up the stairs to bed. He was ready for bed himself but decided to wind down for a further hour in front of *Match of the Day*. It was so rare for him to enjoy these brief respites of solitude, now he was busy as a parent and with work responsibilities. Sally would be fast asleep and snoring loudly by the time he climbed into bed beside her. There had been a time when they wouldn't have slept until they had made love, but their ardour for sex had cooled to Ice Age proportions now that Sally was expecting again.

John awoke late on Sunday morning after a dreamless night's sleep. The sound of wailing downstairs caused him to rise from his place of rest quicker than he would have preferred. He hurried downstairs to find out the cause of the disturbance, establishing that the caterwauling was emanating from an adult, and not a small child. He discovered the source of the lamentations to be his mother. His stomach began to churn as he braced himself for the news of some tragic accident befalling his father.

Sally was sat on the settee with her arm around Maggie Freeman, the television switched on in the background. Sally looked up at John and rolled her eyes.

'What's the matter Mum?' asked John, kneeling down before his mother and taking her by the hand.

'They've killed my princess!' Maggie wailed. 'The French have murdered her!'

'Princess Diana is dead,' explained Sally in response to John's puzzled expression.

'Oh right,' John mused, trying to connect what Sally had just told him with the image of Princess Diana.

They watched the report of the death on the breakfast news programme. All the channels were covering the developing story and piecing together the events that had taken place. Diana had been killed in a car crash that had taken place in the early hours of Sunday morning. The princess and her companion, Dodi Fayed, were being pursued through Paris by paparazzi when their driver lost control of his vehicle and collided with a pillar as they sped through a tunnel.

'They should all be shot for treason!' said Maggie.

John decided to take Kevin out to the park as his mother's hysteria increasingly began to upset him. He took him to a nearby playground and left his mother in Sally's charge.

'Cheers,' Sally hissed in his ear, 'you piss off and leave me to try and console the drama queen back there.'

'I just thought you'd enjoy the break while I went out with Kevin for a bit,' he explained feebly.

'Bullshit!' she snapped. 'Anyway, when did she become the big fan of Diana; she always says she hates the royal family and called Diana black and blue when she did that *Panorama* interview a couple of years ago.'

Sally quickly fell silent as Maggie shuffled into the hallway.

'Come here my little angel,' she said, holding her arms out to her grandson, 'Nana is feeling very sad today. I think I will just go and have a lie down for a bit,' she said sorrowfully to Sally.

'Just give her some of that poteen that Josh gave us if she starts playing up again,' said John, eager to escape the wrath of his wife.

As John made his way down the street, he saw Spike come staggering towards him. He was wearing his old Dr. Martens boots and a pair of tartan bondage trousers, embellished with zips and straps. He wore a Sex Pistols 'God Save the Queen' t-shirt, which featured the iconic image of the Queen; her eyes and mouth blacked out and a safety pin through her nose. He wore his old leather jacket, painted with the names of various punk bands, which included the Snivelling Shits and the Nipple Erecters. He had clearly lost a lot of weight in order to fit into the jacket. The outfit was topped by an incongruous looking flat cap.

'What brings you to this neck of the woods?' John asked amiably.

'I've been kipping down at Cobweb Henderson's place, but his sister is balling about Diana dying, so I thought I'd see what you were up to.

'I never thought I'd see you in that get-up again?' said John, gesturing at Spike's punkish attire.

'I didn't like myself when I was soldier Spike,' he replied, shrugging his shoulders. 'It was much more fun being punk Spike, pissed and proud and all that.'

'Don't you think you're getting a bit old for all that?'

'What's so good about being a grown up? Anyway, I just wanted to come and tell you, I'm going away for a bit. I know some people who are going to stay at a squat in Paris where this band lives. They're called Timmy Tartuffe and apparently they're really big in Estonia.'

'Where?'

'Yeah that's what I said but anyway they're going there on tour and I might just tag along.'

They walked up Garden Lane and passed the Masons Arms on Unwin Road. John wanted to buy a newspaper and an ice cream for Kevin at the Spar on Coxmoor Road. Spike carried Kevin on his shoulders. When Kevin pulled the cap from Spike's head, he revealed a scalp that was shaved on two sides, with an incipient Mohican growth of hair down the middle.

'That's where you'll be going soon,' John said to Kevin, pointing to the primary school across the road.

'I don't want to go to school,' said Kevin sullenly.

'Yeah wait till you've had 11 years of it,' said Spike.

'Oh I don't know,' answered John, 'We had a few laughs to brighten things up. Remember when Mr. Ellis made us get up in front of everyone at assembly when we shouted "Amen!" really loud?'

'I remember nicking a tin of glue from Mr. Mellish's woodwork class and sniffing it in the toilets.'

A red XR3I Escort pulled up beside John and Spike. Loud music emanated from within. A booming bassline that could be physically felt, was accompanied by a rapid Pinky and Perky vocal. Sammy leapt out from the passenger side of the car, while Luke sat in the driver's seat with the window down.

'What happened to the Nova?' John shouted.

'They call these the Ford Clitoris because every cunt has one,' replied Sammy.

'Do you want to walk home, you cheeky bastard?' said Luke.

'I've just been round to your house, looking for you,' said Sammy. 'What's up with your mam? Any one would think someone had died.'

'It's a long story,' replied John, shaking his head. 'So what brings you to this neck of the woods then?' Are you all refreshed and ready for work tomorrow?'

'No fuck that, that's what I've come to tell you; me and Luke are heading off to Ibiza tomorrow; we're going to get jobs over there.'

'It's finished over here,' said Luke morosely.

'Cool!' said Spike.

'What about your notice?' asked John in disbelief. 'You won't get a reference if you just pack in like that.'

Sammy glanced at Luke hesitantly.

'Have you heard yourself!' said Spike in disgust. 'You've turned into your dad; what happened to the John who used to hitchhike to Hull to see GBH play?'

John paused and realised that Spike was right. He had become everything that had been anathema to him when he had been a young punk; admonishing Sammy for leaving a job which wouldn't exist by the end of the year.

'I suppose I'm just jealous that everyone is going off enjoying themselves while I'm stuck here,' he said. 'What are you going to do about money over there?'

'Luke's come into some money,' replied Sammy, 'His uncle gave him a wad of cash that he says he's been saving for him. I've been saving a bit myself; I'll go on the game if I end up skint.'

'Good luck with that one,' said Spike wryly..

CHAPTER TWENTY-SIX

There was a queue of people outside the Town Hall waiting to sign the book of condolence to pay their respects to Princess Diana. I was browsing through *The Fixed Period* at the book stall that regularly stood on the flea market. The couple who ran the stall were discussing the death of Diana with an elderly customer. He came to the stall each week and bought Westerns, returning them the following week, in part-exchange for a new book. He never went out without his tartan shopping bag, pulling it along by its wheels. He would peruse the box marked 'Westerns', always proclaiming that he'd read every title, but always walking away with another dog-eared paperback.

'I think it's disgusting how the Royal family have behaved this week!' he announced to the world. 'I don't think they've got an ounce of sympathy for the loss of that lass.'

The couple who ran the stall shook their heads mournfully in agreement. They weren't prepared to commit any further to the subject. They had learned from bitter experience that it wasn't worth encouraging the old man's polemics. He would stay all day if they gave him the opportunity. I couldn't see what people expected the Queen to do under the circumstances. There was already talk in some quarters that the tragic accident had been instigated by agents of the Crown.

A formidable black prostitute called Lucretia Hall emerged from the Market Inn, laughing uproariously. Onlookers watched with consternation, anticipating divine retribution for the untimely mirth. A Union Jack stood at half-mast above the Town Hall. Beneath the flag, a clock told the wrong time. An escutcheon bearing a coat of arms was placed above a portico of Doric columns. Dawn Townroe appeared from beneath the portico, accompanied by her daughters. I was on my way to the toilets that operated, dungeon-like, beneath the Town Hall. Dawn waved to me and smiled in a way that suggested she might be slowly recovering from her ordeal.

'I bet you're wondering what I'm doing, hanging around on the Town Hall steps,' she said playfully.

Standing on the Town Hall steps had always been a euphemism for plying one's trade as a prostitute in Mansfield. I couldn't recall ever actually seeing anyone engaged in that profession there, but I had known of one or two who operated from the pubs in that area.

I talked with Dawn while her daughters rummaged amongst the Aladdin's cave of busted guitars, Atari consoles and foot spas.

'Have you been to pay your respects then?' I asked.

'Yeah,' said Dawn with a poignant countenance. 'I'm not a big fan of the royals but she came to visit the hospital when my dad was on his last legs. I think it made him really happy, seeing her before he died.'

'You're not planning on going to London for the funeral are you?' I asked. 'I hear there a going to be millions of people making their way down there; it's going to be a nightmare.'

'No I might watch it on the telly; Elton John is supposed to be singing at the funeral.'

'Okay!' I said with a grimace. 'Think I might give that one a miss.'

It was the first time I had really had a proper chance to speak to Dawn since she had been attacked.

'So how are you coping these days?' I asked awkwardly.

'Would you believe, I actually went and visited Andy last week.'

'Wow! That must have been hard. How did it go?'

'Well it looks like he'll be locked away for a very long time. He says he's going to plead guilty to everything he's charged with and tell the police everything he knows about the BFC. He seems very calm about it all; I think he wants to atone for all that stuff he did.'

'Well you're better off without him,' I said, 'You deserve a lot better than that.'

'Well I'm not much of a catch with a face like this. The thing is, I know it sounds stupid, but I think I still love him.'

'Just be careful Dawn,' I pleaded, 'They're dangerous people and…well you know what they're capable of.'

'I don't think they will be bothering us anymore, now Andy's got rid of them. He did all that for me.'

'Is that what he told you?'

'You haven't seen him, he's a changed man. You gave that kid Josh another chance after what he did to your mate.'

'How do you know about that?'

'Oh I figured it out that night when we came to your house and that Sutts bloke said he'd seen him there.'

'Okay you've got me there,' I replied, taking her hand and squeezing it. 'I wish you all the happiness in the world and I hope we can always be friends.'

'I'll never forget the time we spent together,' said Dawn, planting a chaste kiss on my cheek before turning her back and walking away.

After Dawn went about her business with her daughters, I visited the library and sat and read a copy of the *Chad* to see if there was anything in the situations vacant pages. There was little to be found for anyone who didn't have a university degree and the paper was full of local memories of Diana. Amidst all the hysteria about the death, my attention was drawn to a police facial composite of a man suspected of the murder of Nappy Andrews. The *Crimewatch* appeal had jogged a few memories and calls had come flooding in regarding a man who had been seen near the scene of the killing.

The more I studied the picture, the more I felt that it resembled Sutts. I tried to recall whether he had been in jail at the time of the murder but couldn't be sure. I thought back to our catastrophic visit to Trent Bridge, and his preoccupation with the day when Myfanwy had met Edward Towton. He had asked some very specific questions about the movements of Boz and Nappy, questions that I hadn't been able to answer.

I thought about Sutts's reaction when he saw the old photo of Edward Towton and the painful memories it had dredged up. The young man named David Read had suffered injuries, which were the result of an assault that was probably as brutal as the one that Sutts had described. The more I tried to work out why Sutts would have killed Nappy, the more I was drawn back to the day when he and Boz had been in the same area as Towton, when Read's body had been found.

Then I remembered Sutts mentioned that he had visited Myfanwy in 1986. It had been one of the few occasions when he had been at liberty to pay Myfanwy a visit. It was also the year that Boz Bosworth's mutilated body had been found in a dustbin. Myfanwy had confessed to me that he was anxious about Nappy being pimped out by Bosworth when he was desperate enough for money. It began to cross my mind that Read himself might have been offered to Towton by Bosworth.

I rushed home with every intention of phoning the police, if only to establish that I recognised the image in the newspaper as one that resembled Sutts. I started to have doubts about making the call, when I considered that my involvement with Sutts during the incident at the Navigation might be brought to the attention of the police. I was also beginning to feel trepidation about the possible consequences of informing on someone who might possibly be guilty of multiple murders. I had seen what Sutts was capable of when he had shoved a gun into someone's mouth, without any ostensible appearance of unease.

Saturday came and I still hadn't made a decision. It was the day of Diana's funeral at Westminster Abbey. Heidi was planning on watching the obsequies but I had made it clear that I had no intention of spending my Saturday morning viewing the spectacle of a state funeral. I came downstairs at 8:30 and was surprised to hear the postman delivering mail at that time. It was usually nearer to noon when he arrived and I concluded that he must be planning on getting home early to watch the funeral.

A postcard had arrived with a German stamp attached. On the stamp was a sketch of Marlene Dietrich, which contrasted with the disturbing artwork which was presented on the front of the postcard. The card featured an image of a painting by the Dadaist artist Otto Dix, entitled *The Skat Players*. The picture featured three war veterans sat around a table playing cards. The three soldiers were all afflicted with grotesque disfigurements, which they had acquired during the First World War. One of the soldiers sits on his chair without legs, while another's face is badly mutilated. All three are wearing a bizarre array of prosthetic replacements for their injuries; industrial solutions for the casualties of an industrial war.

The postcard was sent from my brother, who had filled as much space with his crabbed handwriting as was possible on the rear of the card. He was living in Berlin and was working as a graphic designer for a German television company. His dreams of success as an artist had been shattered during his visit to the United States. Damian Hirst had received the laurels of the Turner Prize and Ian Swift had walked away into obscurity. He claimed that he was happy in his new role and that he was involved in a relationship with a footballer who played for one of the top teams in the Bundesliga. I was cordially invited to visit him in Berlin and, as a postscript, he asked me to say hello to Dad.

The phone began ringing and I chose to ignore it. I had a feeling that Heidi wanted to persuade me to come and watch the funeral with her and would drive round and pick me up. I made myself a mug of tea and hydrated a packet of dried noodles for breakfast. I settled down to read *The Fixed period* and listened to a compact disc of the *Florida Suite* by Delius.

The phone started ringing again and I obdurately refused to respond. After half-an-hour of peaceful reading, the ringing began again. My doggedness began to falter as I started to imagine that perhaps something might be wrong with Heidi's mother. I reluctantly picked up the phone and instead of hearing Heidi, I was greeted by the sound of an unfamiliar female voice.

'Hello I'm sorry to trouble you but is Nick there by any chance?' said a slightly nervous sounding woman, in whose voice I detected a hint of a Lancashire accent.

'Nick?' I answered with relief, 'No sorry I think you might have the wrong number duck.'

'Oh well I had a piece of paper with a few phone numbers on it and I've tried all the others except this one. Are you Myfanwy?'

'No unfortunately, Myfanwy passed away a while back,' I explained plaintively, 'Who did you say again, Nick?'

'Yeah Nick Sutcliffe, he spent some time in prison with Myfanwy I think.'

'Oh you mean Sutts,' I said, my heart sinking.

'Yeah that's right! I was just a bit concerned about him; I've been trying to get in touch with him for some time but he's disappeared off the face of the earth.'

'Well if you leave me your number, I'll get back to you if I hear anything,' I said, anxious to put down the phone.

I wrote down the number and beneath it wrote down the name she gave me. I was relieved to finally put down the phone; anxious and angry about being drawn into the affairs of Nick Sutcliffe against my will. I glanced at the name that was scribbled on the back of a flyer for double glazing and remembered why the name, Linda Read, sounded so familiar.

I rang her straight back and asked, 'Sorry to bother you again, you just called me; you don't by any chance have a son do you?'

'I had a son name David,' she said, her voice wavering, 'he passed away some years ago.'

'Oh I'm sorry to hear about that,' I replied.

'Why do you ask? Did Nick mention him to you?'

'I think he might have said something about it,' I replied, aware that I was getting out of my depth.

'Did he also tell you that he never bothered to see his son, even when I suggested bringing David to visit his father in prison,' she said angrily.

'Look I'm sorry to have upset you like this; like I said if I hear anything I'll get in touch with you; bye'

I felt a chill as I put the phone down. David Read was the son of Sutts and had died at the hands of a man who had abused both father and son. I was now sure that the murders of Nappy Andrews and Boz Bosworth were both acts of vengeance by Sutts. It then occurred to me that the day Sutts had visited with the intention of seeing Myfanwy, he was bent on discovering whether Myfanwy had been involved in leading David Read to his fate.

I switched on the television in an attempt to distract myself from my fears. Elton John was singing *Candle in the Wind* with customised lyrics for Diana. His hair was cut in a three stooges-type pudding bowl style. His voice wilted amidst the palpable emotional overload that could be felt across the nation. I switched off again after only a couple of minutes. The entire spectacle had taken on apocalyptic overtones, as if Diana's death foreshadowed the Biblical 'End of Days'.

Someone knocked gently on the front door. I went to answer, half-expecting to see Heidi. As I opened the door, Sutts pushed his way into the house, holding a man by the collar of his coat with one hand and pressing his Beretta Bobcat into his back with the other. The man wore an elegant black mourning suit, which might have upstaged the one worn by Elton John at the royal funeral. Sutts, in contrast, was wearing a pair of jeans which were smothered to the knees in mud. He wore a camouflage combat jacket and stank as though he hadn't washed for weeks.

I followed Sutts as he pushed his prisoner through to the living room and roughly shoved him into my favourite armchair.

'Now you just sit there and be quiet Little Lord Fauntleroy or you'll get this!' he threatened, pushing the gun against the captive's face.

'Look if this is about the money I owe King Rasta, tell him I'll get it to him Monday.'

'Shut it duchess!' Sutts said firmly.

Turning around to me, Sutts said, 'Put the kettle on cock, I'm parched.'

I immediately did as I was asked, 'I really need you to help me out here Dean,' said Sutts as he leaned on the kitchen door, his gun still aimed at his companion.

'Who is he?' I said, nervous but still curious.

'That, my son, is the 14th marquess of Straffield, so you'd better have some Earl Grey lying around me old China.'

I was in the presence of Freddy Nordville-Best, the erstwhile companion of Edward Towton. The same man I had seen on *Newsnight* a few months earlier. The good life had clearly taken its toll on Freddy since he had been Edward Towton's favourite catamite. His cheeks were jowly and a paunch spilled out of his morning suit. His accent gave away his Eton schooling and thoroughbred breeding. I sensed that if I didn't do something quickly, another execution was about to take place.

I brought a mug of tea through to Sutts. I had chosen a mug which bore a photo of a semi-clad, nubile young lady. The bikini evaporated when hot liquid was poured into the mug, rendering her naked. In my naivety I thought that the mug might pacify Sutts in some way. I handed him his tea and he placed the mug on the mantelpiece, without giving the girl a second glance.

'Put the telly on, Dean,' said Sutts, 'we don't want the duchess missing the funeral, after he's got himself all decked out in his nice whistle and daisies.'

I switched on the television and the Earl Spencer, younger brother of Diana, was delivering a eulogy. I wasn't concentrating on the words the Earl was speaking, but I watched as the cameras suddenly focused on the huge crowd that had assembled outside Westminster Abbey to pay their respects. Rapturous applause erupted from the crowd in response to something that the Earl had said.

'Is this one of your chums then Freddy?' asked Sutts, 'I bet you and him was busy playing leap frog together at Eton.'

'Actually I've never met the chap in my life,' said Freddy stoically. 'Diana and I met several times at Royal Ascot and–'

'Alright Freddy!' said Sutts irritably. 'This isn't a fucking tea party you know. But I have invited another guest, who you will no doubt want to have a good old catch-up with.'

'Who are we expecting?' I asked, trying to keep Sutts calm.

'An old friend of mine and Freddy's,' said Sutts, waving his gun erratically in the air. 'None other than Mister Edward Towton, Queens Council and buggerer of boys.'

'Really!' said Freddy in disbelief, 'Is this what all this nonsense is all about?'

On the television I watched as hundreds of mourners filed out of Westminster Abbey. I couldn't help but notice that one of them bore a striking resemblance to Edward Towton.

'What time is Edward meant to be calling on us?' I asked innocently.

'Oh he'll be here any moment now,' said Sutts confidently. 'I've made him an offer he can't refuse.'

'Can you tell me what this is all about please?' interrupted Freddy. 'I'm sure we can clear this mess up if we discuss things rationally. What is it I'm meant to have done?'

'Shut it!' Sutts shouted, firing his gun in the air and showering Freddy with plaster.

Freddy calmly brushed debris from his jacket, remaining silent. Someone began knocking on the door and I foolishly imagined it to be Towton, until I remembered that I had seen him a few moments earlier on the television. Sutts was about to leave the room and answer the door, which I calculated might give me time to get Freddy and myself through the back door to safety. He suddenly stopped in his tracks and reconsidered his options.

'Here take this and gut him if he tries anything,' said Sutts, pulling out a fierce looking hunting knife and offering it to me.

'Oh now Sutts, I can't get involved in violence,' I pleaded. 'I'm no good at this sort of thing.'

Sutts looked at me with an expression of extreme disappointment, 'Look Dean, I need you to watch my back here. I looked out for you when those lary geezers started kicking off in the pub, and I sorted you out with that passport.'

I reluctantly took the knife and brandished it before Freddy. Sutts marched down the hallway and I grabbed Freddy and gestured to him to follow me. He leapt up from the armchair and followed me into the kitchen. The key to the back door was hanging on a nail on the wall and I grabbed it with shaking hands.

'Woah, woah! Where do you two think you're going?' Sutts called out before I could even get the key into the lock.

I turned around and instead of being greeted by the sight of Edward Towton, Sutts pushed Heidi into the living room.

'Well I can see I'm gonna have my hands full here now!' he said angrily. 'You've let me down terrible mate, terrible!'

Heidi looked at me with an expression of terror, mixed with incomprehension. Sutts shoved her onto the settee and motioned with his gun towards Freddy and myself to join her. Sutts then began to pace up and down the room, muttering and occasionally slapping his forehead in frustration.

'Was he there when you and Towton killed that boy in Nottingham?' he said, suddenly ceasing his pacing and pointing towards me while staring at Freddy.

'What?' said Freddy, glancing at me with a confused expression. 'I've never seen him before in my life. Is this about the incident in the hotel in West Bridgford? That's all been raked over, time and time again. I never had anything to do with killing that boy. You want to get hold of Towton if you want answers to that debacle.'

'Oh I've got every intention of getting the truth out of that old queen!' said Sutts, laughing manically.

I saw Heidi's hands shaking and held her left hand in my right, 'I forgot to tell you Sutts,' I said, with as much equanimity as I could muster. 'Linda Read phoned earlier; she sounded a bit worried about you.'

This news seemed to disconcert Sutts, 'Linda? What was she after?'

'I think she wanted to talk about David; I don't think there is anyone else who can understand her grief like you do.'

Heidi squeezed my hand to indicate that I should continue in my attempt to pacify Sutts.

'David must have been about the same age as me. You must still have been part of the Kray firm when he came along?'

Sutts appeared to be lost in his own world of thoughts, gazing out of the window, and then said, 'No it was just after everything went pear-shaped for the twins. I legged it up north to get out of the way of it all. I thought I could make a new start up there. Ended up in a place called Clitheroe; I was a big fan of Jimmy Clitheroe when I was a nipper. I met Linda there and it wasn't long before she was expecting David. I couldn't settle down and I had it on my toes before he showed up.'

Sutts lit a cigarette and continued, 'It wasn't long after that, I ended up in Strangeways for a job I did with the Quality Street Gang. She read about it in the papers and came down to visit me; told me she would come again and bring David, but I didn't want him spending his childhood visiting the nick like I did with my old man. I never saw them after that; never even knew about him dying until she turned up and visited me in Pentonville and told me what had happened. The more time I spent locked up, the more I thought what a worthless piece of shit I was. I figured that the least I could do for the boy was to get the bastards that did him in.'

Sutts gave Freddy a look of venomous hatred, 'and here we are, now I'm gonna be judge and jury for a change.'

'Towton's the guilty one in all this!' Freddy desperately interjected. 'I only put up with his hands all over me so I could get hold of his money to buy coke. I swear to God I wasn't in that room with Towton and that boy.'

'So let's hear your story then Lord Snooty; looks like we've got plenty of time seeing as Eddie is running late.'

Freddy took a deep breath and began to recount his version of the events that took place on 12th and 13th July, 1985: 'We'd spent the day watching the test match and ended up in some grotty little pub near the ground at close of play. Edward started talking to some shady looking character with an eyepatch, who said he could sort us out with coke and company.'

'Bosworth!' interjected Sutts. 'Don't worry, he sang like a canary about his role in the whole disgusting business before I bled him like a pig. His mate took some catching before I smashed his ugly head in. It was him who made out he was David's pal before they sold him out.'

'Yes, well,' continued Freddy in a tremulous tone, 'then Bosworth appeared with two fresh-faced looking boys. One of them was a bit too plain looking for Edward, so he chose this blond-haired boy with blue eyes. He said he looked like an angel.'

Sutts lashed out at Freddy with the butt of his pistol, hitting him across the bridge of his nose, 'That was my son, you filthy pervert!'

'I didn't want to have anything to do with it!' pleaded Freddy, whilst clutching his bloody nose. 'I kept telling Edward that they looked too young and he would have the press and the police sniffing around, but he wouldn't listen. I stormed off after he refused to let me have any of the coke and I never even went near his room until it was too late. I wandered around that godforsaken town all day until I ran into Tip Topley, who persuaded me to tell the police everything I knew.'

Another round of percussive knocking on the door began beating out a new rhythm.

'Now we'll see who's who!' said Sutts triumphantly, hopping from one foot to the other. 'Judge Jeffries is here, but I'm the one who's going to be doing the hanging today!'

Freddy breathed a sigh of relief, feeling that the new arrival had granted him a brief reprieve. As Sutts began to advance towards the front door, he suddenly turned halfway down the hallway and span around with his gun aimed at the occupants of the settee, 'Don't get any cute ideas about sneaking out the back this time either!'

We watched in trepidation as Sutts swiftly swung open the door, with the intention of grabbing Edward Towton and dragging him inside. His euphoria was curtailed by the absence of Towton from the doorstep. We watched as Sutts stood, perplexed, in the doorway for a moment, before a voice emitting from a loudspeaker implored him to put down his weapon.

Sutts responded by stepping outside in a rage, screaming, 'I know you're out there Towton, show yourself!'

We heard the report of a gun and saw Sutts stagger and drop his Berretta and clutch his shoulder. A commotion began outside as strident voices ordered Sutts to step away from his gun and step forward onto the street. The three of us breathed a collective sigh of relief as Sutts was overpowered and handcuffed by several police officers.

A firearms officer wearing a ballistic vest cautiously entered the house and ordered everyone to slowly raise their hands.

'I don't suppose this is a good time to ask you to marry me is it?' I whispered to Heidi in a misguided attempt to lighten the mood. She broke down into a hysterical combination of laughter and tears.

EPILOGUE

Elaine and I were sitting in her garden enjoying the pleasant May sunshine. I was keeping her company while Heidi and her father fetched fish and chips from the Barracuda Fish Bar. The plates were warming in the oven and the bread and butter was already prepared.

I watched a pair of blue tits bringing grubs to feed their fledgling brood. Heidi's father enjoyed making bird boxes in his rare moments of spare time. One of his finest pieces of work was mounted on a fence at the rear of the garden. Between the interstices of conifers and fuchsias, one could observe the little birds, disappear and quickly re-emerge from the hole that served as a door to the box. I had spent the whole day watching both parents involved in the pursuit of feeding their young.

The blue tits had arrived a month earlier and chosen the box for their new family. They had then spent a week busily fetching moss and dried grass to build their nest. A feint tone had begun to emanate from the box several weeks later. The sound of the chicks grew more distinct in a few days. As soon as one of the parents appeared with a grub, five or six tiny voices called out for their portion. I found it remarkable, how selflessly the parents spent the daylight hours trying to find sufficient nourishment for their brood.

Heidi and her father arrived, and we sat down to our evening repast. He assiduously tried to tempt Elaine with morsels of food with varying degrees of success. I was reminded of the blue tits and their dedication to keeping their young alive. Elaine had also shown the same dedication to her children but for her, the roles had now been reversed.

Heidi and I had just returned from our honeymoon in Crete. Heidi hadn't wasted any time in getting the holiday photographs developed so she could show them to her father and friends. The water of the Aegean had been the warmest I had ever swum in. I imagined a multitude of antiquities beneath my feet, hidden amongst the golden sand. The detritus left by Venetian fleets, Phoenician merchants and Ottoman galleys.

I think that Heidi's near-death experience at the hands of Sutts gave her a sense of urgency in regard to settling down and raising children. I had somehow imagined that she would never forgive me for that traumatic day, blaming me for bringing Sutts into our lives. When she learned the truth about Sutts's motives for revenge, she felt some pity for him. As I begged her for forgiveness, she reassured me that I couldn't have known about the skeletons in his closet.

In Nottingham Crown Court, Sutts was sentenced to two life sentences with a minimum of 32 years. After attempting to take his own life in Long Lartin Prison in Worcestershire, Sutts was transferred to the high-security psychiatric hospital of Broadmoor. I received a visiting order from him while he was still detained in Long Lartin but decided that it would be wise to stay clear of him in case he decided to escape and pay me another visit.

Exacting revenge upon his nemesis, Edward Towton, had been Sutts's sole reason for living. His failure to avenge his son was the main factor in his mental deterioration in Long Lartin. He might have found some comfort if he had learned that during the time of his transfer to Broadmoor, revelations about Towton's past were about to bring him to the attention of the police. Two 14-year old boys came forward and accused Towton of sexual assault. After fleeing the country on his yacht, police found several hundred pornographic images of minors when they searched the hard drive of Towton's personal computer. After spending time in Spain and Morocco, Towton travelled to the Dominican Republic, a country without an extradition treaty with the United Kingdom.

Heidi initially wanted to have the wedding at the Baptist church where Elaine had regularly attended. The church had played a big part in Elaine's life and Heidi had met some of her best friends through attending the Baptist Youth Group. When she discussed the possibility of holding the wedding there, the minister had suggested that she might think about attending more often, before he thought any more about the matter.

The Church of England was far more accommodating and we were wed at St. John's Church in the heart of Mansfield. As an atheist, I had no preference, but found the surroundings of St. John's Church more conducive to my aesthetic nature. The Victorian church was built in the decorated gothic style of the early medieval churches of England. When restrictions on the Catholic faith were lifted in the 19th century, a revival of pre-reformation architecture began to flourish in the construction of new churches. The pointed arches and flying buttresses of St. Johns were characteristic of the return to a more picturesque age. A paved ramp had been built to allow wheelchair access into the church. As I watched one of Heidi's aunts push Elaine in her wheelchair, I was reminded that I had taken part in the construction of that very ramp during my time on the Employment Training Scheme.

Dawn Townroe was amongst the guests at the wedding. She was still visiting Cuckoo Walsh, who was serving a double life sentence at Wakefield Prison. Since his incarceration, Cuckoo spent more time seeking to atone for his past demeanours. In his first weeks at Wakefield he found succour and spiritual guidance from the prison chaplain. When a fellow inmate lent Cuckoo a copy of a book called *The Walled Garden of Truth*, he began a spiritual journey into the mystical world of Sufism. He earnestly submitted himself to the practices of Islamic mysticism, praying five times each day and purifying his soul.

Dawn was honoured by the company of Jeanette throughout the wedding. The wedding plans of Jeanette had been dashed when Colin decided to cut and run from the prospect of a second term of marital responsibility.

'We're like kindred spirits now,' Jeanette told Dawn. 'I know you always still carried a torch for Colin but you have to understand we're better off without him.'

Jeanette glanced across the pews to where Heidi's brother Andrew was sat alone. She had already made her mind up that she would take Heidi's recently divorced sibling to bed that very night.

John and Sally Freeman were also invited to the wedding. John gave me a postcard from Josh wishing me all the best and reporting that he was now the proud father of a baby boy called Dean. I also learned that Spike had travelled to Estonia with Timmy Tartuffe, before becoming a roadie for the Scorpions. He briefly made a stop in Nottingham when the band played at Rock City, but the hectic schedule didn't allow him the time to visit his friends. During the South American leg of the Scorpions world tour, Spike finally found a soul mate named Elsa Carmagnola in Asunción in Paraguay. He suspended his peripatetic lifestyle and trained as a practitioner of reiki healing.

John continued to pursue a career with Tsucol, attaining the title of 'Black Belt' in the Six Sigma methodology of manufacturing process improvement. After the closure of the Mansfield plant was announced, he decided that there was no turning back once he had sold his soul to the company.

Several months after the closure of Tsucol, the vacant site was leased out to Plataris, one of the world's leading manufacturers of camera film. I returned to the old Tsucol site myself, building cardboard promotional displays for disposable cameras and film. The Plataris factory in Annesley sent containers of film to the new plant in Mansfield, where it was packed into a variety of cartons. The work was out sourced to an employment agency and the workers were all hired on a zero-hours contract. This policy proved to be provident for Plataris, who subsequently transferred the packing work to China. It worked out cheaper for the company to send their film to China for packing and then send it back to the United Kingdom, than transport it from Annesley to Mansfield.

As I washed the greasy plates that had held our chip shop banquet, Heidi and her father were discussing the millennium bug. All the world's computers were forecast to malfunction when the new millennium commenced, with catastrophic consequences. I secretly hoped that the computer crash would take place and give humanity a good kick up the arse.

I had visited the town centre earlier in the day and was shocked by the decimated state of the market. Parts of the market square lay bare, where there had once been stalls trading in every available space. The market square that had once been the heart of Mansfield was becoming a wasteland, populated by drug users. The addicts loitered around the Town Hall lavatories, waiting for their next fix. Blue lights illuminated the public toilets; a strategy aimed at deterring the addicts who couldn't see the veins they wished to inject under the blue glow. Shoppers were now heading towards the new retail parks, seduced by the latest designer goods and American restaurant chain outlets.

There didn't seem a lot to look forward to in the next millennium for the people of Mansfield. At least we seemed to be entering into a new era of peace. The Good Friday Agreement had heralded a great step forward for the people of Northern Ireland. Nelson Mandela had just completed his term as President of South Africa during a decade that had seen Apartheid vanquished. The United States and Russia were negotiating a treaty, reducing their nuclear arms capacity. It seemed as though humanity was entering a new age of peace, finally learning from the mistakes it had made during the 20th century. What could possibly go wrong?

ND - #0284 - 270225 - C0 - 234/156/13 - PB - 9781780915951 - Gloss Lamination